EX LIBRIS

VINTAGE CLASSICS

A NIGHT IN COLD HARBOUR

Margaret Kennedy was born in 1896. Her first novel, *The Ladies of Lyndon*, was published in 1923. Her second novel, *The Constant Nymph*, became an international bestseller. She then met and married a barrister, David Davies, with whom she had three children. She went on to write a further fifteen novels, to much critical acclaim. She was also a playwright, adapting two of her novels – *Escape Me Never* and *The Constant Nymph* – into successful productions. Three different film versions of *The Constant Nymph* were made, and featured stars of the time such as Ivor Novello and Joan Fontaine; Kennedy subsequently worked in the film industry for a number of years. She also wrote a biography of Jane Austen and a work of literary criticism, *The Outlaws of Parnassus*. Margaret Kennedy died in Woodstock, Oxfordshire, in 1967.

OTHER NOVELS BY MARGARET KENNEDY

MARGARET KENNEDY

A Night in Cold Harbour

VINTAGE BOOKS
London

Published by Vintage 2014

2 4 6 8 10 9 7 5 3 1

First published in Great Britain by Macmillan & Co in 1960

Vintage
Random House, 20 Vauxhall Bridge Road,
London SW1V 2SA

www.vintage-classics.info

Addresses for companies within The Random House Group Limited
can be found at: www.randomhouse.co.uk/offices.htm

The Random House Group Limited Reg. No. 954009

A CIP catalogue record for this book
is available from the British Library

ISBN 9780099595489

The Random House Group Limited supports The Forest Stewardship
Council® (FSC®), the leading international forest-certification organisation.
Our books carrying the FSC label are printed on FSC®-certified paper.
FSC is the only forest-certification scheme supported by the leading
environmental organisations, including Greenpeace. Our
paper procurement policy can be found at
www.randomhouse.co.uk/environment

Printed and bound in Great Britain by Clays Ltd, St Ives plc

TO OLIVE AND TONY HALLAM

'Experience had already shown how much could be done by the industry of children, and the advantages of early employing them in such branches of manufacture as they are capable to execute.'
(*William Pitt in asking the House of Commons to reject Whitbread's Minimum Wage Bill. Feb.* 12, 1796.)

'And to what would they be indebted for this gentlest of all revolutions? To what, but to economy? Which dreads no longer the multiplication of man, now that she has shown by what secure and unperishable means infant man, a drug at present so much worse than worthless, may be endowed with an indubitable and universal value.'

(*Jeremy Bentham,* 1798.)

CONTENTS

ix

PROLOGUE: NIGHT

A FEW stones still lie in the heather at a cross-roads on the long southern slopes of Exmoor. They are all that is left of a hut which once stood there, offering shelter for poor people on the roads.

Old Lucy Squires made use of it twice a year, when she took one of her mysterious walks from Abbotsbury, on the Dorset coast, to Minehead, on the Bristol Channel. She had a tryst there with a man who was called Jemmy the Finger, since he had six fingers on his left hand. He earned halfpence for showing it at fairs, where he wore a red mitten to conceal it. In the hut he omitted this precaution: trampers and the Poor People, as the gypsies called themselves, might see it for nothing.

In the summer of 1813 Lucy failed to keep the tryst. Jemmy hung round Cold Harbour for three days, waiting for her. It was understood that neither would wait for the other longer than four, since people were expecting them elsewhere. Jemmy would carry Lucy's news eastwards, while she went on to Minehead. Nobody in Devon, Dorset or Somerset could remember a time when Mother Squires had not been on the roads; when one died, another took her place. Lucy was the daughter of the famous Mary who narrowly escaped the gallows in 1752. Handed down in the family was the same faultless memory for facts and figures. Not a scrap of writing would ever be found on Lucy, should she have the ill luck to be searched. Her pack held no more than a common peddler's wares. The rest was in her head, down to the last barrel of liquor, the last bolt of lace, run up on moonless nights to the

3

Chesil Beach and stored in cellars at Abbotsbury. She knew what goods were there and who had them. When she had carried word inland they were gradually dispersed.

She must be either dead or taken, thought Jemmy, as he sat on the moor and stared down the hill. But if she had been taken he would have heard of it by now. The news would have been out through the country before they had done swearing the constables. In any case she would die game. Her mother had been taken for a robbery committed in Hertfordshire on a day when she herself had been in Abbotsbury. She could have named a score of people, from Parson downwards, who had seen and spoken to her there. She would have kept mum and died on the gallows had not one of them come forward of his own accord. The tale lived on in country ballads describing him as 'Lucy's sweetheart true', a cordwainer, dead now these sixty years.

A person now appeared on the road below, coming up the hill with the aimless plod of one who lives on the roads. It was a woman, but too tall to be Lucy. When she drew nearer Jemmy recognised her. He had seen her often at West Country fairs. Her name was Hannah and she walked with a gypsy called Ptolemy Boswell who sold donkeys.

'Lucy's gone,' she said, when she came up to him.

'Ah! I thought as much. Where?'

'Yarcombe. They sicked a dog on her.'

'She died of it?' he asked in some surprise.

'It brings a weakness that flies all over her and takes her off, seemingly.'

'You was there?'

She shook her head and sat down beside him on the bank, hugging her tattered cloak round her, for the wind was cold.

4

'Word goes out amongst the Poor People.'

'No word from her though?'

'"I'm a-going," she says,' replied Hannah in a whining sing-song. '"My time is come and I must go, like another. These is my last dying words," she says. "Tell them in all the Cold Harbours that Lucy Squires is no more."'

Jemmy did not believe these to have been Lucy's last words, for Lucy was a taciturn old creature. But it was plain that she had tried to send him a message. He sat listening to the chill wind, as it whistled in the grasses, and then he said:

'She was old. Ten years gone they might have sicked a whole pack on her and she'd have been little the worse.'

'Ay, to be sure. She was a very ancient old woman, I believe.'

'You'll bide at Cold Harbour tonight?'

'Who's there?'

'Some people cast away off the Lizard. Making for Bristol inland, for to escape the Press. They've got good mangery.'

Hannah rose and they started up the hill towards the hut.

'And there's Parson Purchiss with his lad,' added Jemmy.

'Him! There's an enquiration for him. At Dulverton.'

'Better keep mum about that, or he'll scarper. Who's seeking him?'

'A Rye in a fine carriage. They say there's a price out.'

'A price? But they can't hang him, I believe, if he be a true parson. What's the price?'

'Ten finches.'

5

A Night in Cold Harbour

Nobody, thought Jemmy, would offer ten guineas for a poor old tramp unless they wished to hang him. Gentlemen in fine carriages were not to be gainsaid. To be taken and hanged by them was a misfortune which might befall anybody at any time, although they were bound by mysterious formalities of their own. First they sent a man before the beaks, and then they sent him up the steps, and then he was hanged, although he might never know why. It was a pleasanter kind of death than some others.

'There's many will keep mum for all that,' he said. ''Twould be thought unlucky.'

'Ay. He has the name of a Holy Man, I believe. He has a book.'

A cheerful noise came from the hut when they reached it. The shipwrecked sailors had learnt how to look after themselves. They had brought up some faggots from the copses below and lighted a fire. Their mangery, as Jemmy had promised, was good; their forlorn tale softened the hearts of cottage wives and they got better pickings than gypsies or trampers received. Amongst them they had collected half a cold pease pudding, some green bacon, some turnips, the heels of three loaves, and two hares. They did not know that food was not common property in Cold Harbour, nor was there any need to tell them. Hannah was welcomed civilly and given a place by the fire. At a hard glance from Jemmy she produced from her bundle a red spotted handkerchief containing bread and cheese. This prize, some labourer's dinner which she had picked up under a hedge, she would have preferred to reserve for the next day, and to sup tonight on the sailors' food. Jemmy was determined to create an atmosphere of fellowship and good will. He

6

contributed some rum himself, produced an iron pot, and offered to skin the hares.

'It's all for one and one for all,' he muttered, as he reached across her to put the pot on the fire.

He jerked his thumb over his shoulder to a corner where a trembling old man crouched beside a lad of about fourteen. This was the crazy creature whom they called Parson Purchiss. Nobody knew his real name. It was said that he was a true parson, but at war with the Quality. He had got his name from a book which he carried with him, and from which he would sometimes read out stories of travels in strange countries.

He did not beg but made shift to live in various ways, although very poorly. He baptized the gypsies' children, thus protecting them, as it was thought, from smallpox. He would read and write letters for those who had no schooling, and this service was valued by cottagers who had kindred at the wars, or on the sea. Being a true gentleman, he would keep a secret, and was therefore more trustworthy than some know-all-tell-all neighbour who might have a little schooling. One could be sure he would set down the meaning plainly, finding words for those who were tongue-tied. He never turned out a letter so elegant as to be incomprehensible. And, crazy though he might be, he sometimes gave his clients good advice. He knew, or had once known, something about the laws. He knew how money might best be sent, or safely laid up. He could break bad news gently, and an angry letter became milder when he had written it.

For these services he was more often paid in food and shelter than in coin, but Dickie, the boy who went with him, could play the fiddle, which was a source of income.

7

A Night in Cold Harbour

Although they had not been on the roads for very long they were well known in the West and were regarded with friendliness, mixed with a kind of awe. It was asserted that Parson Purchiss could change a man's luck. Any striking encounter with agony or wretchedness threw him into a passion of weeping, and some people believed that these tears worked a charm. Amongst them was Jemmy, who was convinced that they had cured him of gangrene. A bite from a farm dog had set up a sore in his leg which would not heal. It began to look ugly. His whole leg swelled to an immense size so that he could no longer walk. He had been obliged to cut off his boot and cram his leg into a great fisherman's boot, covered with green mould, which he had found rotting in a ditch. Even so he could not walk, and was lying in unspeakable torment by the roadside when Parson Purchiss came by, beheld him, and wept. In a little while the pain eased. The leg, in due course, healed pretty well. Jemmy roundly testified to this miracle everywhere and once fought a man at Newbury who maintained that he might as well declare that his leg had been cured by a mouldy boot.

Had the old man been less kindly, simple, and innocent, these powers might have been ascribed to a sinister source. But nobody could suppose him in league with the devil. It was felt, rather, that his tears had power to move Somebody Else. Fear as well as gratitude prompted Jemmy to deal honestly with one who had so powerful a Friend. This view was likely to be shared by many. Ten guineas might be a temptation but there was no knowing what lay in wait for the man who took them.

The sailors were less dependable than gypsies or trampers would have been. They might, with luck, never hear of the reward, for they were avoiding large towns and villages. As merchant seamen they would be clapped into the navy immediately, if taken before the Magistrates for vagrancy. They kept to by-lanes, never begged from the prosperous, and were slipping as quietly as they could up to Bristol where they had friends. They might, of course, see some bill posted, but Jemmy was sure that four out of the five of them could not read. The fifth, a spare, sly little man called Hughes, seemed to have had some schooling, although he was not likely to inform the rest of ten guineas which he could hope to secure entirely for himself. The hares had been his contribution to the supper; he declared that they had been given to him, which nobody believed. He was not likely, by the looks of him, to believe in luck and Holy Men. He had money of which his companions knew nothing. When they first arrived at Cold Harbour they had removed their boots and bathed their tired feet in a nearby ditch. Hughes went a little apart from the rest to do this, upon which Jemmy plagued him by coming too, and making conversation, until it became clear that Hughes had some very good reason for sticking to his boots when anybody was by. With such a man on the roads it might be better that Parson should lie hidden for awhile.

Jemmy went over to his old friend but got no return to his enquiries save a dazed look.

'He's poorly,' said the boy. 'He took a fever lying in the wet one night. He does naught but shiver and shake.'

'He should lie warmer than this. Mother Dicker, over by Watersmeet, would give him a bed. She owes him a good turn. He wept for her grandchild.'

'I doubt I could get him so far. 'Twas all I could do to bring him here.'

9

'He might do better for a taste of rum. There is reasons he should lie snug for a week or so. Tomorrow we'll make shift to get a pony.'

'I've a guinea. A gentleman at Glastonbury gave me a guinea for to go away, since my fiddling broke his lady's sleep.'

Jemmy laughed.

'That's a sweet way to get a guinea! I'll take to the fiddle myself if gentlemen will give me guineas so I don't play upon it.'

Between them they got their patient to swallow a little rum. Jemmy then took the hares out of the hut to skin, for he wanted to keep an eye on the road. Presently the boy slipped out to ask what was blowing. Upon hearing of the reward and the gentleman in the carriage he gave a despairing groan.

'They're coming up with him. I knew they would, at the last. We should ought to have stayed in Ireland. I was against it, but he took a fancy to come back here, seeking his book.'

They both looked uneasily southward, at a sombre world sinking into night. Questions were never asked in Cold Harbour, but Jemmy now ventured on a few, since the confidence about the guinea showed that the boy put trust in him.

'Are you kin?'

A shake of the head, followed by:

'He's Quality. I'm a whore's bastard.'

And a lord might have got you for all that, thought Jemmy.

'You been walking together long?'

'Five years. We was in Ireland at first, and we wan't on the roads then.'

'Who might be after him? D'ye know?'

'The gentry. They turned on him when Miss Jenny died. She was good to us. We was snug enough along of Miss Jenny. When she died we were forced to scarper.'

'He's a true parson?'

'To be sure he is.'

'They can't hang him then. Might it be you they're after?'

'Me! Never! Keep out of the way is all they ask of me.'

'There's a smell of Quality about you.'

'Never!' cried the boy again. 'I've but one thought in my heart.'

'And what's that?'

'To be even with 'em. To pay 'em back in the coin they've paid us.'

Jemmy laughed and began to skin the hares.

'That's proof enough,' he said after a while.

'Proof of what?'

'Even with 'em! Not one of us would harbour such a hope. You're Quality enough to get yourself hanged before your beard sprouts. Even with 'em!'

The boy muttered something about the French and a guillotine.

'Much good that did the Frenchies, poor sods! A gilliteen don't fill empty bellies. You'd best get back and play your fiddle to the sailors.'

'Them! What would they give me?'

'Good will. You might need it before the night is out. Here's the meat. Take it.'

He flung the hares to Dickie and spread the skins to dry on a flat stone behind the hut. They were worth a trifle, if Hughes forgot to ask for them. Inside the hut the fiddle struck up *Billy McGee*.

The night was falling fast over the great amphitheatre of country below. There had been no sunset. A cloudy sky boded rain before morning. A light or two twinkled out in cottage or farm windows. There was no movement discernible on the roads, yet Jemmy smelt trouble. If our Benefactor should drive over the moor tonight, he thought, we should see his carriage lamps a long way off.

The epithet held no irony in Jemmy's mind. Benefactor was a fine name which the Quality bestowed on themselves; he had never heard it used in an attractive context. This strange species had sometimes shown him kindness. Gentlemen had tossed him a coin to drink their healths. And there was one who, seeing him very lame from that scarce healed leg, had given him a lift in a curricle, chatting affably, as one man to another. But people of that sort were not given to announcing themselves as benefactors. The word was oftenest heard from those who put man-traps in their woods, kicked stray dogs out of their way and preached repentance to condemned prisoners in Newgate.

The interior of the hut was now quite dark, save for the flames of the little fire. Faces, clustered round it, watched the bubbling stew. The stench was such that even Jemmy flinched for a moment before going in. The rum had put the sailors into a cheerful mood. They were singing *Billy McGee* as they watched their supper cooking. Hannah was now bending over the old man.

'He's a-going,' she said to Jemmy. 'He'll not last the night. Feel of his skin. Hark to his breathing, how it do roar and whistle.'

He was inclined to agree with her. The scheme to get a pony and seek shelter with Mother Dicker would never answer. Nor could he linger long, for he must be on his way, carrying news of Lucy's death to those who were waiting for a word from her. Yet he did not like to go. He remembered the roadside where he had lain howling, and a moment of unmeasured bliss which had come to him when those tears fell, as though he had risen up and floated away into some other existence. Some part of him had been touched which had nothing to do with his leg. He sometimes felt that, ever since, he had been a slightly altered man.

'It might be for the best,' he said. 'Better than that he should be taken.'

He took the hot shrivelled hand and felt a faint pressure.

'D'ye know me, sir?' he whispered. 'Jemmy? 'Tis Jemmy.'

A faint reply was drowned by a bellow from the sailors.

'His horse has found a warmer stable.
Billy McGee McGaw!
His dog has found a bigger kennel.
Billy McGee McGaw!
His mort has found a better mate,
And we shall get some grub to ate!
So they all flapped their wings and cried:
Caw! Caw! Caw!
Billy McGee McGaw!'

'When you've eaten,' he said to the boy, 'go you and watch the road. Give word if you see carriage lamps.'

'They'll never come tonight!' protested Hannah.

'My mind mistrusts me. This Cold Harbour is well known. No profit to enquire by day. 'Tis after dark they might hope to find folks here.'

'And what might you have done with them skins?' said a voice at Jemmy's shoulder.

It was Hughes who had slipped quietly up to them.

'On a stone behind there, if you want 'em.'

'To be sure I want 'em. What's to do here?'

Hughes bent over to look and exclaimed sharply:

'The man's dying.'

'No, he an't.'

'I say he is. He must go outside. There's no luck to be had sleeping with a corpse. It won't hurt him to die on the heath and we can sleep in peace.'

'You may sleep in peace on the heath if you choose,' said Jemmy. 'He'll bide here.'

'I'll have you to remember there are five of us. You'll do as we say. Take him out. Take him a mile off at the least, so we shall have no trouble tomorrow. When they find a dead man in Cold Harbour they bring back all those that were with him to speak before the Crowner.'

'You know too much for a sailor,' retorted Jemmy, 'nor you don't speak like a sailor. Must have been the fear of the gallows drove you to sea. He'll bide here. Unless you want that your cullies should know what you've got in your boot.'

Hughes started and changed colour.

'Have it your own way,' he said hastily. 'Since you set store by the old fellow. Who might he be?'

'One that passes for an honest man with the Walking People. If you want to see Bristol you won't cross us.'

Hughes retreated.

'That Gaujo means no good,' said Hannah.

'He'd skin his own mother for tenpence,' agreed Jemmy.

14

The pot was lifted from the fire and all gathered for the meal, spearing out pieces on their knives.

Jemmy took pains to establish cordial relations with the sailors. He gave them advice as to the safest lanes eastward, told them of a good barn where they might spend the next night, and amused them with stories. All that he said impressed upon them the importance of winning favour with the Walking People. He told them about the Bottle Man, at Shaftesbury Fair, who had filled a large tent with people paying sixpence apiece to see a six-foot blackamoor get inside a pint bottle and there to sing a song. After waiting for near an hour they tore the tent to pieces. The blackamoor and his barker helped them to do so since, in the interval, one had washed his face and the other had assumed the disguise of an old woman. So great was the riot that a record number of pockets had been picked. But later a reward was put out and the conspirators were taken. One that knew them, explained Jemmy, turned informer, not being accustomed to the roads but making their acquaintance in a Cold Harbour, as it might be this one, and by trade a seaman, as it might be one of the company. No detail was spared as to the ultimate fate of the informer at the hands of the Walking People.

All the time, as he talked, Jemmy's heart was as heavy as lead. He could not forget the life ebbing away in the corner. No death had ever affected him as this one did. When the sailors began another song he went back.

'He's trying for to say something,' murmured Dickie.

Jemmy put his ear to the trembling mouth and caught a whisper:

'Trouble for you . . . Coroner . . . put me . . . in a ditch . . . for Billy McGee.'

15

'No, no, Parson. We'll stay by you.'

'Dickie!'

'I'm here. Holding your hand.'

'Learn. . . . Don't stay on the roads. . . . Eccles. . . . Go to him . . . tell him . . . from me . . . he will help you. . . .'

The voice fell silent.

'Go back to the door,' said Jemmy to the boy. 'And don't blubber. He'll go so quiet I believe the rest won't know unless we tell them.'

The boy went to the door and cried out immediately that the lights of a carriage were coming up the hill.

An uneasy silence fell upon the hut. Presently they heard the distant ticking of hooves, the rattle of wheels. The sound came nearer. As the carriage clattered past a ray of light from a lamp looked in for a moment at the open door. It went on but, just as a sigh of relief broke from the listeners, it stopped.

'No matter what questions is asked,' said Jemmy urgently, 'we knows nothing.'

Voices were shouting outside.

'It's here or hereabouts.'

'I believe we've passed it.'

Then came a quieter voice in the accents which they had most cause to fear:

'Don't turn. I can walk back. I think I see it.'

A door slammed. Quick footsteps approached the hut. The vagrants within huddled close together as if for protection and Hannah threw her cloak over Parson Purchiss. A tall man appeared in the doorway. Flinching, as Jemmy had flinched, from the stink, he paused on the threshold. A cluster of faces, lit by the dying fire, stared

at him. To his greeting, which was civil enough, Jemmy
returned a mutter which might serve for all.

'Is this the place they call Cold Harbour?'

'Ay.'

'I believe that some of you good people might be able
to help me. You are all travellers, I take it?'

'Travellers and Poor People,' whined Hannah. 'What
does the kind gentleman want with the likes of us?'

'I'm seeking two people who may be wandering in the
country hereabouts. I believe they lodge very roughly.
An old gentleman, the Reverend Dr. Newbolt, and a boy
called Richard Cottar. Have any of you heard of such
people?'

There was a general murmur of dissent.

'Are you sure? They might not go by those names.
But any person who has seen them would, I think, remember them. The boy carries a fiddle. I am offering a
reward of ten guineas to anyone who may bring me to
them. So keep your eyes and ears open.'

'Might we know your name, sir? In case we should
hear of them later?'

This was from Hughes. Dickie made a quick movement.
He had whipped out a knife before Jemmy caught his
arm with a firm grasp.

'My name is Brandon. Of Stretton Priors, Severnshire.
For the next few days I shall be found at the Dolphin Inn
at Porlock.'

The silence and stillness in the hut seemed at last to
daunt the stranger. He paused, as though at a loss, and
then said:

'I trust you will help me, if it is ever in your power.
Meanwhile, perhaps you will drink my health.' He tossed
a coin towards Hughes, who had at least made a civil

17

reply. 'And remember! I intend to be the benefactor
of any person who brings me word of them.'

With this unfortunate statement the scene closed. He
wished them good night and turned up the road again.
Everybody stirred and sighed. Not one of them, not even
Hughes, hankered after a benefactor in any shape or form.

They heard the carriage door slam again. The horses
started forward. The hooves clopped and the wheels
rattled for a long time in the still night, but at last they
could be heard no more.

PART I

A YOUNG GENTLEMAN IN A RAGE

I

ROMILLY BRANDON, born in 1777, was reckoned by the neighbourhood to be a child of singularly good fortune. As an only son he was heir to a considerable property. A large sum of money had also been left to him by an uncle, of which he was to have absolute control when he came of age. His excellent parents doted on him. His five sisters were expected to defer to him in everything. His tastes were considered, his opinion asked, at an age when most children are told to hold their tongues. In person and capacities he deserved his reputation as the handsomest and liveliest young man in the county.

He knew no check, was balked of no desire, until his twenty-first year, when Jenny Newbolt wantonly broke his heart. She was a distant connection, the daughter of the Rector at Stretton Courtenay, and they had been sweethearts as long as they could remember. They had agreed to announce their engagement and to marry as soon as Romilly was twenty-one, when his uncle's bequest would make him perfectly independent. But, six months short of the date, Jenny suddenly took it into her head to wreck this delightful scheme. It had been, she said, a childish fantasy which must now be given up. They must wait, for some years perhaps, since her mother had died and she could not abruptly abandon her father at such a time.

Romilly was furious. Whatever the claims of her family might be, he insisted that her earlier vows to himself should have priority. When she refused to listen to him he broke with her completely and fell into a fit of the sulks which culminated, before the year was out, in a bitter quarrel with his father, since it became clear that he intended to put nothing of his private fortune back into the Stretton Estate.

Old Mr. Brandon had always assumed that he would do so, and had relied on it. Debts had piled up. There had been a succession of bad harvests. Marriage portions for five daughters must some day be forthcoming. It was only fair that Romilly, who would some day inherit Stretton, should take some notice of these responsibilities, and his refusal was never forgiven. He made no secret of the fact that he disliked country life, found the local society insufferable, and wished to settle in London. He meant to spend his own money in his own way. He hoped, in elegant and cultivated surroundings, to become a patron of Art and Literature. It was a great grievance with him that he had never travelled or seen the world, never taken the Grand Tour. This right had been denied to him by the barbarous custom of fighting the French, for which his father's generation must be held responsible.

To London, in the end, he went, and in London he remained for ten years. Thrice, during that period, he went home — to bury his father and to attend the weddings of a couple of sisters, but he never stayed longer than three days.

At the age of thirty he had got through a good deal of his money without having done anything in particular for Art and Literature. He began gradually to think that he might patronise them quite as effectively living on his own property, and spend a good deal less. He grew quite sure of this during a visit to his friend, Scrutty Phelps, of Long Bickerton. Scrutty was neither cultivated nor elegant, but more respectable friends, whose company Romilly had sought on first going to London, had now grown cool or dropped him; for want of better he was driven to the society of an idle rake with whom he had nothing in common. Having lost money to Scrutty every night for a week, he decided that boredom at home would be cheaper, and set out for Severnshire, in pouring rain, on a morning in May.

He took with him a young naval lieutenant called Edward Latymer, a cousin of Scrutty's, whom he had met at Long Bickerton. He had been rather sorry for the young man, who was too poor to share in the amusements of the house, or even to secure the civility of the servants. The maids, known through the county as 'Scrutty's Seraglio', famed for their complaisance to his guests, had no smiles to spare for such a shabby visitor, and purposely omitted to bring him shaving water. Nobody knew what he did with himself all day. When he appeared at dinner he was boisterously greeted and immediately forgotten again. On an impulse of good nature Romilly decided to take him to Stretton, lend him a fishing rod, lend him a horse, and generally play the patron.

As they drove in the rain over the Cotswolds he learnt that his protégé was the son of a clergyman in Yorkshire. Both the parents had died during his absence at sea. An only sister had married and gone to the West Indies. He had left a happy home, a united family, which he was never to see again. Home now, on leave, he had gone up to Braythorpe to attend, as he put it, to the graves, and had probably spent more than he could afford on tombstones. Then, having no other kinsman, he had betaken himself to Scrutty, with whom he had been on good terms in boyhood.

'It's not his fault, you know, that we have so little to say to one another now. He's very good-natured. He invited me to stay there as long as I pleased.'

'He's got twenty bedrooms,' commented Romilly, 'and can't always fill 'em. But had you no friends, down in Yorkshire, with whom you could have stayed?'

Latymer flushed. There had been friends, he admitted . . . a family from whom he had expected a welcome . . . but certain circumstances . . . an alteration of feelings . . . there had been changes, in the course of seven years. Yorkshire was now the last county which he could visit in comfort.

Few young ladies will wait seven years for a penniless lieutenant, reflected Romilly. It's pathetic enough. But family tedium might be just the thing for him at the moment. The girls can take him for picnics and my mother can take him to church. I shall endure it better myself if it does him any good.

He then remembered that Stretton Priors was not so full of girls as it used to be. Charlotte and Sophy were married. There remained but Bet, who was too plain and stupid to put Yorkshire out of any man's head, and a couple still in the schoolroom — Amabel and Ellen.

'I've spent very little of my time in Severnshire these last ten years,' he said. 'I had, formerly, a strong aversion from it. I don't know if I shall like it any better now. That remains to be seen.'

Latymer glanced at him and then looked out of the window down which the rain sluiced continually.

'It will clear in a few minutes," he observed. 'Wind's sou-west. Ten years is quite a period.'

His tone, which was a little dry, nettled Romilly, who would have liked to hint, with a sigh, that his own history might have been quite as pathetic as Latymer's. He could not do this, however, at the top of his voice, and the drumming of the rain on the window panes obliged them both to shout.

In a few minutes it slackened. Splashes of light dappled the hills to the west, as a few isolated trickles ran down the panes. Eastwards a misty shadow rolled away over England. Now there was an opportunity for a sigh, but Latymer got one in first, a long breath of pure pleasure.

'I never watched a squall at sea go by,' he said, 'without thinking of this kind of scene — how the colours change on the hills and fields when the sun comes out, and the smell of the soil after rain, and the way the birds strike up. That fellow in front must have got very wet.'

'He's paid to get wet.'

'Do they expect you at Stretton tonight?'

'They don't expect me at all.'

'I thought you said you'd sent a servant on.'

'Not to Stretton. I sent him home for a holiday.'

This piece of good nature Romilly was already regretting. It had been prompted by the fear that Markham, who was a good valet, might find Stretton very slow, and refuse to settle there. Nor was the scheme for patronising Latymer quite so attractive as it had been when they set out. It seemed that he had enjoyed himself at Long Bickerton; he had hired a pony and explored the countryside. At Severnton, while they were changing horses, he insisted upon looking at the cathedral. A person so determined to be in good spirits could hardly be endowed with pathos.

The sun was shining as they crossed the great tract of hilly forest which lay between Severnton and their destination. Emerging from the trees, they saw beneath them an expanse of rich fields, prosperous farms and shadowy woods. With more emotion than he had expected Romilly thought that all this was his. Latymer lowered a window glass and looked out. Immediately at the foot of the hill a river wound through an oddly smudged and blackened tract of country. There was a clutter of hovels, too many for a village, too few for a town, amidst great sheds, squat chimneys and mounds of grey-white earth.

'What's this? A pottery?'

'Observant fellow! Yes. That's Cranton's. The land used to be ours, but my father sold it. There's china clay there, and lead, and coal to be got in the forest.'

'Cranton's china? I've heard of it. What a pleasant spot it must have been before, though!'

'It was. Luckily there's a rise in the ground which hides it from us at Stretton.'

The sale of this land had been a grotesque blunder which Romilly generally managed to forget. Cranton's offer, at first contemptuously refused, had later become a blackmailing threat in the course of the quarrel between father and son.

'Very well, Romilly! Very well, sir! If you won't, you won't. But I warn you I may be obliged to close with Cranton.'

Having said this a dozen times the pig-headed old gentleman began to believe it. In the end he parted with the land as much to punish Romilly as to enrich himself. Nor did anybody imagine that much would come of it.

Cranton might have secured the valley but it was supposed that a good many years must elapse before he did anything with it. Mr. Brandon did not expect smoking chimneys to rise during his own lifetime, though they might do so to plague Romilly after his death. They rose within a very few months. A tatterdemalion horde known as 'Cranton's people' came swarming through the forest to build their huts round the kilns. There was no remedy save to ignore the very existence of the place, which was easy for the Brandons, since rising ground and thick plantations lay between the river and Stretton Courtenay.

The eyesore vanished when the carriage had taken the second turn down the hill. Thereafter the prospect indicated order and prosperity. They saw well tilled fields, fine timber, thriving farms and neat cottages. As they approached Stretton their consequence increased. They were no longer mere travellers in a post-chaise. Romilly was the most important creature within a radius of ten miles. He looked about him and thought that his neglect did not seem to have done his people much harm. Giles, his steward, maintained the family tradition of treating them well. Should they fall into trouble his mother and old Newbolt, the Parson, supplied soup and blankets.

The village was very pretty. On its wide triangular green some boys were playing cricket. Others sat watching under the trees. This pleased Latymer, who leant out again to look, and heard, above the noise of the carriage, the sounds of a summer evening, when the shadows lengthen and folk turn from work to play. He heard the caw of homing rooks, the smack of a ball on a bat, and a lazy cheer from the group under the trees.

'I think I could still enjoy a game of cricket,' he said.

27

'Could you?'

Yawning, Romilly reflected that he had this fellow on his hands for the best part of a fortnight. But I won't play cricket, he thought. I draw the line at that. Ellen can play with him; if I'd thought of it in time I could have bought her a cricket bat in Severnton. I suppose I should have bought presents for all of them.

Ellen, whom he remembered as a long-legged rosy child, was his youngest sister. Now that he was bowling along beside the walls of his own park he began to picture his arrival — his mother's exclamations and her probable tears. She would ask why he came, how long he meant to stay, yet would give him no time to answer. He must endeavour to be patient with her, to listen to her budget of tedious news, and to kiss Bet and Amabel with some attempt at cordiality. Ellen was the only one of the girls for whom he felt any affection. He wished that he had brought her a pretty work box. To pinch her round cheek and to make her laugh was not a duty but a pleasure. She would hardly regard Latymer as much of a present.

They were at the lodge gates. An old woman opened them, bobbed a curtsey, recognised Romilly, and bobbed another with an audible squawk of surprise. They bowled through the park, crossed a bridge spanning an ornamental canal, and drew up before the honey-coloured façade of Stretton Priors.

Partridge, the butler, had the door open before they had alighted. He was too well trained to squawk, and contrived to look as though his master had just returned after an hour's airing.

'How d'ye do, Partridge? I am come home, you see. Is all well here?'

'Very well, thank you, sir.'

28

'Here is Mr. Latymer come with me. You had better get a room ready and all that sort of thing. Where is my mother?'

She should have been in the hall already, fluttering and exclaiming. Partridge, in a tone of apology, explained that Madam was from home.

'She's dining out?'

'No, sir. She has gone to Hereford, to Mrs. Sykes, for a fortnight, and taken all the young ladies with her.'

Mrs. Sykes was Sophy, Romilly's second sister. When he heard the news he burst out laughing, and turned to Latymer.

'We might as well have stayed with Scrutty. Here's another bachelor's hall.'

He awoke next morning in excellent spirits. This was so unusual with him that he put it down at first to the fact that he had not been obliged to drink too much, the night before, or to lose money at play. Then it struck him that Stretton Priors might be a very agreeable place could he always have it completely to himself.

For a fortnight he would not be obliged to play the central part in an intricate pattern, devised and ordained long before he was born. To fly from it had hitherto appeared to be the only course, since he might not alter it by a hairbreadth. He might receive deference, give orders, but he had never thought it possible to escape from the life which his father had led before him. If he lived at Stretton Priors at all he must take his place on the Bench, confer pompously with Giles, visit the local bumpkins, and eat his dinner at four o'clock.

Now, sipping his morning chocolate, he asked himself why these plagues should be obligatory. After some reflection he decided to make a list of important reforms, immediately to be set on foot. To head such a document with the word *Object* was in itself stimulating: he often thought that he might be a happy man could he but find a satisfactory *object*.

A French cook. (Supper last night abominable.)
Dine at six o'clock.

Water closets. Tell Partridge I'll have no jordans
in the sideboard.

Throw out pictures. Replace with better.

Library?

Cellars? Probably adequate.

These pleasing projects could only occupy him as long
as he was able to fancy that his ladies had gone to Hereford for ever. Their return within a fortnight was not
propitious to his Object. His mother's conversation
would ruin any meal, even though it were dressed by a
French cook. He could not inflict it upon the kind of
company which he meant eventually to discover and
collect, in place of local bumpkins who might continue
to demand jordans in the sideboard. The wives of these
bumpkins were his mother's oldest aquaintance: she
might, with justice, refuse to drop them.

What, he wondered, did other men do with their female
relations? Scrutty had a mother and a sister or two who
had fled to Bath rather than share a roof with the Seraglio.
But Scrutty was no model for elegant seclusion. Other
men seemed to put up with this nuisance until they
married, when the problem was solved by some convenient
dower house.

There was such a house on the Brandon property,
which had stood empty since the death of his grandmother. He remembered it as a very pleasant place. For
a party of ladies no house could be more suitable than
Corston. It stood on a river bank, opposite a fine wooded
hill. Established there they could entertain whom they
pleased. They could, besides, take the present cook with

them. There need be no painful dismissals. They could take any servants they chose, so long as they left Partridge. Corston would answer perfectly if suggested in some way which could not possibly hurt their feelings.

He thought that he had better inspect it immediately. According to his father it afforded 'the prettiest peep' in all Severnshire. The river there ran very smooth and clear; it reflected every leaf on the wooded hill opposite. If one crossed the bridge, there was the house, dreaming upside down against the clouds. It had always looked more beautiful, that house in the river, than any real house could hope to be. He and Jenny, as children, had devised some curious legends concerning it and the person who lived in it. They had a name for it which they had got from some old book belonging to Dr. Newbolt. This name now escaped Romilly's memory, but the mythical owner had been, he thought, called Lord Carn. These memories, however, must be dismissed if he was to revisit Corston. Fear of them had kept him away for ten years. He rang the bell for his boots.

The penalties of good nature were brought home to him when no Markham answered the bell. After a very long delay a hobbledehoy appeared who disclaimed all knowledge of boots.

'Find out!' snapped Romilly. 'And tell them I want a horse. Two horses. Stay! Take my compliments to Mr. Latymer and ask if he would choose to ride with me this morning.'

The creature gaped and vanished. Romilly looked about for his clothes which must have been unpacked and put away by some demented devil. He was still hunting for a shirt when the half-wit returned, breathing heavily:

'Your boots is a-bringing, sir. And Mr. Partridge

says for to say the other gentleman have et enough breakfast for six, these three hours gone, and we don't none of
us know where he be now.'

'What d'ye call yourself?' asked Romilly, amused in
spite of his vexation.

'George, so please your honour.'

'I should have said what's your service?'

'Second-man-on-approval, so please your honour.'

'The devil you are! What's become of . . . of . . . the
other fellow . . .?'

'William is gone with the ladies, sir.'

Partridge here appeared with the boots, swept George
out of the room and helped Romilly to dress. He explained
that this lubberly fellow was cousin to Mrs. Flinders, the
housekeeper, who had begged Madam to give him a trial.
He was new to the work and would have been kept out of
sight, had William not gone to Hereford. Romilly had
forgotten old Flinders and her innumerable cousins. They
could all go to Corston, he thought, as Partridge knelt to
put on his boots. A clean sweep. I'll have decent people
about me.

When asked whether all the horses had also gone to
Hereford, Partridge became regretful and apologetic.
Not much in the way of a mount, he admitted, could be
produced for his master that morning. Romilly enquired
sarcastically after the cook, and learnt that she had gone to
Bristol. Some underling called Dolly Skeate had produced
that abominable supper.

'Mrs. Flinders? Where's she? At John o' Groats?'

'No, sir. She and the maids are taking the opportunity
to clean the library.'

'What? D'ye mean to say I can't sit in my library?
Upon my word, it has all been very ill managed. When

I come home I don't expect to find half my servants gone off and half my rooms unfit for use.'

Partridge bowed his head, accepting the reproof, attended his master downstairs, and saw him onto one of the errand horses.

This contrast between the real and the imagined return amused Romilly, although he kept up a scowl. It served him very well to have a grievance. As he rode off he delivered a neat ultimatum to the apologies which his mother would be obliged to offer on her return.

'My dear ma'am, why should you not visit Sophy whenever you please? But you must admit that these upheavals won't do if I am to be living in my own house. I can't be left with no horses, no cook, and nobody to clean my boots. Yet it would be a melancholy thing if my return were to restrict your freedom. Were I married, you would, of course, enjoy all the advantages of your own establishment. . . .'

Things could hardly have fallen out better. This neglect was far more propitious to his Object than any anxious attempts to please and content him.

Occupied with these reflections, he rode on towards the rise in the ground separating Stretton from the river valley. Here, where the track led through a plantation, he began to take some notice of his surroundings. There had been, he perceived, a loss of brightness in the day, a dimming of the sunshine. His nose now protested against an acrid smell. The air was full of smoke. Ahead he could see great clouds of it, inky black, drifting through the slender trees. Then he was in the midst of it. This was no heath fire! It was not wood smoke.

With a slight shift in the wind it veered aside. He could see the plantation ride again and noticed that all the

eastward sides of the trees were slightly blackened. Then
the dense cloud poured down on him once more, so that
he could scarcely see a yard ahead. He was half choking
when, with the next wind shift, he saw the track leading
out of the trees and up over Corston Common. The great
wall of blackness rolled away on his left. Now he rode
in sunshine, but even here the grass and bushes had a
scorched smutty look.

Cranton! The explanation burst on him. This was a
Saturday, when they burned coarse salt in the kilns,
leaving the ovens to cool over Sunday. His mother often
complained of the smoke as a great evil, although it
seldom blew as far as Stretton.

Hopes of Corston began to decline when he remembered
its situation, so close to Cranton's. A Saturday there
would be unendurable. With mounting anxiety he
reached the top of the rise and went a little way down a
rutted lane. He knew exactly when he should first catch
sight of the house. They had ridden over there so often
in the old days; he, Jenny, her brothers, Charles and Frank,
his sisters, Charlotte and Sophy, a party of children in
the care of an elderly groom. Down this lane they went
to Corston. The rest would raid the famous strawberry
beds. He and Jenny would run across the footbridge to
look at the house among the clouds.

Here was the turn in the lane where one could look
over a gate. He drew rein and looked. The blackened
house was still there, rotting away beside a river which
could never reflect anything, so thick it ran with scum and
clay deposit from the pottery above. He stared long
enough to know that everything down there, the weedy
lawns, the young green foliage, the mellow walls, now
bore the same squalid smear. Then he turned his horse

and rode away. So much for Corston! He had, he knew, been a little afraid of seeing it again, but he had never dreamt that nobody would ever see it again.

Ten years rolled away, as the black smoke rolled when the wind shifted, leaving him defenceless against pain. He might be feeling his loss for the first time. It drove like a keen pure blade into some part of him which he had hitherto contrived to protect.

She had never been a beauty. She was too tall, her face was too long, she had no complexion, and her dark hair could seldom be kept in curl. Yet there had been a time when the handsomest women in the country looked insipid beside her. They were all determined to please him, all hoping that he would fall in love with them. She never altered. She said what was in her mind, and that mind was completely congenial to him. She had been, still was in memory, superior beyond comparison to any other woman.

With what exquisite tranquillity could he go down a dance with her! He knew himself to be the target of so many smiles, the object of so much conscious flattery, and exulted in his secret immunity. Only once, for a week or so, had his heart wandered. A very lovely girl came to visit a neighbouring family. She had all the enhanced interest of a complete stranger. His head had been a little turned until he chanced to overhear her scolding her maid and felt that a wasp might make as good a wife. Only with Jenny could a man hope to be safe from shocks of that kind.

The celebration of his twenty-first birthday was to culminate in a great ball. It was then that he meant to announce his choice to an astonished world. She had fallen in with the plan, just as she had shared his choice of Corston as the only house in which they could possibly live. They had but one mind between them until that unspeakable day when she faced him, dressed all in black save for an apron as white as her face, and insisted that everything was now quite changed. It was a wintry day, very soon after her mother's death. There had been a heavy frost, he remembered, on the day that they had buried poor Mrs. Newbolt.

Again the familiar pall of resentment rolled over him, numbing his grief. The past was the past. Nothing could recall it. He must make as much of the present as he could. He had an Object. Every day should see some step forward in the transformation of Stretton Priors. As soon as he got home he would give orders that dinner must, in future, be served at six o'clock.

On second thoughts he decided, for Latymer's sake, to postpone this particular reform for twenty-four hours. Poor Latymer, expecting to eat at four, might grow confoundedly hungry if kept waiting till six. But the more elegant timetable should certainly be ordained for tomorrow.

3

AT four o'clock, therefore, they dined. Romilly came to the conclusion that Dolly Skeate must be a descendant of Mme de Brinvilliers, the celebrated poisoner. Latymer, however, swallowed all that was set before him with the greatest satisfaction. It appeared that he had been fishing all day.

'And when I came back,' he said, 'I made the acquaintance of a very pretty girl.'

'You've lost no time! Pray where did you find her?'

'Playing the pianoforte in your drawing room.'

'*Here?*'

'I heard her as I came in and wondered who it could be. When I had changed my dress I ventured to peep in, and there she was, hard at it. As lovely a girl as ever I saw.'

'But who is she?'

'A Miss Newbolt. The daughter of the Parson here.'

'Good God!'

'Your mother told her to come here whenever she likes to practise her crotchets and quavers. But you must know her?'

'To be sure I do. And you think her . . . handsome?'

'Anybody must think so. On the tall side, of course, and not one of these rosy girls. Something pale. Don't you admire her, then?'

'I've not seen her for a long time. Go on!'

'I introduced myself and begged her to continue, which she refused to do. She said she must be going home, so I walked with her across the park.'

'Did she know that I . . . that we were here?'

'To be sure she did. We talked about you on all the walk. She's wild with curiosity to see you, and asked a great many questions, most of which I couldn't answer.'

'What sort of questions?'

'Your habits. Your tastes. The books you read. I fancy she might be a trifle bookish and poetical. But there's no harm in that if a girl is pretty.'

Romilly was stunned. If this was true the change in Corston could be nothing to the change in Jenny. The indelicacy of such an intrusion, forcing herself into the house although she knew him to be there, would once have been impossible to her. She knew his tastes. She knew what books he read. Or had that been a delusion? Had she been no more than a posturing cheat, like all the rest? Or had she sunk to this after breaking with him? Despite his resentment he had been, in his own way, faithful to her for ten years. He had always thought of her as superior. Must he now learn to despise her?

'I could only tell her,' said Latymer, 'that you would be at church tomorrow.'

'And why did you tell her that?'

'You will, won't you?'

A moment's reflection forced Romilly to agree. Not to be seen at church on a Sunday morning would be eccentric. He would, however, break with the family tradition in one respect. He would not walk up the path to the porch between lines of bowing and curtsying yokels, who waited until the party from the Priors had made its entrance.

Next morning he took Latymer across the park to a small gate giving access to a lane behind the church. Thence, by another small gate, they slipped into a secluded corner of the church-yard, close to the hedge which divided it from the Parsonage garden.

'We'll wait here,' he said, 'until the bells have stopped.'

'I caught sight of quite a mob on t'other side of the church,' said Latymer. 'I believe they are waiting to see you.'

'I daresay. Come behind this great yew. I don't care to be seen.'

The ringers were doing their best to celebrate Squire's return. The bells brawled beneath the summer sky. Romilly and Latymer hid behind the yew tree, while two sparrows mated negligently on a flat tombstone at their feet. Latymer began to laugh.

'Gulls!' he said. 'We were all lined up once to receive some Admiral that was coming aboard. Stiff to attention, you know, round a square of white deck left clear for my lord's party. And two gulls knew no better than to . . .'

He broke off. There were voices behind the Parsonage hedge.

'Ladies in the offing,' he muttered.

Two women hurried into the church-yard, unaware of the lurkers behind the tree. The elder went on. The younger paused for a moment to put on her gloves. Romilly felt an instant's dizziness. It was Jenny!

It was not Jenny! Here was the long face, but with a symmetry in the lines of cheek and chin which made it strikingly lovely. The pale skin had a transparent freshness, like the petal of a flower. The dark hair curled snugly under a flat straw hat. There was a suppleness and grace about the tall figure of which he had no recollection.

40

This was not Jenny. This was the beauty which she had missed, as he now saw, by a very narrow margin.

As she stood, fitting every crease of the glove over her slender hand, an enormous silence fell upon the world. The bells had stopped. Into it a voice broke (*Jenny's voice!*) calling:

'Venetia!'

'Coming!' replied the beauty, as she moved forward and vanished from their sight.

'The bells have stopped,' said Latymer.

'But that is not . . . she is not . . .'

'We shall be late. I'm going.'

Latymer started on and Romilly followed. Venetia? So like! So unlike! A sister? Had she a sister?

By the time that they reached the church door he remembered that she had. Ten years ago the Parsonage nursery held a mob of little creatures with whom he had no dealings. He had come to remember them all as boys, but one might have been a girl. Seven years old then? Now seventeen? And Jenny, he reminded himself, must be thirty. He and she were of an age. Thirty! Then that other . . . that old . . .

The disappointed mob was now inside the church and upon its knees, repeating the General Confession. The tardy appearance of Squire caused considerable disturbance. For a few seconds the chorus ceased, save for the voice of the clerk bellowing the acknowledgement that: 'We have left *h'un*done those things which we *h'ought* to have done.' The latecomers made their way up the aisle through a battery of staring eyes. Their progress was impeded by an old woman whose office it was to open the pew door for them; she was determined to get there first and ran round them like an efficient sheep dog.

At last they were safely shut into a high walled box round which ran a cushioned bench. It also contained several hassocks, two arm-chairs, a small stove, and a table littered with fans, devotional works, smelling salts and a tin of biscuits. Once inside they were hidden from the rest of the world unless they stood up. They could have played a hand of whist in there and nobody would have been the wiser save Dr. Newbolt, when he mounted his three-decker.

Latymer knelt. Romilly flung himself into an arm-chair. Could that other woman have been Jenny? He had scarcely looked at her — had received an impression of the sort of woman at whom nobody ever looks. But he could make sure when they stood up. The Parsonage pew was just across the aisle. After the Lord's Prayer, he remembered, there would be a passage between Newbolt and clerk, in the course of which everybody would stand up. Latymer would know. Latymer did. He suddenly shot to his feet. Romilly got out of his chair.

Heads, bare heads, wigged heads, and summer bonnets, were appearing above the high walls of all the neighbouring pews. A glance across the aisle, however, was disappointing. Nothing was to be seen save a pale curved cheek under a straw hat, and beyond it a great ugly bonnet which completely concealed the wearer. Both ladies were intent upon their prayer books. Every other eye in the building was fixed unwaveringly upon Squire.

Old Newbolt had not altered at all. His pink face, between white puffs of wig, looked like strawberries and cream. The gloom of the psalm, which he was now reciting, did not appear to have affected his spirits in the least. He beamed upon his flock as he announced that his days were consumed away like smoke, his bones burnt up as it were a firebrand, that he sat alone on the housetops like a sparrow, had eaten ashes, mingled his drink with weeping, and was withered like grass. There never was an old gentleman from whom such statements could be more unlikely. He took the psalms at a great pace, starting a new verse before his clerk had half finished the response. He disliked the metrical versions, so Romilly remembered, and would therefore never allow the psalms for the day to be sung.

This was as well, since the Stretton choir had always been abominable. As a small child, unable to see beyond the walls of the pew, Romilly had believed that a free fight broke out immediately after the third Collect. Jenny, at the same age, had thought so too, as they discovered later, with some amusement. They had not understood that this hullabaloo purported to be music; they thought that angry people were roaring and screaming at one another.

The actual singing might now be a trifle improved, but the accompaniment, a serpent, a fiddle and a small pipe, was as bad as ever. It was a relief to sink out of the general gaze and to lounge at peace, during an optimistic sermon on the infallible effects of Grace.

Here, thought Romilly, pulling one of his mother's fans to pieces, was an old fellow whom one might really believe to be happy. The living was a good one. The Parsonage was handsome and well appointed. Mrs. Newbolt might be dead, and the sons scattered, but two daughters remained to keep their father company. He was fond of his dinner. He liked to entertain. His flock was contented and well behaved. All loved him, from the children whose heads he patted, to the greybeards whom he confidently despatched to a better world. The old boy could not have

43

a thing to plague him save perhaps an occasional reminder that he must soon be taking the same journey himself.

And I don't believe, thought Romilly, that he likes that notion any better than the rest of us. To be shovelled into a dirty hole, under a stone that's mighty convenient for sparrows . . . but he'll die in his bed with all his pious family weeping round him . . . that *is* the Newbolt grave, under that yew tree. I remember it at her mother's . . . It might not be Jenny at all. She might be away, visiting one of the brothers. This might be an aunt, or something of that sort. We must take care to be coming out of this loose box when they leave theirs. Then they must face us.

This manœuvre succeeded, when the Morning Service was over. The beauty came out first. After her came a terrifying, faded, withered creature who had indubitably usurped the name of Jenny Newbolt since, replying to his bow with a slight curtsy, she gave him a brief glance from eyes which he could never forget. Thirty? She looked nearer fifty.

They all walked down the aisle, the rest of the world waiting respectfully until they had passed.

'We must be off,' muttered Romilly to Latymer as soon as they were in the porch, 'if we don't want to spend the morning saying how-d'ye-do to people.'

Upon this both ladies looked at him. From one he got an unmistakable smile of complicity and approval. From the other a glance of startled distress. Between them they fixed his resolve to defy tradition. He might not otherwise have had the courage to walk off without a word of greeting to neighbours and tenants, after so long an absence. It was stimulating to know that one pretty rebel supported him. A hint of protest from the hag settled the matter. At the moment he quite hated her, for

44

she had destroyed a confidence, never fully acknowledged but never relinquished, that he might, if he chose, forgive her sometime, and in the twinkling of an eye abolish the past.

He bowed again and hurried off with Latymer, who asked eagerly, as soon as they were out of earshot, if he did not think Venetia very handsome.

'Oh yes. But I've never seen her since she was out of the nursery. I thought you meant the other one. Her sister.'

'Her sister! No wonder you were surprised. They are alike, of course, but I thought it was the mother.'

'Should you like to see your beauty again? Shall we call at the Parsonage and continue the good work?'

'What good work?'

'Mending your heart, my dear fellow.'

'Hearts don't mend at such a pace. One must allow time for these things. But I should like to see her again.'

Romilly was not sure whether he should like it himself. But a call at the Parsonage was, in any case, the kind of social obligation which even he could not ignore. He could then decide whether the beauty or the hag provided the more painful parody of his lost love.

He strode back to his Object. All his pictures were either to be banished or rehung. Enlisting George and a step-ladder he worked very hard for some hours. By four o'clock he was unpleasantly hungry. But the elegant timetable was now in force. To wait until six would be a penance. He told George to fetch him some bread and cheese.

4

THEY paid their call at the Parsonage next day, taking the more formal approach through the village. At the front gate they encountered a great bonnet — not the bonnet which had concealed Miss Jenny Newbolt's face in church, but a shabbier affair of the same sort, with fewer trimmings and narrower ribbons. She was carrying an enormous basket. When she saw them she halted, smiling politely.

'Good morning!' said Romilly. 'I'm come to repair my sins of yesterday. Allow me to present my friend, Mr. Latymer.'

Latymer bowed. Jenny curtsied, the basket bumping against her shins. When asked whether her father was at home she said, in a flat hasty voice:

'Oh yes. At least . . . no . . . I believe not. I believe he's gone to the mill. But he'll be back quite soon . . .'

Latymer took the basket, which threw her into astonished confusion.

'Oh pray . . . not heavy at all . . . I'm only taking it a little way . . . across the green . . . pray, Mr. Latymer . . .'

'We can take it for you,' said Latymer. 'It's much too heavy.'

'Not at all,' she expostulated, trotting after him. 'Only some broth . . . a few things . . . there's sickness . . . pray don't . . .'

Gentlemen offering to carry baskets did not, it seemed, often come her way. Romilly fell into step on her other side. She used not, he thought, to talk so much or so fast. He hoped it might be a symptom of agitation but feared it was habitual. She was agreeing rapidly with Latymer as to the best diet for the sick poor: he seemed to know a good deal about it.

'Much better take it cooked,' he said. 'They have such scanty means of dressing it.'

'Yes indeed! Often but one kettle for all purposes, and firing is not so plentiful. A good nourishing broth should simmer for several hours.'

'My mother had a famous scheme. She'd start a broth on the fire and then put it in a box full of hay, where it simmered away of its own accord.'

Jenny's exclamation, which had a faint echo of the old eagerness, shook Romilly a little. She questioned Latymer about the hay box as though it had been of the greatest importance, demanding every detail of the process, and declaring that it would be a great boon to poor people. Not only would it save firing: it would set their sole kettle or pot free for other cooking.

'Very few of our women took to it, I believe,' he said. 'They'll do nothing that wasn't done by their grandmothers.'

'They get so much advice,' said Jenny, 'from ladies who have never cooked a potato. They suspect that what we say must be foolish.'

Then, as if remembering her manners, she turned her vague friendly smile upon Romilly and said something about a fringe frame.

'Mrs. Brandon's fringe frame,' she explained. 'We promised to return it on Saturday. But now she's gone

47

to Hereford, and to tell the truth we should be very glad to keep it a little longer. New fringe, you know, for my father's curtains. How long does Mrs. Brandon expect to be away?'

'For a fortnight, I believe.'

'Oh that would be more than . . . in that case I'm sure she won't mind if we keep it a little longer. I hope she's enjoying herself at Hereford. It must be delightful to hear these famous singers from London. And a grand performance of the *Messiah*!'

'I heard nothing about that. Only that they were gone to stay with Sophy. What's all this music?'

'Oh, the Festival in Hereford Cathedral. The girls begged to go, and no wonder! I can imagine nothing more charming. But Mrs. Brandon was against it at first. When she heard that Lady Baddeley was to be there she changed her mind. Oh, here we are! This is the cottage. Thank you so very much, Mr. Latymer. I must confess it is a little heavy. Bottles, you know. I believe that my father might be at home by now.'

She vanished with her basket into a cottage.

'Partridge never told us any of this,' fumed Romilly, as they crossed the green again. 'Lady Baddeley is my eldest sister. She lives in Berkshire, thank God. It makes my flesh creep to know she's as near as Hereford.'

'A very sensible woman, the older Miss Newbolt,' said Latymer. 'Too bad she doesn't go to Hereford too. One can see she's fond of music. Making fringe can't be much fun.'

Romilly thought bitterly that it was her own choice. For ten years he had wondered what she would say, if ever they met again. He had imagined some very unlikely topics but he had never hit on a fringe frame. To have

48

thought it deliberate would have been comforting, but he was obliged to reject that idea. Artifice of any kind must still be utterly foreign to her nature. She was, and always would be, truth itself. To this narrow compass of hay boxes and fringe frames had her mind now dwindled. She had only herself to thank.

Dr. Newbolt was still away, and they were conducted into the Parsonage garden to wait for him. Here they found the beauty, sitting under a tulip tree with a volume of Marivaux. She received them with an assurance remarkable in a Miss of seventeen: Romilly might be the most important young man in the country, but she did not show that she knew it. Her voice was low and distinct, but she spoke a little too slowly, which gave to all her utterances an air of formidable deliberation. After five minutes he set her down as the most artificial creature he had ever met.

What she said was lively and amusing enough, but she had no wish, apparently, to exchange or to communicate ideas, her remarks were like a succession of small physical taps or blows, each designed to provoke a particular emotional response. They were pleasant little taps, but he had a notion that she would use a stiletto rather than make no impression at all. This amused him. It was a game which he had played with many women. Let this chit make him jump if she could!

'This is an excellent opportunity,' she said, after the first civilities were over, 'to tell you something which has been on my mind for ever so long. I think you should know it.'

She paused and he looked attentive.

'You are said to be fond of antiquities.'

'Indeed? Who does me that honour?'

'One of your sisters. I forget which.'

He doubted this, and doubted whether he was expected to believe it.

'I've found one which must be yours,' she explained, 'since it's on your property.'

'What sort of thing? Coins?'

'No, no, nothing of that sort. Since I don't know what it is I can't very well describe it.'

'What does your father think?'

'I've never told him about it. He might think it very wicked and destroy it immediately.'

Latymer, who was new to this game, started violently and repeated '*Wicked?*' in some consternation. Romilly preserved a civil composure.

'A small tablet of lead, with writing scratched on it.'

'In Latin?'

'No. English. But very difficult to make out. First there is a name. Katharine Sewell. Then a list of names. I can't remember them all. The first ones are Hasmodeus, Geroint and Ishtaphar.'

'Those are the names of demons,' said Romilly.

She opened her eyes very wide, but he was sure that she had known this already.

'No! Are they? Then there are these words: "That the person shall banish away from this place and countery at my desier. J.Q."'

'And where did you find this object?'

'Do you remember Corston?'

'Yes. You found it there?'

He could not be sure. He had the impression that she was probing and guessed Corston to be a vulnerable spot. Jenny was no longer to be the only person in the world with whom he shared a secret about Corston.

'I went with your sisters last summer to see if any strawberries grow there now. But they are all withered away. The smoke, I suppose. We wandered over the house. I went into one of the garrets; it must have been a servant's bedchamber, and I noticed that a floorboard was loose. Some whim prompted me to pull it up. This object was underneath.'

'And where is it now?'

'Still there, so far as I know. I put the board back and left it there.'

'What an odd thing!'

'I thought it odd. And since then I've remembered that there's a cross-roads near Corston that the country people call Sewell's Cross. You know it?'

'Oh yes. They say a suicide is buried there.'

'The old women hereabouts have it that she was a servant at Corston in Queen Anne's day. She fell into a melancholy and made away with herself, nobody knew why.'

'Served her right for meddling with spells,' said Latymer, who did not like this story.

'Oh, but she was the victim,' exclaimed Venetia. 'It was J.Q. who put it secretly in her bed-chamber. And it was Katharine Sewell who "banished away".'

'If I had found it,' declared Latymer, 'I should have thrown it in the river.'

'It might float,' murmured Venetia.

Romilly jumped, in spite of himself. A sudden, inexplicable shiver ran over his body. For a few seconds the warm sunshine lighted some pictured scene from which he was excluded.

'Whatever it may be,' said Latymer, 'it's associated with malice and ill will. That's always wicked.'

'Should you,' she asked Romilly, 'call it an antiquity?'

'Not exactly. These relics of our rude forefathers don't deserve such a respectable name. But I'll look for it sometime when I'm at Corston.'

He rose as he spoke for Jenny had come out of the house and was scuttling towards them as though on some kind of errand. But it appeared that she merely intended to join them and to chaperone Venetia. They then all sat down again.

Their bench was not very convenient for social intercourse. It was circular, running right round the tree trunk. Three could sit there talking together. Four could not, since those at the end of the row pretty well had their backs to one another. They were obliged to converse in pairs. Jenny bombarded Latymer with all the questions commonly asked of a sailor. She seemed to have developed the catechising vein often adopted by shy women who find it difficult to sustain a conversation.

Venetia, by silence, invited Romilly to introduce a topic and he asked if there were many balls in the neighbourhood. She said that there were scarcely any.

'We have no men, you see, save one family — the Freemans, they are five brothers, but it's possible to grow tired of dancing with the Freemans. Now that we have you and Mr. Latymer your sisters must give a ball as soon as they come home. For all our sakes, Mr. Brandon, pray stay for it. Don't go back to London without dancing with any of us.'

'I'm not going back to London.'

'So everyone says. But I fear you will, in the end. You are reputed to be so very fond of pictures, and at the Priors you must continually be looking at a prodigiously long horse who hangs over your dining-room sideboard. He must spoil your dinner horribly.'

'The Brandon Arabian? I mean to remove him.'

'Impossible. He was your grandfather's horse. I'm sure no horse was ever so long. The painter put an extra leaf in him, like a dining-room table.'

'I think of throwing him into the canal.'

'Never! You'll never get him off that wall.'

Romilly had already failed to get him off that wall. George declared him to be too heavy, and they were waiting for William's return from Hereford.

'And how many ships are there in a squadron?' demanded Jenny, who was giving Latymer a heavy time of it.

'But I hope you'll promote some of your pictures,' said Venetia. 'In one of the bedchambers, the yellow room, you have a charming landscape. Tall trees and fountains and sunlight.'

'How our tastes agree!' exclaimed Romilly. 'I mean to put it in place of my poor long horse, if it don't turn out to be too small. Have you any idea of the painter?'

'Oh, I know nothing about pictures. I've been nowhere and seen nothing, you know. But I like it.'

'I must compliment you for doing so.'

'It reminds me of one I saw in a great house near Bath, to which we were taken when I was at school. It was something the same. The painter was Fragonard.'

'Fragonard!' cried Romilly, becoming genuinely enthusiastic. 'Exactly! That's my guess too. You must have a very keen eye. As to the history of this picture I know nothing. I must try to find out. But I went to Paris for a short time, during the Peace, after Amiens. And I saw there a great Fragonard . . . trees, fountains, sunlight . . . I believe that mine is a sketch for it. . . .'

At this point the quartet on the bench was broken up by the appearance of Dr. Newbolt, overflowing with welcome. The two girls were dismissed and the visitors driven indoors to the study.

This was a darkish room, smelling of books, the light obscured by a large cedar too close to the window. Romilly, looking round it, remembered a ceremonial visit paid on the eve of his Confirmation. He had come here in great trepidation, because his father insisted that it was the thing, but unable to guess what might be expected of him. Old Newbolt had behaved like a gentleman. He gave his young caller a glass of wine and discussed dry fly fishing. At the very end of the visit he said hastily:

'And tomorrow? Eh? I'm sure you feel as you ought. You are to be done first. Bow to the Bishop immediately upon rising, remember! Then the other children will perhaps follow your example.'

Glasses of wine were offered now. Nor was conversation difficult, for their host undertook the whole of it. He told them why Buonaparte was certain to lose the war, why dairymaids never caught the smallpox, and why Cranton burnt salt in his kilns on a Saturday.

'But we don't suffer much from the smoke over here. They're a ruffianly-looking lot Cranton has working for him; but he keeps them so hard at it they've no time to get into mischief. They cause us less trouble than we feared when first they came. And his wares are pretty enough. Venetia was for buying one of his dinner sets. But we scarcely need it now that we are such a small party. All the boys gone, you know. Frank is with the East India Company. Charles is a banker. Harry is at the Bar, and Stephen has taken orders. I have only

Venetia left, nor can I hope to keep her for ever. I must give her up some day, no doubt. Nor shall I grumble when the time comes, though I shall miss her sadly. She will be the last to go. I shall then be quite alone, save for Jenny. . . .'

When he pauses for breath, if he ever does, thought Romilly, I shall jump up and go. We must have been here an hour.

He suddenly remembered another visit to this room. Jenny, long, long ago, had brought him there on tiptoe to show him the passage about Lord Carn. He looked over at the corner where they had found the old book and spelled over the text, for it had been early in their reading days. He wondered if it was there still.

'You used,' he said suddenly, 'to have an old travel book . . .'

'Ah yes!' exclaimed the doctor. 'A great treasure. But I've lost it. A most vexatious thing. I never had the original. I made a copy in my own hand once from a folio, and got it printed. A whimsical thing to do, perhaps. And now, it's a shocking story . . .'

A servant mercifully appeared with the news that the horse doctor had called to see to the mare. Excusing himself, Dr. Newbolt bustled off, and his visitors could escape without having to hear the shocking story.

5

O N Tuesday Latymer offered to lend a hand with the pictures. Amongst them they got the Brandon Arabian down from his wall and propped him against the dining-room fireplace. Upon hearing from George that a-many big old pictures did be laying up in the attics, Romilly had them all brought down. By dinner time every chair in the house had a picture propped against its back, and all felt that much had been accomplished.

On Wednesday they rode to the other side of the county, in order to escape from the sight of what they had done. Returning just before five o'clock they were struck by something altered in the aspect of the house as they trotted up the drive. It looked less empty and somnolent. This impression was confirmed by the sight of the stable-yard, full of carriages, horses and servants. Mrs. Brandon, Bet, Amabel, Ellen, the governess, William, the coachman, a groom, and two maids, had suddenly come home. They had, moreover, brought with them Lady Baddeley, three of her children, and four of her servants.

'What in the world can they mean by it?' fumed Romilly. 'People should not turn up like this without warning.'

He strode out of the yard in a fine rage, followed by Latymer who was trying not to laugh. Between the

stables and the house they met Ellen, grown out of all
knowledge, a blooming young creature of fifteen.

'Rom!' she exclaimed. 'Thank heaven you are come.
We are all so hungry and Partridge won't let us have
any dinner until six o'clock.'

She had no business to call him Rom. Even Charlotte
and Sophy had ceased to do that. He said severely that
he had not expected them home so soon.

'And we had not expected you at all!'

Latymer gave a smothered guffaw, at which she burst
out laughing. Romilly crossly introduced them, and
demanded the meaning of this invasion.

'Sophy's children have got the scarlet fever. Since
we have not had it Mama thought we had better come
away, and Charlotte came with us, because she was
staying with Sophy too.'

'Charlotte has a house of her own.'

'She's afraid of the infection for little Creighton. He's
so delicate. She left him behind in Berkshire. If the
others have taken the fever it will be safe for him if they
have it here.'

'In my house!'

'How could we know that you were in it? Poor Mama!
She was moaning and bewailing on all the way home at
the pother there would be, with Mrs. Edwardes gone to
Bristol and Flinders in the midst of spring-cleaning. She
said we should get no dinner. Nor have we. Is it true
that we are always to dine at six?'

'I dine at that hour. I gave no orders as to schoolroom meals.'

'But we all of us, always, dine with Mama,' protested
Ellen.

'Not when I am at home. Come, Latymer. . . .'

57

'Has Mr. Latymer had the scarlet fever?'

'Yes,' gulped Latymer.

'Then he is safe. But not you, Rom. Mama says you never had it. I daresay you will catch it from us. We may sicken at any time: Amabel was very unwell coming home.'

'Where is my mother?' demanded Romilly.

'Walking about looking for a chair to sit on. There seem to be pictures . . .'

Romilly stormed into the house. His mother was in the drawing-room, walking up and down with a plate of bread and butter. She, at any rate, showed some contrition.

'Oh, my dearest Romilly! Could anything be more unlucky! Five days! I'm afraid you must have been very . . . and you brought a friend with you! Friday evening! And we went off on Friday morning, little knowing. It so happened that there was this delightful . . . the girls were wild to go and Sophy quite pressed us and Charlotte was to be there too . . . Music Festival at Hereford. And they say you brought no servant!'

'I should have managed pretty well,' said Romilly, returning her kiss, 'if you had left me a cook.'

'Ay, that's the worst of it. Poor Dolly Skeate! Yet at the time it seemed an excellent . . . poor Edwardes was so anxious to go to Bristol. Her daughter, you know, lying in with a first child. That partly decided me. . . .'

She paused to take a bite of bread and butter, giving Romilly time to suggest that these mishaps must never recur.

'Oh, no. As for the pictures! I never gave orders. Flinders must have run mad. But George and William are hard at work putting them back again. They have got the horse up, and several more. They might as well, you know, since we are not to dine till . . . so here you see me eating bread and butter! To tell the truth we have none of us ate anything since breakfast, save for some wine and cake we had in the carriage with us.'

She paused to take another bite.

'My dear ma'am . . .'

It was an excellent opportunity for a first hint of the benefit to be derived from separate establishments. But he was frustrated by Charlotte who now walked in, greeted him casually, and turned her back on him whilst complaining that Latymer had got the room she had designed for her children.

'I think he had better be moved to the North room.'

'I think not,' said Romilly. 'This is my house, you know, and my friend . . .'

'Yes, my love,' cried the flustered Mrs. Brandon. 'We can't very well ask Romilly's friend to . . .'

'He has been asked. He's moving his clothes now and Ellen is helping him.'

'Give orders in your own house, Charlotte. . . .'

'If they take the fever they must be near me. We should in that case be forced to stay here for a good many weeks.'

She had always treated him with very little deference, and had encouraged the others to do so. Now, having married a baronet, she was worse than ever.

He stalked out of the room. The house was full of bumping, banging doors, maids calling from room to room, and children bawling. In the corridor upstairs he collided with the governess who carried a sinister-looking basin from Amabel's room. Bet poked a fat red face round a door. She grinned at him, vanished, and announced to somebody behind her that 'His Lordship is in a tantrum'.

Dinner, which was not served until a quarter to seven, suggested that this crisis had completely overpowered Dolly Skeate. Partridge and William waited, with gloomy faces, as if ashamed of the dishes they handed. Mrs. Brandon, at the head of the table, sent terrified glances of apology to Romilly at the foot of it. Amabel, still indisposed, remained upstairs in the care of the governess. Conversation was carried on by Charlotte, Bet, Ellen and Latymer.

'If they should take the fever,' said Charlotte, 'I doubt if Patty can manage. Is there a nurse to be got in the village?'

'You could send for Jenny Newbolt,' suggested Bet. 'She's a capital nurse.'

'Oh yes. I'd forgotten her. It's strange how one does.'

'Very little to remember,' said Bet. 'A pair of hands. A pair of feet. That's the sum total of Jenny Newbolt.'

'I should feel perfectly easy if she would . . . but would she sleep here? Could her father spare her?'

'He could spare her for ever so long as he has his doting piece . . . oh, by the way, Mama, did you give Venetia leave to come and play on our instrument whenever she pleases?'

'I . . . I don't remember,' stammered Mrs. Brandon, aware that anything she might have done would probably turn out to be wrong.

'Flinders says she walked in here one morning, as cool as a cucumber, and sat playing for hours.'

'I expect Amabel told her to come,' put in Ellen. 'They are great friends nowadays.'

'I don't approve,' said Charlotte. 'She'll make Amabel as idle as she is herself. We all know that Venetia spent five years at boarding school and came home with nothing to show for it.'

'Except,' suggested Romilly, 'a remarkably good French accent.'

There was a startled silence. For the first time his ladies began to wonder what he might have been up to since Friday. Their faces fell.

'You called at the Parsonage?' suggested Mrs. Brandon.

'Naturally.'

'And talked French with Venetia?' cried Charlotte.

'We discussed Marivaux.'

'Oh indeed! At her age she should not have read Marivaux.'

'I daresay she never has,' put in Bet. 'She can talk as if she had read everything.'

'A marked accomplishment,' said Romilly. 'So many girls talk as though they had read nothing.'

Even Charlotte was silenced.

The meal ended in an unusually long wait for some course which never appeared. Dolly Skeate must have thrown up the sponge. Mrs. Brandon, meeting the eye of Partridge and receiving no encouragement to linger, jumped up and fled, followed by her daughters. Romilly, pushing the port decanter towards Latymer, apologised for the dinner.

'But I like all this,' said Latymer. 'A large family party . . . children in the house . . . though I hope they won't take the fever, and it's a shame she should miss her frolic.'

'Who?'

'Your youngest sister. Why did you tell me she is only twelve years old?'

'She was when I saw her last.'

They did not stay over their wine for long. Latymer
went off to join the ladies by whom he was cordially
received. Ellen, whilst helping him to move his clothes,
had learnt something of his situation and had told the
others. Their hearts were softened. His cheerful good
nature in so readily changing his quarters had already won
their approval. Even Charlotte smiled at him when she
heard that he had offered to take her little boy on a fishing
frolic.

The master of the house fled from it, having no refuge
within, no place where he might be safe from bustle and
hostility.

The evening was beautiful. He sauntered down to the
bridge and watched the fading sunset clouds reflected
in the canal. Behind him a moon, near full, rose over the
woods towards Corston. He perceived that his situation
was ridiculous and that he had only himself to thank for
that. Why should his return to Stretton Priors be welcomed by anybody? His absence had suited them much
better. After ten years they had come to regard the house
as their own, where they might do as they liked.

He could not avoid the suspicion that some of the
neglect with which he had been treated arose from
deliberate policy. Charlotte and Bet meant to exasperate
him into departure, and his mother had not the character
to withstand them. In that case he must expect further
assaults upon his consequence and comfort, which he must
parry as best he might until Charlotte went back to
Berkshire. She must do so eventually, and then they
should know who was master.

The moon sailed clear of the woods, turning the park
to black and silver. There were lights in most of the

windows of Stretton Priors where they were all, doubtless, still making Bedlam, stampeding from room to room and squalling at one another.

'Good evening!' said a voice at his elbow. 'It's a long time since we've seen the old house look so lively.'

'Dr. Newbolt! Ah . . . Good evening.'

'I've come to bring my daughter home. It's too late for her to be walking alone across the park.'

'Is she there?'

'She ran up to see Amabel. Ah, here she comes.'

A tall white figure had emerged from the shadows and was floating towards them.

'I never knew you were here!' exclaimed Romilly. 'When did you come?'

'Oh, I've been upstairs these two hours with Amabel. We heard that she came home very unwell, so I ran up to see how she does.'

'You must be careful. There's some risk of . . .'

'Fever? It's nothing of that sort. Travelling always makes her unwell.'

'You were in the house, then, when we were at dinner?'

'Yes. When I come to see Amabel I slip in by the side door and up the back stairs. Do you think you should have guessed?'

'Perhaps,' he murmured. 'By the pricking in my thumbs.'

She heard him and laughed. They all three began to walk down the drive, and Romilly complained that there should be nightingales.

'They've all been scared away by the fever,' she suggested.

Dr. Newbolt asserted that nobody need be alarmed by scarlet fever. Romilly was impressed by his confidence and

63

almost believed it, but then remembered that the old boy would say the same thing about smallpox, gangrene, or a broken neck.

'Not this fever,' agreed Venetia. 'Amabel assures me that Sophy's children have nothing worse than nettle-rash.'

'*What?*' cried Romilly.

'Ssh! Listen!'

From a lonely tree came four long sweet notes and a fine roulade. If Newbolt now quotes Milton, thought Romilly, I shall knock him over the head.

'Most musical, most melancholy bird,' quoted Dr. Newbolt with diabolic promptitude. 'But I see nothing melancholy in a nightingale. There is often some confusion between the melancholy and the solemn.'

He discoursed on this theme at some length, without much taxing the attention of his companions. Romilly was convinced that Venetia knew the Brandon Arabian to be back again on his wall, that she was laughing at him silently, and that she despised him for not turning Charlotte and her brats out of the house.

He, for his part, was planning to turn the tables very neatly. Venetia might, he began to think, supply him with an effective threat, should his ladies remain insubordinate. Nothing would alarm them more than the notion that he might be going to marry her. Nor would it be difficult to suggest such a possibility. She was undeniably a beauty; any man must admire her. But it was obvious that they all disliked her, with the possible exception of Amabel whose particular friendships seldom lasted longer than a fortnight. They would compound for anything, they would dine at midnight, sooner than see Venetia set over them as mistress of the house. He had already made a start; he had frightened them by praising her at dinner. He would continue to frighten them. He would call every day at the Parsonage. By marked and public attentions to Venetia he would bring them all, even Charlotte, to heel.

At the gate into the lane he parted from the talkative old gentleman, made his bow to the silent young lady, and walked back to the field of battle. A dozen nightingales were now in full chorus, tossing long cadenzas from tree to tree. There were too many, and they made too much noise, for which he was not sorry since one alone might have evoked too sharp a reminder of former days. He was able to continue his plan of attack. That Venetia deserved no consideration was a signal advantage. Had she been a candid, artless young creature he must have had scruples: his attentions would arouse expectations in the whole neighbourhood, and when they came to nothing her situation would be unenviable. The world would say that she had failed to catch him. She might even fall in love with him. But he need fear nothing of that sort in Venetia's case. She was a sly little schemer, and he doubted very much whether she had a heart to lose. She would be mortified, but that would do her no harm.

I should think twice about it, he decided, if it was in the least likely that she ever helps Jenny to carry a heavy basket. Or even takes a turn at the fringe frame. I believe she does nothing all day save sit with a book in her hand, some book which she ought not to be reading and has not, in fact, read. But I must take care that she don't creep in by the side door and deposit some horrid little antiquity under the floorboards in my bed-chamber. Those who cross her might, I fancy, be liable to 'banish away'.

PART II
THE VICTIMS

I

I<small>N ONE</small> of the Parsonage garrets lay old Tibbie, formerly autocrat of the Newbolt nurseries, now palsied and senile. The servants, who were supposed to tend her, did so grudgingly. Four times a year Dr. Newbolt climbed the stairs to take Tibbie the Sacrament. No other member of the family went there except Jenny, who ascended daily in order to make sure that Tibbie was kept clean and comfortable, to persuade her to swallow her pap, and to listen to her grievances. Of these the most persistent was irritation at Jenny's own folly.

'You might have been lady at the Priors these ten years if you hadn't gone and ruinated yourself by keeping that promise to your poor Mama. Nobody a penny the better for it. Not that you should have refused the poor dear aught in her last dying moments. I never says that. If she went easier for hearing you swear you'd stay by your poor desolate Papa, you was right to swear it. But once she was gone . . .'

Jenny no longer troubled to reply that a promise is a promise, whether given to the living or to the dead. Had she known how to refuse that plea, gasped out in such mortal agony, she would have refused. Since she had not been able to do so there was no more to be said. She scarcely listened to Tibbie and heard her now very much as she heard the squeak of the pump handle in the yard below; it was one of the morning noises at the Parsonage.

She merely waited for another opportunity to insert a spoonful of pap into Tibbie's mouth.

'She never gave you your place. The boys was her pride, and Venetia was her dote. She never made no favourite of you. She didn't care to believe young Squire was sweet on you. "'Tis nothing," she'd say. "A mere boy's fancy. He'll never wed Jenny. He can take his pick of the handsomest women in the country, and she's no beauty. Which is a comfort to me," she'd say, "for I daresay she'll never get an offer, and her father will need her when I'm gone. He could never endure to be solitary and if Jenny an't by he'll put some stepmother over my lambs." Which is true enough. But it would have been all to one a better thing if your Papa had married again. He'd have thought more of his new lady than he ever has of you. And who's to say she would have been unkind to the children? What's this spoon? This an't my spoon. What's become of my good silver spoon?'

'Oh, Tibbie, don't you remember? You had me put it away in your chest after it had been taken down to the kitchen by mistake one day.'

'In my chest? You're sure?' asked Tibbie suspiciously.

'You saw me put it there yourself.'

'I don't like to eat from a pewter spoon. I want my own spoon, that's solid silver, that I had from my Granny.'

'Tibbie, your pap will get cold if I look for it now.'

'I must make sure 'tis still there. Wait now till I give you the key.'

When Tibbie failed to find the key under her pillow she declared that some thief must have stolen it and demanded the constables until Jenny found it in her Bible box.

'Some unaccountable person must have put it there.'

'Won't you take your pap before I unpack the chest?'

70

'Not with a pewter spoon. A labouring person's kind of spoon. Not fit for a gentleman's house. There's no stepmother could have bested Venetia. That might have been seen, if your Mama had cared to see it. And who's the better for it all? You've had no thanks for it. They think nothing of you. You're but a servant that asks no wages. Who's the gainer?'

Jenny, unpacking the magpie hoard in the chest, might have said that Tibbie was a gainer, since nobody else would have put up with her. But the kind of reflection likely to prompt such a reply was a danger which Jenny avoided as much as possible. Thought of any kind was certain to be painful, as she had long ago discovered. She fled from it. Bet Brandon had not been far wrong when she said that a pair of feet and a pair of hands provided the sum total of Jenny Newbolt. To keep both in continual action was a measure of defence against thought. There was always, luckily, a great deal to be done.

'Young Squire, he flew off in a rage. No wonder! Never knew a check in his life before; it took him all in a drawback. What's that you have there?'

'Your Paisley shawl.'

'Give it me here. I'm feared of the moth.'

As Jenny brought the shawl the church bell tolled a single doleful:

BONG!

'Eh!' cried Tibbie in high glee. 'Who's passing?'

'I think it must be Goody Tompkins.'

'You don't say so! Mary Ann Tompkins! I never thought she'd be taken so young. Why wan't I told?'

She had been told, but recent events made no impression on her.

71

'What ailed her?'

Jenny was about to say old age, since Goody Tompkins had been over eighty, but changed this to a chill on the lungs.

'Eh dear! Well! She was a flimsy kind of creature all her life.'

BONG!

'Here's your spoon, Tibbie.'

'What's that?'

'Your silver spoon. Now you can eat your pap.'

'Nay, I did but want to be sure it was there. Put it away now, careful, with the rest of my things.'

'But your pap!'

BONG!

'Did Parson take her the Sacrament all according?'

'Yes. He was there on Thursday.'

'Ah well . . . we must hope she's gone to a better world. Mary Ann! She was married a Shrove Tuesday and lay in before Easter. That child got a good taste of his mammy's wedding cake, as the common people say. But loose talk of that sort I won't have in my nursery. Little pitchers has long ears.'

Tibbie's pap was the first item in the morning programme. Dinner must then be ordered. Jenny was still in the kitchen, talking to the cook, when a maid called Kitty, whose services were pretty well monopolised by Venetia, came running in breathless from some errand to the Priors. Venetia had contrived to send her there every day, since Romilly's return, upon one excuse or another, and she always brought back a budget full of news. On the first Sunday she had been able to tell them that Squire

72

would never choose to dine before six o'clock, that he had tried, and failed, to take down that great old horse in the dining-room, and that he was making a rare to-do over a picture called Froggysomething, in the yellow room. It was Jenny who had deduced Fragonard, and had stuck to it that there was such a painter; she had seen a Fragonard once in some great house to which she had been taken when at school. This episode had been transferred to Venetia's schooldays by Monday, when Romilly and Latymer called, and Fragonard stood high in her esteem, which Jenny might have thought a little odd had she not decided that it was always wiser not to think at all.

What must be done next? she asked herself as she went from the kitchen. What task demanded hands and feet? The poultry yard? Her father's newspaper? Had they brought it from the village? She looked into the study to make sure, He had it, but produced another errand for her.

'Tomorrow is Sacrament Sunday,' he said, 'and there may be an unusually large party from the Priors. They will, of course, communicate before the rest of the congregation. Should they all stay, they will make up a complete row. The chancel is so narrow. As a rule you and Venetia make up a row with the Brandons. In this case you must wait. The Arbuthnots come next. Should you not have a word with Mrs. Arbuthnot, explaining that you girls will join them after the Priors party have communicated? They are very worthy people, the Arbuthnots, but they might not like to come forward until you have returned, since you go, as a general rule, before them. Yet it would be a sad waste of time for all of us if you girls were to be making a row by yourselves, eh?'

73

'I'll call on Mrs. Arbuthnot now, and explain it.'

'Pray do. Of course there is no knowing how many of the Brandons . . . it will be a tight fit if Romilly and the other young man were to take it into their heads . . . but that's not very likely.'

Communion once a month, in Dr. Newbolt's opinion, might do very well for women. Men who turned up more than four times a year were liable to brand themselves as enthusiasts.

'Mr. Latymer,' said Jenny, 'might stay. He goes back to sea on Thursday, and may not get another opportunity for a long time.'

'Oh ay! In his case it would be a wise precaution, poor fellow. At least in time of war.'

Off into the village went Jenny, at the rapid pace, almost a trot, which had become habitual to her. As she went she turned her blank faded face from side to side, lest she might pass acquaintance without duly smiling at them.

Mrs. Arbuthnot was a widow with two daughters. All three were in the parlour when Jenny appeared, although the two girls generally beat a retreat on such an occasion. Today, however, they were agog for news, since Romilly's attentions to Venetia were the talk of the village. They heard with some impatience of the problems created by a narrow chancel on Sacrament Sunday, and answered as briefly as possible Jenny's conscientious questions concerning their health, their garden, and their relations. These enquiries represented Jenny's idea of social intercourse; to make them and to get answers was a duty, not a pleasure; their general effect was often to make her victims feel that even their own affairs were singularly dull.

74

The Victims

At last Louisa Arbuthnot rebelled.

'Do you think that Mr. Brandon will run off from church tomorrow, as he did last Sunday, without saying anything to anybody?'

'What could he have meant by it?' asked Maria. 'Does he know, I wonder, how much offence he has given?'

Jenny flushed unbecomingly, as she always did when something disapproving or critical was said in company. She hastened to find excuses for the offender. Last Sunday, she suggested, Mr. Brandon might have found it difficult to remember his neighbours' names, since he had been away for so long. Tomorrow he would have his mother to remind him. Perhaps he had been waiting for that.

'You are the only family to have seen anything of him,' suggested Louisa. 'He called again at the Parsonage yesterday, so we heard.'

'Yes,' said Jenny.

'What is he like? You must remember him before he went away. Is he much altered?'

'No more than one would expect, in ten years.'

'What does he talk about?' pressed Louisa.

Jenny tried to remember.

'I was not there all the time,' she said, upon which the three exchanged glances. 'I think . . . he talked about Mount Vesuvius.'

She rose to take her leave, since her fifteen minutes were up, and left them to fruitless speculation. Had she been extremely discreet, or could she be so simple as to have observed nothing, conjectured nothing? The world, they all agreed, held not a better creature than poor Jenny Newbolt. She would do anything for anybody. She had never been heard to say an unkind thing. But she put one out of spirits.

Her next task was to visit a cottage where a new-born child must be inspected. To hear Romilly discussed caused her no agitation. His return meant nothing to her. This stranger had no more in common with the lover, vanished ten years before, than she had with the girl who had lost him. Both were gone for ever. He had dissolved immediately, when he refused to listen, refused to forgive, refused to wait until the children at the Parsonage were old enough to do without her. She had never doubted that he would, in the end, agree that she had no choice. He might be angry and jealous that she should recognise any claims save his own. But he would, she was sure, ultimately allow that she could not refuse a promise demanded in such circumstances, nor fail to keep it, once given. When it became clear that he expected her to break her word, he vanished. She had never ceased to love and mourn him, but as a creature inhabiting some other world, now lost.

Her cottage errand was soon despatched. Mother and child were doing well. With poor people she was popular. She only came amongst them to make herself useful. She never advised them to be contented with their lot, nor did she preach at them, or scold them, as most ladies did. They could not suppose her own lot to be very delightful, which gave them a fellow feeling for her.

Her path from the cottage led across a common and here her pace slackened. She fell into a fitful stroll and at length sat down upon a log. Pulling off her bonnet, she flung it on to the withered bluebells at her feet. For a while she stared fixedly at the ground. Then her face changed. She looked about her like a person awakening from sleep in a happy place, smiling with a relaxed simplicity, as very young children smile. She had indeed taken a trip backwards over twenty years and more; she was safe for a while in a region well on the further side of calamity.

This respite was granted to her occasionally. Her existence otherwise would have been intolerable, solitary and comfortless as it was. She could not have found the energy to continue in it. Tibbie had told no more than the truth. Nobody valued her, save as she might serve them. Nobody cared to hear what she might say. She had no money and no hope of liberty; when she left Stretton Courtenay, presumably upon her father's death, it would be to live, dependent and useful, with one of her brothers. She lived as a nun, but unsupported by knowing herself to be a member of a community. Yet her mother had not been mistaken when, the dire promise given, she whispered that God would send the strength to keep it. He had done so. He sent her these hours of release, thus sparing her the guilt, the shame, of vices, drink, laudanum, the hysteria, spite, and malice, to which she might otherwise have been driven. Suffering had withered her body and dulled her mind, but her soul had been preserved from evil.

This mysterious euphoria had first come to her soon after her mother's death, when she had indeed believed herself to be lost. Fits of uncontrollable weeping and sobbing took her. By no effort could she check them although everybody scolded her, pointing out that her father's loss was infinitely more severe and that she should endeavour to comfort him. She grew very thin and began to cough. A physician, brought from Severnton, talked of a decline. A change of scene and sea air were recommended.

She was despatched on a visit to an old school friend at Clifton. After two months she was thinner than ever. Her father then took her for a ramble to the Cheddar Gorge, a wonder of nature which he had always wished to visit. It was interesting and awful, but Jenny still wept, perhaps because it provided no sea air.

Thence they went to explore the Somerset coast and took a fancy to the great wooded cliffs east of Countisbury where the streams of Exmoor plunge through narrow gullies into the sea. Wandering in one of them Dr. Newbolt fell into conversation with a stranger, a lodger at a farm nearby, and Jenny went on down the ravine by herself. Sometimes the stream vanished beneath curved and twisted rocks, although she could always hear it falling, falling, towards the black sea floor far below.

Presently she could go no further. She sat down and fell into so violent a fit of weeping that she thought her lungs must burst. The spasm relaxed suddenly. After a period of complete exhaustion she looked about her, and discovered that she was in Xamdu.

This was a name which she and Romilly had formerly given to the house in the river at Corston. But it had an earlier association. The first Xamdu had been suggested by a screen belonging to Romilly's grandmother. A landscape with no distances went up and up from the bottom to the top. Nothing was near. Nothing was far away. All objects were the same size. A belt of clouds lay across it at intervals, and then it continued as before. Trees writhed and rocks curved over a stream falling for ever down to a flat grey sea where people in round hats were fishing in a boat like a basket. Other people wandered in the gorge or sat cross-legged looking pensively at the stream.

78

In those early days she and Romilly had tried to believe it possible that they might, by some spell or charm, get into that place. Corston itself only became Xamdu when they grew old enough to relinquish that first wild hope. But now, without effort, she was there.

A loud hallooing from above assailed her ears but she took no notice of it at all. She sat where she was. She was in Xamdu and her father, shouting for her, was on some other planet. Presently he came scrambling down with his new friend, looking as near to being angry as his habitual good humour allowed. When he saw Jenny, however, his expression altered. Both men looked at her very oddly. She rose to greet them, announcing placidly that this was Xamdu.

Hastily they agreed. Of course it was Xamdu, but would she not come back with them to the carriage? Between them they pushed and pulled her up the steep slope. She saw that they thought her mad and began to explain what she meant, describing the screen at Corston. The stranger exclaimed that he knew exactly what she meant. He had seen such landscapes himself in Eastern screens. But why did she call it Xamdu?

'Ah!' said her father, 'she has got that name from a book of mine. A great favourite. I am seldom without it; I have it in the carriage with me up above.'

He explained about the copy he had made from an old folio, and how a printer fellow in Severnton had made a very neat affair of it. The stranger expressed a strong desire to read it. Since they were now on a clear path they left Jenny to her own devices and, all the way back to the carriage, discussed strange landscapes, alligator holes in North Carolina, and wonders of that sort. When they reached the carriage her father pressed the loan of his book upon the other, promising to call for it later. They parted with the greatest cordiality.

As soon as they had driven off, however, Jenny got the severest scolding she had ever heard her father give to anyone. Her bellowing and bawling, down in that ravine, he said, must have been audible from Minehead to Lynmouth. The stranger had evidently believed her to be mad. She must promise never so to expose herself again. And that had been the last of her wailing fits.

Dr. Newbolt put down the improvement of her spirits to the sea air and took her on a very rough trip to Lundy Island in order to increase the dose. But he never got back his book. He called on his new acquaintance once, taking with him all the particulars and terms of the Severnton printer, and thought that the fellow seemed to be a good deal less cordial, although he had expressly asked for these particulars. He made no effort to conceal the fact that the visit was unwelcome and a bore, and stared so glassily that at last he drove the intruder away.

Shortly afterward the Newbolts got news of an accident to one of the children at the Parsonage and set off for home in a hurry, forgetting the book until they had gone too far to return for it. At the time this oversight gave Dr. Newbolt little uneasiness, even though he had forgotten the borrower's name. His own bookplate was on the title page and he was confident that his property would be returned in due course. It never was — an omission which deeply shocked him. He would seldom allow that there could be any really wicked people in the world but he now came to the conclusion that there must be one — the scoundrel who had got his book.

Jenny continued to enjoy, at intervals, all the ecstasy of Xamdu. She came to recognise it, not as a place but as a state of being into which she passed occasionally. On these excursions time signified little and facts were altered. All was reshaped and re-interpreted according to another kind of perception, suddenly bestowed and as suddenly withdrawn. She felt it to be a better and a truer world and she still gave to it the name devised by herself and Romilly for a fancied existence which they had hoped to discover. They had been right so to hope. Its felicities were absolute. A green leaf could satisfy her completely by being simply itself — a green leaf. There was no gulf between promise and fulfilment, and every object perceived carried its own clear meaning.

She also came to realise that these moments of exaltation must be concealed. The values, judgements, and motives then prevailing with her would have been thought inexcusably singular by everybody in Stretton Courtenay. Her good was not their good, her necessities not theirs. They would say that nobody had any business to feel as she did until they had gone to Heaven and that, even there, one ought to feel differently. For her own comfort, and for the comfort of those about her, she kept her heretical notions to herself.

Since those about her seldom paid her any attention she had been pretty safe until Venetia came home from school. Concealment thereafter became more difficult. Venetia's sharp eyes missed nothing and she soon spied enough to disturb Jenny's security. With no one else did Venetia give rein to her temper. When displeased she generally preserved her composure, although she saw to it that the culprit was paid out sooner or later. Only with Jenny did she fail in self-command, as though the close proximity of a creature so unlike herself was more than she could bear. An odd kind of conflict had sprung up between them — all vindictive attack on Venetia's side, and on Jenny's a passive but effective withdrawal.

On one occasion, when irritated because Jenny had forgotten to mend a torn flounce for her, Venetia struck home.

'I should have known better than to expect it. You have been in one of your transports.'

'What . . . what do you mean?'

'You know very well what I mean, although you try to hide it. You depart into the clouds, and must pass an agreeable time there, for you don't answer one, and never know what o'clock it is, and behave generally as though you were half-witted.'

'I might sometimes be a little absent . . .' said Jenny, beginning to tremble.

'Completely absent!'

'But this flounce . . . I think it's the first time I ever . . .'

'Oh, I don't say that your . . . *absences* . . . cause anybody much inconvenience. We get on very well without you. We ain't so much dependent on you for our comfort as we say we are. But it's the thing to say, you know, about any woman of thirty who has not got a husband: *What would her family do without her?* It's for your own sake you'd better be careful. It doesn't do to be so very eccentric.'

Jenny was in part shielded from this onslaught by the fact that self-consequence, which might have been wounded, had, in her case, long been mortified out of existence. She did not mind attacks upon her vanity; she had none. But she took warning and kept out of Venetia's way when seized by a transport. If possible she invented some errand on the far side of the parish and vanished for a time.

The Victims

She now sat smiling in the wood, looking about her at the clouds and the trees, and listening to the sound of an axe in a distant clearing. She felt herself to be a part of it, as though she were one instrument in some great orchestra.

When she returned to the Parsonage she slipped in by the kitchen door. She put some apples, some lumps of coarse brown sugar, a piece of bacon, some bread and cheese, and a book or two into a large bag. Before slipping out again she told the cook that she must go over to Corston Common and that she might be away for some time.

2

THERE was a farm called Millthorne, above Corston, on the edge of that region which had come to be known as 'the black fields'. Crowther, the farmer, was said to be hard with his people. Giles would have got rid of him, had it not been for the difficulty of finding another tenant. Millthorne lay too near to the smoke, which was thought to damage the crops.

A listless line of women and children were hoeing a field that Saturday. When noon struck from Stretton Church they threw down their hoes and trooped to a shady spot where they had left their dinner. All went save one, who turned and went slowly across the field to a gate on the farther side of it. He had seen Miss Jenny leaning on the gate, watching him, and hoped that she might have brought him something to eat. She was waiting for him under a hedge, on the other side of the gate.

His name was Dickie Cottar and he was nine years old. He lived with his grandmother in a tumbledown cottage belonging to Crowther. Of his mother, who had left the country soon after his birth, nobody had heard news for a long time. Amongst the dozen fathers bestowed upon him by local gossip, one was always mentioned in undertones. Romilly, during the interval between his breach with Jenny and the final quarrel with his father, had taken to keeping very disreputable company. There was, however, some reluctance to believe the child his. Bessie Cottar, at one time barmaid in an alehouse at Slane St. Mary's, a rendezvous frequented by all the young rakes of the neighbourhood, gave herself airs enough without that. The Brandons themselves ignored the story.

For Jenny the child had a strong affinity with her playmate of twenty years back, whom she remembered, perhaps, better than anyone else did. Romilly had been taller and sturdier, he had lived better, but in all else the likeness was astonishing. She had come, in a way, to think of the child as her own. She should have been his mother; she would have been, had she and Romilly married when they planned.

He had been about three years old when she first caught sight of him, peeping at her from under a bed in his grandmother's hovel. That look had taken her back to a very early memory. An infant herself, she had trotted behind her mother on a visit to the Priors. They were taken to a great room where Mrs. Brandon lay in and where a number of tall ladies bent over a cradle containing the new-born Sophy. Jenny had spied a pair of bright eyes looking at her from under the bed flounces; little Romilly had crept there into hiding. She crept in beside him and they lay in that great dark cavern, listening to the ladies talking and waiting for the delightful moment when they should be missed. It had been the first of their joint escapades. She had later been whipped for it. Romilly had not — a distinction which they both thought very natural.

Romilly! she thought, meeting the eyes of the little creature under the cottage bed.

From that time she had taken him under her care. She gave him food, made little shirts for him, and later taught him to read and write. Her visits caused less gossip than might have been expected. Old Mrs. Cottar thought it best to say very little about them to her neighbours. Parson might not like so much notice to be taken of the boy, should he come to hear of it. The food and the shirts were very welcome, since Bessie had never sent home a penny for the child's keep.

Jenny, when Dickie joined her, silently spread out the food upon the grass. There was no need to ask if he was hungry. He was always hungry. He fell upon the food, while she watched him. Presently she asked if he had learnt any new tunes for his fiddle. He shook his head.

'I han't played that this long while.'

'Oh Dickie! What a pity!'

It was a fiddle which she had contrived to get for him, a couple of years earlier, upon learning how much he longed for one. An old man, living close to Corston, had promised to teach him. She had sold a brooch and bought him a little fiddle in Severnton; for a time it had given great delight to both of them. He learnt quickly and showed some talent.

'My Granny, if she hears me play that, she clouts me for wasting time.'

'But a child must have time for play!'

'I'm no child. This will be my last summer at haysel, Master Crowther say.'

'He'll put you to a man's work!'

'He'll put me to no work. He don't want no more men at Millthorne.'

Jenny sighed and picked up the book from the grass, upon which he said, almost angrily:

'I can't stay to read, Miss Jenny. If I'm not back at my hoe with the rest I'll get the stick.'

86

Her look of sorrow made him impatient. For some years they had been close friends but now he felt that he had outgrown her company. He was a man, with a man's cares, of which she understood so little that she did not even ask what he was to do if Crowther had no work for him. His grandmother would not keep a lubberly boy of nine; she had said sometimes, contemptuously, that Miss Jenny was crazy, and he began to believe it. Yet, with a faint contempt for her, he also felt some remorse. She had been very good to him. He relented and took the book from her.

'Maybe I could read a little piece. There's none stirring yet. But I must go back when they do.'

'Yes. Read just a little. It would be such a pity if you were to forget it all. You have taken such pains.'

'It an't much good to the likes of me,' he muttered.

At one time he had taken very great pains, for it had seemed to him that some schooling might help him to look after himself better. He lived in horror of coming upon the parish, for then he might be despatched as an apprentice to the mills in the North. He had once seen a wagonload of such children go by, and he had never forgotten it. There had been a good proportion of idiots amongst them since the parish authorities generally stipulated that a certain quota of idiots must be taken off their hands in return for supplying a cargo of cheap labour.

Fear had spurred his studies, but he also liked reading for its own sake. When doing so he dropped the country accent with which he generally talked, and copied Jenny's voice when reading to him, which she had done for many years. At such moments he not only looked, but sounded, like the lost Romilly.

Opening the book at random he began at the top of the page:

> 'Yea, Truth and Justice then
> Shall down return to men,
> Th' enamelled arras of the rainbow wearing.
> With Mercy set between. . . .'

Jenny, as she listened, sat smiling expectantly at the great white clouds floating lazily across the summer sky, as though, at any moment, they might part to send Truth, Justice and Mercy down to set a sorry world to rights.

To her they were not abstractions, although they dwelt in another place. They were as solid and personal as herself, or Dickie, or any of the people munching bread and cheese on the far side of the field. She knew their faces and could recognise their voices. Truth and Justice might have frightened her had they not been ruled by that appointed companion. Without Truth no facts could be scanned, without Justice no verdict passed. But the last word, she was confident, would for ever rest with Mercy.

3

I KNEW that he was good and religious, thought Ellen triumphantly. I could never love a man who is not.

She and Latymer were the only members of the Priors party to stay for the Sacrament. Mrs. Brandon, Charlotte, and Bet had hurried out with Romilly, determined that, this time, he should greet his neighbours civilly. Rumours of last Sunday's performance had greatly shocked them. The governess, whose soul was apparently at the disposal of her employers, had been ordered to take the children home. Amabel had cried off church on the plea of a headache.

The uneasiness, the antagonisms, which had filled that small enclosure during Morning Service, dissolved as soon as Latymer had shut the pew door on the last of them. All now was security and confidence. The two young creatures knelt in their high walled seclusion, listening to the voice of the unseen Dr. Newbolt, and whispering responses. Latymer thought of the cold little church on the moors at Braythorpe, and of his father's voice, now silent for ever. Ellen thought that her companion had been very nearly perfect before; this proof that he was good and religious removed all possible doubt.

They stayed there for a long while after they should have gone up to the altar. It did not occur to her that he was waiting until she made a move. As the youngest of the Brandons she had never led the way, but had followed where others went. Dr. Newbolt waited for a minute or so, expecting to see the Priors party emerge. Venetia then settled the matter by sailing up the aisle, Jenny and the Arbuthnots in her wake. Others followed. Their slow footsteps echoed through the silent church. Latymer at last whispered:

'Should we not go?'

Ellen jumped up in confusion. They stepped out of their pew into a group of poor people coming up the aisle from the free benches at the back. These had waited until all the Quality had received the Sacrament, and the tardy appearance of a lady and gentleman caused some confusion. Some drew back. Others scurried forward. At the altar rail Ellen found herself separated from Latymer, and felt a stab of disappointment. On her way back, down the chancel, she saw that the intruder had not been one of the Stretton cottagers; she got a glimpse of an unfamiliar face, gaunt and pallid, under an apology for a widow's cap. None of our people, she thought, would have pushed in like that. Nor would they come to church looking so! She is almost in rags!

On emerging from church she saw the stranger again, shuffling off down the village street.

'One of Cranton's people,' commented a good-wife to whom Ellen had just said good morning.

'Oh? I thought they never came to church.'

'Best not, if they can't come decent.'

A shadow of uneasiness fell upon Ellen's sunny mood. Nobody visited Cranton's people. They were not parishioners. They were not tenants. Nobody knew what went on in that black valley. Who cares for them?

she wondered. Poor people need somebody to care for them. Their lot would be too hard else.

This qualm of doubt subsided when Latymer offered her his arm. It was the first time that any gentleman had done so. There were so few of them in her life, and their arms were always laden with more important women. Now she had one all to herself; there was not even an older sister on the other side to monopolise the conversation. She might still be in the schoolroom, she might be wearing a close bonnet, but she had taken a marked step towards maturity. She waited for him to say something, which was unusual with her, since she loved to chatter. But he walked on in silence, rather faster than was necessary. The arm on which she hung grew stiffer and harder, as though some barrier was rising between them.

He was, in fact, struggling with a desire to kiss her, an impulse of which he felt heartily ashamed. Only a scoundrel would entertain such a notion so soon after kneeling with her at the altar. She was too young to be kissed. She was too old to be kissed. He must be more guarded in his conduct. In four days he would be gone, never to see her again or hear of her again, for he doubted whether Brandon would care to keep up the acquaintance. Had she been his sister . . . but he could not help preferring that she should not be his sister. Had she been three years older . . . What if she had? He was too poor, too friendless, to entertain hopes of that sort. He sighed.

Ellen, hearing the sigh, nearly burst into tears. In four days he would be gone to a life of forlorn solitude, away on the sea, with no Mama to write him letters.

'But you have a sister!' she exclaimed.

Startled, he turned to look at her.

'She'll write to you. But not from home. Only from Jamaica. She won't be able to say that the snowdrops are out or that the hay is all in.'

'Yes, yes! That's what one wants from home. News of the garden and the neighbours and the dogs.'

'Is there nobody . . . down in Yorkshire?'

'Nobody now. But I'm luckier than many. Plenty of fellows get no letters at all, not even from a sister in Jamaica.'

'No letters at all? How shocking!'

'They can't read. Their families can't write. They must get a friend to write for them and that's not the same thing. I remember one . . . he brought me a letter he had had, and asked me to read it to him. It was to tell him that his wife was dead, and their first child with her. Some pompous fool had written the letter. It was full of fine phrases . . . melancholy occasion . . . pious resignation . . . the dear remains . . . and so forth. But I don't think he minded it as much as I should have in his shoes.'

'Oh dear! How very sad.'

She pictured the little scene, pitied the poor man, but thought him lucky to be in the same ship with Latymer.

'Should you like it,' she asked suddenly, 'if Mama were to write to you?'

'Oh, I could never think of troubling . . .'

'It would be no trouble to her. She loves writing letters. Especially to people who will answer. She even writes to Romilly, who never answers. I know Stretton is not home. But it's a place in England and you've seen it. You know how it looks, and who all the people are.'

And I should hear of you again! thought Latymer.

'We could tell you all the news. We can tell you if
that wicked man, who has got Dr. Newbolt's book,
repents upon his death bed and sends it back. We can
tell you . . .'

We! We!

'If it would give you pleasure, I'll suggest it to her.'

'Nothing could give me greater pleasure.'

Careful! Something a trifle unguarded about that?

'I mean . . . I should be delighted . . . too kind of
your mother . . . but it would be asking too much. . . .'

'No indeed. Consider what we owe to you! If it
were not for you I daresay we should all be ground down
under the tyrant's heel. Like Europe.'

Latymer, with great complacency, accepted credit for
the entire British Navy. If Mrs. Brandon were to write,
his conscience would be clear. If *we* meant that Ellen
slipped in a note or so, her mother would know of it and
could discourage it if she disapproved. Nor should anybody accuse him of negligence in reply. Such a corres-
pondence might give him an excuse for coming back.
On his next leave . . . preferment . . . prize money
. . . no longer so very ineligible . . . and Ellen would be
older.

His arm grew less stiff. He looked at the distant house
with affection. It was not home. It was more than home,
since it sheltered the dearest creature in the world. Even
had that first home at Braythorpe still existed he might
now be more eager for news of Stretton.

Whatever might lie before him, he was aware of one
great gain. He had been cured of the illusion that a
Miss Mary Baines had broken his heart. She was not, she
never had been, the fancied creature whose image he had
cherished for so long. He thought of her now, a little

apologetically, as 'poor Mary' as though she had been a
deceased acquaintance, remembered with good-will but
without distress.

'You'll want to know how Rom goes on,' continued
Ellen. 'How long do you think he will stay here?'

'I don't know him very well, remember. He seems to
be fond of changing his mind.'

'He never knows what he wants. That's the trouble.
It's very tiresome, having him here, though it's a shame
to say so, poor Rom! Everybody wishes he would go,
even Mama, though she won't own to it. She's so afraid
he will marry Venetia Newbolt.'

'Should you be telling me this?'

'You must have seen as much for yourself.'

'She's very handsome . . . Miss Venetia. And clever,
I imagine?'

Ellen hesitated and then said:

'A lady should never criticise another lady to a gentleman. Especially if she is very handsome. The other
lady, I mean.'

'They do sometimes,' remembered Latymer.

'They'd better not. The gentleman is always likely to
take the side of the handsome lady. You would, I'm
sure.'

He protested rather half-heartedly.

'Female jealousy, you'd think. So it's of no use to tell
you that Venetia is quite horrid. She's completely selfish.
It's all scheming and pretence, whatever she says or does.
Even Amabel is beginning to see it, though she was taken
in for a while, because she's a bit of a schemer herself,
and people of that sort, you know, deceive one another
more easily than they do us. Now . . . say *it!*'

'Female jealousy!'

He jerked her arm so as to give her a little shake. They both laughed.

'But I'm sure Rom knows it. He don't really like her. He pays her attention so as to scare us all into perfect submission.'

'He'd better look sharp then. I fancy the lady knows what she's about, even if he doesn't.'

'I'm not so sure. In some ways she has behaved very stupidly. She was so insolent to Mama yesterday that she gave Charlotte an excuse for ordering her out of the house. She's been told not to come here any more unless she is invited. I don't call that clever, do you? Not if she's really after Rom.'

'Does he know of it?' asked Latymer thoughtfully.

'Oh no. And nobody is going to tell him, naturally.'

'Still . . . if he finds out . . . he's so much inclined to oppose Lady Baddeley, whatever she does . . . might he not . . .?'

'Insist on bringing Venetia back? I suppose he might. And that would be quite a victory for her. Oh dear! You don't suppose that Venetia got herself turned out on purpose? In order to . . .'

'Oh no!' said Latymer. 'I never meant that. But I think Lady Baddeley has played into her hands.'

'It would be just like Venetia to do it on purpose. She's horridly clever. And Rom is so easily . . . he's just the sort of man to marry a very disagreeable woman, quite by mistake. I've often wondered why so many of them do, when they have a large choice of agreeable ones. But I begin to see.'

'Yes,' said Latymer. 'There's nothing in the world safeguards a man's happiness so well as to be quite sure . . . perfectly sure . . . of what he wants.'

Ellen looked at him. Their eyes met. Flushing scarlet he turned his head away to stare, with fixed intensity, at the canal. His arm became quite rigid. Only a scoundrel would exchange glances with a tender young creature in a close bonnet.

4

ROMILLY had intended that morning to grin and to shake hands, on his way out of church, with a grace and affability which should erase all former impressions. He had no wish to distress his mother or to be known through the neighbourhood as a boor. He merely wished to do these things at his own time and in his own way.

Thanks to Charlotte the whole business was conducted in a manner calculated to enrage and humiliate him. She gave him no chance to take the initiative. She and Bet planted themselves half-way down the path, so that he could not possibly get by. Having thus cut off his retreat they beckoned people forward whilst his mother, in frightened undertones, reminded him of their names. It was made plain to the world that his family were forcing him to behave himself.

When, at last, they let him go he flung off to the stables, got a horse, and set off at a gallop towards the Welsh hills. Some time passed before he grew calm enough to remember that there was nothing to be hoped for, in the way of dinner, west of Stretton. The villages were small and the inns wretched. Nobody of any consequence lived in that direction except the Freemans. They would be glad enough to see him, they were always glad to see anybody, but he would have to be civil to them, and some hours must elapse before he could put on a civil face again.

He turned and made for Slane Forest. Gradually his pace slackened as he debated means for getting even with Charlotte. This was no new occupation. They had squabbled in their cradles. Many follies which he now regretted had been provoked by her domineering ways. The fact that she always came off victorious did not, even now, discourage him.

The scarlet fever scare seemed to have subsided, yet she showed no signs of going. He was beginning to doubt whether attentions to Venetia were really the most effective form of attack. His ladies were obviously much alarmed; they knew exactly how often he called at the Parsonage and how long he stayed there. But this very panic might have determined Charlotte to remain, in case they needed support. He must take active steps to render her sojourn uncomfortable whilst giving her no grounds for declaring it necessary. He would drop his visits to the Parsonage but, in future, any order given by Charlotte should be reversed as soon as he heard of it. She should be obliged to ask his leave before taking so much as a donkey chair round the park. If she wanted to visit the greenhouses she must come to him for the key. He would, moreover, support his mother and the girls, whom she bullied abominably, in any gesture of rebellion.

He had ridden far into the forest before he realised that any scheme for dining in Severnton must be given up. It was much too far away. He was growing very hungry, nor was he certain of his direction. The only good road went up the hill by Cranton's pottery. He had entered the forest by a lane several miles to the south of that point. It was a rough track but it seemed to be leading somewhere, since it was clear of weeds and rutted by wheel marks. Sooner or later he might reach a hamlet where he could ask the way.

He went on and let the charm, the silence, of the forest soothe his irritation. He had always loved these trees. They seemed to be so old, as though they had stood there for ever and owned no man as master. Presently he began to laugh a little at himself and Charlotte and the morning's fiasco. She could not stay for ever. Baddeley would want her back, or think that he did: if he did not she would be off in a great bustle to discover why not.

The track plunged downwards. He could smell wood smoke. There must be houses down below, he thought, and then got a glimpse of them. A few cottages clustered at the bottom of a deep ravine. Slane St. Mary's! He remembered it now, though it was not a spot which he cared to remember. But he went on because there was nothing else to do. He would have recognised the lane before had it been in better repair; ten years ago it had looked more like a road. Plenty of roaring company used to clatter down this hill when old Knevett was alive, but nobody was likely to come there now, and the Manor House was deserted. The present owner preferred to live elsewhere, which was not surprising.

Knevett's death had been very horrible, for his creditors had invoked the law to refuse him burial until his debts were paid. All the servants fled, leaving the corpse on the great bed upstairs. When, after some months, matters were settled, it was found that the rats had left very little to bury. Nobody could speak of Slane St. Mary's without a shudder.

There was nothing astir in the village when Romilly came down to it, no evidence of human life save a thread of

99

smoke from a chimney or two. The cottage walls were crumbling, the thatch weedy and broken, and the little gardens full of broken earthenware, ordure and rags. They had always been a brutish lot down there; little better could be expected with such a squire. Nor had they any resident parson. The living was held by an absentee, who sent a curate over occasionally to gabble Divine Service in a dank and empty church.

There had been an inn, by the bridge. It was still there, the Knevett arms hanging crooked by the door, but when he peered through one of the broken windows he saw that it, too, was deserted. He remembered it as a lively sort of thieves' kitchen. The servants of the Quality visiting the Manor House used to carouse there, night after night, along with half the village whores in the county.

The lane went up again to Slane Bredy, over the hill. A few minutes later he passed the gates of the Manor House but did not linger as the whole region smelt abominably of pigs. It was hard to believe that he had, at one time, often turned in at those gates. He had been numbered among Knevett's boon companions who were mostly either old and dirty or young and callow. For that folly he had mainly Charlotte to thank. She had incited his father against him and promoted attempts to choose his acquaintance for him. Slane St. Mary's was forbidden, a by-word, never mentioned without disapproval. Thither therefore he went, so soon as the old man tried to curb his independence. He had, in truth, liked Knevett as little as he had liked Scrutty Phelps, ten years later, but the same perversity drove him to both. The debauchery of Long Bickerton, however, had been elegant, refined, compared with the rustic saturnalia of Slane St. Mary's. Scrutty's guests were drunk every night. Knevett's guests were never sober. Scrutty's Seraglio had at least been introduced to soap and water. The forest nymphs, occasionally summoned from their roost in the ale house, were for ever scratching their heads. It was a short-lived folly. A few months, between his break with Jenny and his departure to London, saw the beginning and end of it.

As he left the place behind he thought of Stretton, and for the first time in his life felt some gratitude to his father, and his father's father, for preserving so fair an inheritance. He could himself take no credit for it but he began to be glad that he had contrived to look like a respectable squire after church that morning. If the women would but refrain from hints and covert reproaches he might, in time, go further. To improve the lot of his people might well become an Object and, once he set about it, he would certainly outshine his stick-in-the-mud forebears. He might study the newest methods of agriculture and come up with suggestions which would startle old Giles. There must be a great deal, in that way, to be done. The thought of it compensated for the fact that he had, as yet, done nothing.

The smell of pigs still hung on the air but grew fainter as he inwardly defended himself. He might so far have done no good in the world but he could not allow that he had done any harm. His folly, idleness and occasional dissipation had hurt nobody. No victims would rise to accuse him at the Last Day. He might, moreover, have been more actively good had he not been so totally out of sympathy with his seniors. He was, at heart, a reformer. To preserve the *status quo*, even though it was pretty tolerable, would never satisfy him: for them it was the whole duty of man. His mind must inevitably run on changes, on improvements. To change anything at Stretton was an unpardonable crime.

Old Newbolt now, he thought, whistling a little tune as he rode, Old Newbolt now . . . an excellent man in his way . . . but never wanted to leave things better than he found them. Content to see that they grow no worse. Shuts his eyes to any alarming evil. Enthusiasm! With him that's another name for lunacy. Now I, by nature, am an enthusiast. That's my trouble . . . in a nutshell. Yes . . . yes . . . education, rank . . . the age . . . bid me flinch at the word, but I'm an enthusiast. Once an Object appeals to me . . . if there had been anyone who entered into my thoughts . . . my feelings . . . no *companion* . . . I have always been very solitary . . . *Oh once I had a kind companion* . . . even now they don't know me. They've not the least idea . . . *Oh go and leave me if you want to! That will never trouble me* . . . Ellen, perhaps, might in time become a companion . . . *a kind companion* . . . I shall take her out of the schoolroom. She shall come with me on these rides. I shall talk to her . . . tell her . . . *and in my grave I'd sooner be.*

Over the noise of his own voice, proclaiming this defence to his inward ear, that word *companion* had been ringing like a descant, chanted in another voice — artless, plaintive and rustic. It figured in the tune that he whistled and had struck up when he saw the inn. Some person there, one of the sluts there, used to sing ballads very prettily. She had been something of a favourite with him on that account, although he could remember nothing else about her. Molly? Betty? What did it signify? She had been no better than the rest, save for a voice which had taken his fancy.

The Victims

Last night when you were sweetly sleeping,
Dreaming in some soft repose,
I, a poor girl broken . . . broken hearted,
Listened to the wind that blows.

The voice faded. His thoughts sank away. The forest
was very silent. Last year's beech mast, still thick on the
track, muffled the sound of his horse. Yet he had an
uneasy notion that he was being watched, subjected to a
vengeful stare from no human eyes, but from the beings
to whom this silent wilderness belonged. He remembered
something read once, a myth of the ancient world, of
dryads, unseen by the traveller, who stared so hard after
he had gone by that he dared not look round. In this
place, if anywhere, such beings might linger on; he understood for the first time why men had been afraid of them.

They stared at him until he came within a mile of Slane
Bredy where he found an inn which provided ham and eggs.
Whilst eating he chatted with the landlord. Very few
people, so the man said, now lived in Slane St. Mary's.
These worked for nobody. They raised pigs on the wasted
Knevett property and talked a lingo which nobody could
understand. Services were no longer held in the church.
They were a heathen lot and cared little for parsons.
Their children, frequently got in incest, were often
fourpence in the shilling and sickly-looking. All those
with a spark of energy or intelligence had moved away;
the rest were dying off and were buried, without ceremony,
in the forest, which was rapidly encroaching upon Squire
Knevett's fields.

'The forest,' explained the man, 'she comes back
amazing quick, once folks are gone. Fight enough we
have here in Bredy against them trees. Stands to reason.

They was here first and they mean to be here last, I reckon.'

This epitaph upon man's effort depressed Romilly. As he rode home he reflected upon the superior wisdom, the tranquil felicity, of those who are content to do nothing at all. Leisure for its own sake was considered by the poor to be the greatest of the privileges enjoyed by their betters. He remembered an old labourer sitting on a bench in the sun by a cottage door, who had explained that he no longer worked because his children supported him and had insisted upon 'making a gentleman' of him. What better occupation could a man have than to ride at ease through the plantations towards Stretton, smelling the sweet scent of hawthorn, listening for the nightingales, observing the warm hues of the summer dusk? I might myself have asked for no more, thought Romilly, if I had some companion. I was not always so solitary.

Of a sudden the twilight was full of her, sharing every mood, every thought, silent when he was silent, sunk in the same reverie, exclaiming when he exclaimed, startled by an identical discovery. Oh come back! Come back! he cried to her. I can't live without you.

A moment later he saw her walking towards him through the trees. He felt no amazement. He drew rein and waited.

The dusk was kind to her, wiping out the changes which had so wrung his heart. The restless, hurried gait was abandoned; she walked slowly, as she used to walk long ago, swinging her bonnet from her hand. He sat very still, scarcely daring to breathe, as she drifted towards him like a phantom from the past. She came very close to him. He could see her face — her smile, pensive and serene, neither young nor old but timeless. Then she went on. She passed him by and vanished into the shadows. She had not seen him there. He began to believe that she would not have heard him, had he called to her. She had not come to him, drawn by his need of her. Some other power now possessed and ruled her; she had but passed him on her way to some other, more abiding, joy. She had left him and his world far behind her, and those outward changes which had formerly shocked him scarcely signified at all compared with this one.

All bitterness against her subsided as he perceived the truth. Having once fully beheld her he could think of her with awe and tenderness as one whose company he had never deserved and might not presume to keep.

He rode soberly home. His mother was alone in the drawing room, looking so forlorn that he suddenly offered to play backgammon with her. He was already aware that this mood of exalted resignation would not last for very long. It would not for ever protect him from Charlotte. He had yet to discover that it might, at a lower pitch, recur and let him in for a good many games of backgammon.

5

THE ragged stranger in church had been a Mrs. Hollins — one of Cranton's people. Dr. Newbolt learnt these facts from his clerk, who always managed to know everything. He observed to his daughters at dinner on Monday that he thought it his duty to visit her, since the black valley was still, presumably, within his parish.

'But my dear sir!' exclaimed Venetia. 'Suppose they should all take to coming to church? There are hundreds of them. You could never possibly visit them all.'

'In that very unlikely event, I should be forced to engage a curate.'

'Which we have been begging you to do for years. As it is, you exert yourself more than any other clergyman I ever heard of.'

'In the meantime this poor creature is undoubtedly one of my flock.'

'I hope she'll be grateful. Her appearance was discouraging.'

'A word or two of advice might alter that. They are very rough people down there, you know. I shall ride over one morning this week.'

Jenny now interposed to point out that nobody working for Cranton would be at home in the morning, adding that the hours at the pottery were from six-thirty in the morning until seven in the evening, on a short day.

'Jenny knows everything,' laughed Venetia. 'You don't need a clerk, Papa.'

'Mrs. Tawney told me,' said Jenny. 'She had thought of sending Peter to work there, but she thought those hours too long for a child.'

'They would never force children to work for those hours,' asserted her father. 'It would be inhumane.'

'She's a foolish creature, Mrs. Tawney,' said Venetia. 'The boy must work, you know, and all apprentices work hard.'

'Goody Cottar, over at Millthorne,' said Dr. Newbolt, 'thinks of putting that grandchild of hers to work at Cranton's.'

'What?' exclaimed Jenny. 'Dickie? Dickie Cottar?'

'Ay, that's the lad. Old enough to keep himself now, and Crowther has no work for him.'

'Not at Cranton's! Not at Cranton's!'

'It's not a pleasant place, to be sure. But he'll work under shelter, which is more than many do. I expect he'll bless himself, in the winter, to be working snugly by those great warm ovens.'

'No,' said Jenny again. 'He must not.'

'That's for his grandmother to say. This is very good mutton, my dear. May I trouble you for another slice?'

It was Jenny's business to carve, but she made no move to do so. She sat quite still, as though thunderstruck.

'Dickie Cottar,' said Venetia, 'has always been a great favourite with Jenny, I believe.'

'He's very clever,' said Jenny, finding her tongue again. 'He can read and write. I think it might kill him to work in that place, I do indeed.'

'Shall I carve a slice for you, Papa?'

'If you will, my dear, since Jenny seems to think more of young Cottar than of our dinners.'

After a few minutes' silence Dr. Newbolt added kindly:

'One is sorry to see these little creatures put to work so early. But we must remember, Jenny, that these things are ordained by Divine Providence. Some are born high. Others humble. Some to labour. Others to rule. It is the duty of every man to be content with his lot, with the station in life to which God has called him.'

Jenny burst into noisy tears.

'I don't believe it,' she sobbed. 'I don't believe God ever called any child to die of potter's rot for two and sixpence a week. It's we who say that such things have to be. We could change them. I'm sure we could, if we wished. I don't believe that God is pleased at all. I daresay He's in the greatest of a rage about it.'

Her tone and manner so much startled them that they scarcely listened to her words. All her anxious diffidence was gone. She not only used the terms, she spoke in the high defiant voice, of an angry child. Venetia began to laugh, upon which Jenny jumped up, slapped her face, and ran, bawling, out of the room.

'This is no laughing matter,' said Dr. Newbolt rather sternly. 'I'm afraid she must be very unwell.'

Venetia looked grave and agreed. Poor Jenny! She had been quite unlike herself. This was not the only instance of eccentricity which she had been obliged to observe. She mentioned others.

'She exerts herself too much, always going about amongst the poor people. Might not a change of air and scene . . .?'

He thought that it might. It was, he remembered, ten

years since Jenny had spent a single night away from Stretton, and he had a notion that, on some former occasion, she had made him uneasy and had been cured by a change of air. They agreed that she must be despatched, as soon as possible, upon a long visit to Charles or Stephen, whose wives could scarcely object, since Jenny would be certain to make herself useful, wherever she went.

'I had meant to speak to you of this before,' said Venetia. 'I thought you should know. It's such a very great pity that she should take any particular notice of *this* boy, or give him notions above his station.'

Her father frowned, and she managed to blush. He had always refused to listen to the stories about Dickie's birth; it was, he thought, indelicate of her to refer to them. But, though blushing, she persisted.

'Just now we are a good deal more intimate with the Brandons than we ever were before. Amabel and I are very great friends. And ... Mr. Brandon ... comes here so much. ...'

Half smiling he took her point, although he said nothing. Trouble over Dickie Cottar might be unpropitious. There was no doubt that Romilly admired Venetia. All the Newbolts would rejoice if it came to a match.

'Jenny will forget about it, once she is away,' said Venetia. 'Until she goes we can set her mind at rest by promising that the boy shall not be sent to Cranton's.'

'We can't promise, my love, and break our word.'

'No indeed, sir. In any case, Cranton's is too near. But I believe they send children from here, sometimes, to the cotton spinners, down in the North.'

'No children from Stretton,' he said quickly. 'I don't like that business at all. The parishes binding the children can procure a settlement for them at the end of forty days, and so be rid of them for ever. In that case the poor children would not have a single human being to protect them, supposing they should be misused. If Dickie is ill-treated at Cranton's he can always come to me.'

'Very true, sir.'

With a lighter heart, convinced that matters could easily be smoothed over, he left her and went to his study. He found Jenny waiting for him. She had dried her tears but she still spoke at a higher pitch than usual and she looked at him steadily, without ducking her head and glancing sideways. All this disconcerted him.

'Papa, I'm very sorry for my conduct at dinner. It was wrong. But Dickie must not be sent to Cranton's. Many of the children die there very soon.'

'You mean the potter's rot. They don't get that now. They have a machine, I believe, for grinding the flints.'

'The children put to be scrubbers are all as white as millers with the flint dust, Mrs. Tawney says, and breathe it into their lungs. And there is poison from the lead . . .'

'Don't talk nonsense. If there were any truth in this, no parents would allow their children to work there.'

'Mrs. Tawney refused. But . . . my dearest father . . . I have a request. . . . You told me, some weeks ago, that I might engage an extra servant here, some boy for the knives and boots and to run errands. . . .'

He checked her with a raised hand.

'No, my dear! Impossible. Not young Cottar. Any other child in the parish . . . you must know what I mean?'

She nodded sadly.

'I don't like to raise such a point. If we should take particular notice of the child, just now, there would be talk. That would be most unfortunate at a moment when we all hope that Romilly has come home to settle. Those old stories should be quite forgotten. Personally, I never . . .'

He was about to say that he never had believed a word of it, but could not, since he was a truthful man. He had not believed it originally; for the past couple of years he had never caught sight of Dickie without regretting the particular cast of his eyes, his nose, and his mouth.

'Poor Bessie Cottar, you know, was a woman of very bad character. But I would be less resolute, since you feel so strongly, if we hadn't Venetia's comfort to consider. Have you thought of that?'

'Oh yes,' said Jenny simply. 'She means to marry Romilly.'

This was not the way to put it. He frowned.

'It's too early to . . . but you must have observed . . . he pays her a great deal of . . . if anything comes of it we must all be delighted. The sort of match she deserves.'

'Do you think that the Brandons will be delighted?'

'They are all very fond of her. Want of fortune could be the only . . . but there I think we shall surprise them. You've all been scolding me for keeping no curate. In that, and in many other ways, I've had Venetia in mind, ever since your dear mother's death.'

'I know that, sir.'

'I've been a careful man. A saving man. With a good living, thrift, and your mother's fortune kept intact, I have been able to lay by a good deal. When Venetia marries she will have twenty thousand pounds!'

Jenny knew so little of money that the sum meant nothing to her. She supposed it was all that he had got, but she could not guess what impression it might make on the Brandons.

'She can marry whom she pleases!' declared the old man joyfully. 'But this . . . this is better than anything we could have hoped. If it should be so! She won't be torn from us. She'll live no more than a mile away. We shall see her every day.'

'I know that would make you happy, Papa.'

'You too! Our beloved child! Such a marriage would make me perfectly easy in my mind, not only on her account but on yours. I shall have her near me while I live. When I die she can give an agreeable home to you.'

'You mean . . . live . . . at the Priors . . . with . . . with . . .'

'Where else? This marriage provides for you both. At my death you must have gone to one of the boys. But the Priors will be an even pleasanter home for you. A sister is always dearer than a sister-in-law.'

The injustice to herself in this scarcely struck Jenny. Since she had been so improvident as to catch no husband she must expect to pay for it. She knew that penury and dependence lay in wait for most old maids and that many more women might remain unmarried could they hope that some provision would be made for them other than a dowry. Nor did she know how to fight for herself.

Of what she could be capable, when fighting for another, she now discovered fully for the first time. After a short pause she heard herself say:

'Then you won't help poor Dickie?'

'I don't think I should be justified in doing anything.'

'Then I must write to Romilly.'

'*What?*'

'I must tell him what is happening to a child, on his own land. I don't suppose Romilly knows of Dickie's existence. He had gone away to London before the child

was born and I'm sure none of the Brandons will have
mentioned it. And he's not been back here long enough,
or met enough people, to have heard of it anywhere else.
He's not ungenerous. Not a monster. When he knows
that his very existence injures poor Dickie, he'll take steps
to prevent it.'

'Have you gone mad? The indelicacy . . . a young
woman . . . a lady . . . writing to a gentleman. . . .'

'I'm not young. And if Romilly cared for delicacy he
and Bessie Cottar would never have met.'

'Venetia . . . have you no regard . . .'

'She can fend for herself. A child can't.'

'I forbid you to do it. I solemnly forbid . . . promise
now that you will never do such a wicked thing!'

'I don't think it's wicked, if there is no other way.'

'I shall never forgive you . . . never speak to you . . .
I shall . . . I shall . . .'

What should he do? Disown her? Turn her out of
the house? Deprive her of all indulgences such as . . .
such as . . . at the moment he could not remember what
indulgences in particular were accorded to Jenny. There
must be a long list of them, since he knew himself to be
a singularly indulgent parent.

'Go!' he said at last. 'Go upstairs. Go to bed.'

To dismiss her as though she had been a naughty child
was all that he felt able to do; she was looking un-
commonly like one.

She went upstairs, but not to bed. The contest had
sharpened her wits. She was always powerless against
Venetia but this was chiefly because she had made it her
maxim never to think if thought could be avoided. She
never defended herself by foreseeing or avoiding possible
onslaughts; to forestall them would have entailed too

much reflection. On Dickie's behalf, however, she was willing to think. She saw at once that some effort would be made to get her out of the way. Communication with Romilly would be put out of her power. She had better, therefore, write to him at once. The letter need not immediately be sent to him, but she must have it composed, written, addressed and sealed, in case of an emergency.

To count fifty was, she had discovered, a soothing exercise in moments of agitation. She did so now. Then, smiling, sure of herself, she sat down at her desk and took up her pen. Venetia, seeing her just then, would have diagnosed a transport. Without hesitation she began:

Dear Romilly,

Somebody should tell you about Dickie Cottar. I fear that nobody will. He is a boy of nine years old. He lives on your land. And he has no friend. His mother was Bessie Cottar. She used to be a barmaid in Slane St Mary's. She went off, nobody knows where, soon after Dickie was born. He was reared by his grandmother, who lives on Corston Common.

At nine years old, you know, poor children are expected to keep themselves. Dickie cannot get work from any of your people. He will, therefore, be obliged to go to Cranton's. Have you ever been to Cranton's? Before you say: 'Why should he not?' pray go there and observe the children who work there. Many of them die. But not all suffer, while they live, as Dickie will. He's a clever child. He can read and write. He will feel it more. Observe the children and don't say: 'They look as though they were dull-witted creatures. They are probably fit for nothing better.' Think of yourself at that age.

He will be lucky if he dies soon. He will but live to be a maimed and tortured creature. Or else he will run away, thirsting for freedom, and fall in with wild, lawless people, and end on the gallows. I think it is a longing for freedom which oftenest makes people break the laws. It is wrong to break laws, but we must never have the minds of slaves. God ordained our need for liberty.

He has a remarkably good ear for music. I believe he might do well if apprenticed to a musical instrument maker. I would do this for him, if I had any money.

Nobody will speak of this to you because it is said, amongst the village people, that Dickie is your son. To take notice of him might, it is thought, offend your family. But for this story my father would, I believe, give him employment here. People are so much concerned with a possible injury to you that they forget a certain injury to Dickie. Yet which of you suffers most from such a story? It's a cruelty which you would set right, I am sure, if you knew of it.

I have a schoolfriend who is a relation of the Broadwood family. I can find out from her what it would cost to apprentice Dickie to such work as that. I could let you know the cost. If you think you can afford the sum, you can give it to me, and I will arrange it all. Will you let me know what you think of this scheme?

It would be cant to say that these measures will make Dickie perfectly happy. He's too clever to be happy. Nor can we, in this world, do anything to secure happiness, for ourselves or for others. But we must challenge misery, even though it is always too strong for us. We must still defy it, and cry out against it.

Ever your affectionate friend
JENNY NEWBOLT.

This letter she folded, sealed, addressed, and hid in a place where Venetia would never find it.

Next morning, the transport over, she wondered at her own boldness although she could not repent of it. If she were now to attempt such a task she would most certainly waste a week in miserable indecision over the very first words: 'Dear Mr. Brandon'? 'Dear Sir'? 'Sir'?

She would be confused by the stranger now at Stretton Priors and would torment herself with fears lest he should fail to respond. Such an appeal could only be penned at one of those moments when Truth, Justice, and Mercy sat solidly amongst the clouds and when she knew, without the least shadow of doubt, that he was not changed — that he would recognise a command from those voices and instantly obey.

PART III

THE ENTHUSIAST

I

No appeal to Romilly, on Dickie's behalf, proved to be necessary. Jenny's letter was left in its hiding place. Within a week Dickie was established as knife-and-boot-boy at the Parsonage.

Dr. Newbolt decided to pay his pastoral call on the disreputable Mrs. Hollins at a late hour on Wednesday, when he might hope to find her at home. He did not mean to stay above fifteen or twenty minutes, and expected to be back again before dark.

People were trooping home from work when he came to the scattered collection of hovels in the black valley. They stared at him, but answered more civilly than he expected when he asked for the house. How he found it he could not afterwards remember, but he must have found it, and found a post to which he could hitch his horse. During this visit he received a shock which was to change the whole course of his life, shatter his well-being and drive him, in the end, to a hard death in Cold Harbour. It had, at first, the effect of some physical injury or blow. He was, for some time afterwards, dazed and confused. Some incidents were erased completely from his memory.

Daylight was gone when he emerged from a strange aching fog to find himself sitting in a small room lit by a rush candle. He was asking, rather testily:

'Poised? What does she mean by poised?'

119

'She means kicked, sir.'

Mrs. Hollins spoke in a hoarse whisper. She had formerly worked as a scrubber and the flint dust had affected her throat.

Poised? he thought. I never heard the expression. North-country perhaps. Could there be a connection with *pieds*? I must make enquiries. What's the French for kicked?

He leant forward to examine huge bruises on a skinny little back.

'I was feared for her ribs, sir. But I believe they're sound.'

The child, who had flung her gown over her head to show him the bruises, now pulled it back again. Her sharp little face peered up at him under a mop of filthy hair.

'But why did he poise you, my dear?'

'He sent me for a candle. I ran as fast as I could but they hadn't no candles to spare in the muffin room. I had to go to the saggers. He said I was a lazy bitch and he threw me down and poised me.'

'They gets very fierce, the jiggers,' whispered Mrs. Hollins. 'It's hard for them. They're paid by the piece. If it's said a piece is spoiled they get naught for it, though Cranton may sell it later.'

The wizened child climbed on to a pallet beside two smaller creatures who were fast asleep.

'The jiggers, they all poise us,' she said with some pride.

She opened her mouth wide. Mrs. Hollins, who sat in front of the bed, on a stool, a bowl of soup in her lap, put in a spoonful. The other two were then roused and forced to swallow a little, although they whimpered and protested.

Dr. Newbolt wondered how long he might have been

there. He need not have waited for the evening to call on Mrs. Hollins. In that house only the children worked.

'Do they all work for jiggers?' he asked.

'No, sir. Only Sukey. Polly's a dipper. Tommy, he's a mould runner. Ah now, Polly, rouse up and get your victuals!'

'They are too much exhausted to eat!'

'But they must eat, sir. At six in the morning I'm forced to rouse 'em again and drive 'em off to work. Sukey! You leave that alone! That's Tommy's sup.'

'Tom don't want no more, Mam.'

'He must get his victuals.'

Something should be done, thought Dr. Newbolt. I came here to . . . I came here to . . . why did I come here? Her pastor . . . I had intended to tell her . . . what? . . . Her dress on Sunday . . .

'You are a church woman?' he said.

She explained that she had been country bred and had gone to church as a child, a long time ago. She could not account for her sudden appearance at the altar at Stretton Courtenay. She had, she said, taken a ramble for once, and had heard the bells.

'I must speak to Mr. Cranton,' he said.

This terrified her.

'Oh no, sir! Pray don't, sir! We'd only be turned off, and then what should we do? If we was to come upon the parish the children might be taken from me and sent . . . sent . . .'

'But this whatdyecallit? This jigger!'

'He's no worse than many, sir. Maybe Sukey was slow. She might have run faster. Nor I'm not the only one. There's plenty places where the children get work, and men and women is turned off. Children comes cheaper, you see. Sukey! If you try for Polly's sup again . . .!'

'Polly don't want it. She'd sooner sleep.'

'They must get their victuals. They can sleep Sunday. Polly! Polly! Eh dear! I can't wake her. . . .'

In despair the wretched woman began to cuff and claw the children violently, cursing them because they could not take their victuals. Dr. Newbolt rose and took the bowl from her.

'Rest a little,' he said. 'Let me try. Polly . . .!'

He felt more certain, now, of what he had come to do. He did not leave the house until the soup had been shared equally between Sukey, Polly, and Tommy. Then he rode homewards through sweet moonlight, the smell of hawthorn all about him.

'Very late,' he thought dreamily. 'As near as nothing too late. Poised? I never heard the word before. But I must get home before the moon comes nearer.'

The moon was growing in size. It was coming down out of the sky. The light was intolerable, burning him to the quick. That passed, and he was lying under a hedge with hawthorn petals on his face. His horse on the greensward nearby cropped peacefully.

Alarmingly late, he decided. I was nearly overtaken by Perpetual Light, I believe, and I am far from ready for it.

People were standing round him, calling out that it was Parson, and asking what ailed him.

'A light,' he muttered. 'A command . . .'

Had he fallen? Was he hurt? Was he sick? Had any person attacked him? What light? What command?

'Feed my lambs!' he shouted suddenly, and fell to weeping as though his heart would break.

2

A<small>T</small> the Priors, that night, they were dancing. Ellen had sought out her brother, soon after breakfast, and wheedled him into a genial mood.

'Mr. Latymer . . . it's his last night and . . . and he loves dancing . . . and he has not danced once, his whole time ashore. If we could collect eight couple . . .'

'Impossible! Not in this desert.'

'Oh yes. We don't want for girls, and then there are all the Freemans. It's so obliging in that family to be all men. And you. And Ed . . . Mr. Latymer . . .'

'Not I. My dancing days are over.'

'Really? Charlotte said so, but I refused to believe it.'

'Ho? Charlotte said so?'

'Oh yes. She's all against it and said that you would be against it too. And Mama . . . you know how it is? She is sorry for Mr. Latymer, and would like his last night to be cheerful. But she's afraid of Charlotte. So . . . if you are against us too, there's an end of it!'

'I never said I was against it, only that I won't dance. Charlotte has no business to interfere. Collect eight couple by all means. The scheme has my blessing.'

'Oh, Rom!'

'But not if you call me Rom.'

'Oh, brother!'

'That's going a little far the other way.'

'How good . . . how very good of you! It can be managed very easily. Jenny and Miss Wilson will play for us by turns. If you'll be so kind as to speak to Mama, I'll send word of it to the Newbolts.'

'I will,' he said, returning to his book.

'There's no time to be lost,' she persisted. 'Pray go to her now. We must send a message to the Freemans at once, if they are to know in time. It's a long ride for them, but they are always ready for a frolic, and they'll have a full moon to light them home.'

Ellen's bright eyes were impossible to withstand. Romilly shut his book with a bang, got out of his chair, and promised to lose no time. The thing, if done at all, should be done handsomely. Could they not get a fiddler? A governess at the instrument sounded a trifle tame. Ellen, in ecstasy, declared that there was an old fiddler near Corston.

'We'll have him over. And then . . . supper? White soup? Syllabubs? All that sort of thing?'

'Charlotte would never . . .'

'Confound Charlotte. She shan't send my guests away hungry. Don't be uneasy, child. I'll see to everything.'

Having sponsored the enterprise he found that he had let himself in for a troublesome day. Innumerable difficulties emerged, most of them, he suspected, contrived by Charlotte. No servant could be spared to carry a note to the Freemans. The fiddler was said to drink. There was no stock for white soup.

Doggedly he fought down all these obstacles. By eight o'clock the long saloon was cleared for dancing. The fiddler was reported to be in the kitchen, cold sober. The Freeman boys came whooping and galloping up the drive.

The Arbuthnot girls were upstairs, removing cloaks and adjusting ribbons.

'We shall be one couple short,' declared Ellen, doing a swift *chassée* down the whole length of the saloon. 'One man too many, without Venetia. So we will excuse you, Romilly, if you really don't care to dance.'

'What? Are the Newbolts not coming?'

'Jenny is here. She's upstairs with the Arbuthnots. But she never dances: she'll play any tune we may call for if the fiddler gets drunk.'

'But what has happened to her sister?'

Ellen looked embarrassed.

'I scarcely know. She won't come. Charlotte . . .'

'Charlotte *again*?'

'I believe Charlotte dropped her a hint not to come here unless she was invited. I suppose she has taken huff.'

'But she has been invited. By my mother. You said so, surely, in your note?'

'Oh dear! I never thought it necessary. I wrote: "We are to have a little ball tonight. Pray come. . . ." She must have known we had Mama's permission. But perhaps she's offended.'

'I don't wonder,' said Romilly. 'I shall go down this instant to the Parsonage and bring her back with me.'

Ellen began a protest, but checked herself. To argue with him was always fatal.

'If you can persuade her to come,' she said doubtfully, 'it would be much pleasanter. It seems quite unkind to be dancing without her. But what shall we do? We are to begin in a few minutes, and you may be ever so long before you come back. She'll need to put on another gown if she comes. Yet we can't begin without you.'

'Oh yes. You are a couple short, in any case, unless she comes.'

'But you are the host! Oh dear! I wish Charlotte was at the bottom of the sea.'

'I should be quite content if she was in Berkshire.'

He hurried upstairs to change his shoes and then set off. The fiddle struck up as he left the house. *St. Leger's Round!* For a moment he forgot his irritation and smiled to think of Ellen frisking away with Latymer. She was a good little creature. The thought of her put him out of humour with his errand, for he had no real concern for Venetia's feelings. He was only going in order to defeat Charlotte.

Half-way across the bridge he hesitated. Should he turn back and content himself with the innocent victory already secured? Thanks to his intervention Ellen and Latymer might skip up the middle and down again, and that was an excellent achievement. To introduce Venetia might impart a flavour of hemlock to the syllabubs. Nobody would be the happier. But then the earliest nightingale, whistling four times from a distant tree, settled the matter. *Nettlerash!* he remembered furiously. He went on.

She was sitting in the Parsonage garden on that round bench under the tree. Without any great appearance of surprise she rose to greet him, explaining that her father was from home, visiting some person over at Cranton's.

'I've come,' he said, 'to persuade you, if I can, into accepting poor little Ellen's invitation. She'll be quite miserable if you don't come, and so shall I. There seems to have been some misunderstanding . . . she wrote on my mother's behalf of course. But she's very young. Unused to these things. I'm sure you'll forgive her.'

Regretfully she shook her head. She was sorry, exceedingly sorry, but the other ladies of the family had made it so clear that she was unwelcome. . . .

'No, no,' she finished. 'Believe me, I'd better not come.'

'It's all Charlotte's doing. You know what she is. I'll engage she shall be civil to you, if only you'll come.'

Venetia smiled and sat down again.

'I don't intend to take any risks. It must not be said that you forced me upon your family.'

He sat down beside her, looking obstinate but unable, for the moment, to discover any compelling answer to this. After a while she went on:

'If I come with you . . . only think what a tale the world would make of it! Everyone believes that I'm trying to catch you. Everyone can see that you pay me marked attentions. I don't take them seriously. It's all to serve your own ends: a kind of threat to your family. I shall have served my turn if they come to heel. Your attentions will then cease. If you fail, you'll go back to London. In either case, every person within thirty miles of Stretton will believe that I have suffered a signal disappointment. I'm not at all sorry for this opportunity of showing my indifference. If you go back now without me . . .'

She laughed a little. Romilly, disconcerted, protested that she must think very badly of him.

'Not as well as I did,' she said ruefully. 'At first I thought you a match for Lady Baddeley. I really believed you might contrive to be master in your own house. Now . . . I doubt it.'

'I'm determined to take you back with me.'

'Only to satisfy your own vanity.'

'And nothing will satisfy yours, short of . . .?'

'An offer?' She laughed. 'What would that be worth? You'd never be allowed to marry me.'

And yet, he thought, they had much in common. She had no heart. His was a burden rather than a blessing. Only a wife, it seemed, could rid him of the Brandon Arabian. She had taste. Fragonard! That was a striking piece of natural insight. She was a beauty. She would adorn his dinner table, although he might not want to see her face on his pillow when he woke up in the morning. She could keep her own quarters, which he would visit whenever he felt inclined. She would, he was sure, be content with marriage unhallowed by tenderness.

'I believe,' she said, 'that you are debating Mrs. Malaprop's great maxim: It's always best to begin with a little aversion.'

'Where do you stable your broomstick?'

'In the church vestry.'

Once married to her he might hope to be safe — from memory, from Ellen's bright eyes, from his mother's forlorn looks. He might hope to end this miserable indecision which swung from schemes for their banishment to evenings at backgammon. Venetia would deal with them. She would cure these onslaughts of feeling so liable to invalidate all the pleasure of self-indulgence.

'Come back with me,' he said. 'We'll tell the whole country that I have offered and you have accepted.'

'Without a word to my father? Oh no! That would never do.'

'He'll consent, won't he?'

'Probably.'

'When do you expect him home?'

'At any moment.'

'Then I'll wait and ask him. We'll get him to come back with us. Will that satisfy you?"

She laughed and he asked again:

'What more can I do?'

'You seem to be very sure of my answer.'

'I am. You mean to marry me, if you can, and I think it might do very well.'

'You'll have to marry me if you insist upon speaking to my father. And you'll have a sad time of it. Charlotte will forbid the banns. My four brothers will rush to my defence. Charles and Harry will come from London, in a post-chaise. Stephen will come by coach from Dorset. Frank will set sail from India. Charles will call you out. Harry will bring an action. Stephen will denounce you from the pulpit. There'll be nothing left of you for Frank to thrash.'

'What devoted brothers! Why are they so fond of you?'

She continued in this strain, laughing at him and refusing to take him seriously. But, for all that, he thought he could detect a certain tensity; she was listening, while she laughed, on the alert for sounds of her father's return.

He said at last, in order to make her jump:

'I think Dr. Newbolt must have got his boots off by now. He'll be in his study, I take it? I'd better go to him.'

'Why . . . he's not back yet.'

'Oh yes. He came back ten minutes ago. I heard his horse in the lane.'

To his delight, she jumped. They went to the study which was dark and empty, since Romilly had heard no horse in the lane. Venetia could scarcely conceal her vexation.

'I can't think what keeps him,' she exclaimed. 'He never stays longer than fifteen minutes unless they are dying.'

'Shall we go to the gate and see if he's coming?'

'Yes.'

She hurried out of the front door declaring that if her father did not show up soon Romilly must positively go back to the Priors without her. He must do his duty, and dance with poor Louisa Arbuthnot. And then, in the midst of a sentence, she broke off with a cry of surprise:

'Who are all those people? How strange they look! Good God! My father's horse!'

A little knot of people was trooping towards the Parsonage. One of them led the horse. The rest supported Dr. Newbolt, who shambled along amidst their encouragements and exhortations. At the sight of the couple by the gate several voices broke out:

''Tis Squire. . . .'

'Oh Miss. . . .'

'His Reverence. . . .'

'A sad accident. . . .'

'A seizure. . . .'

'We don't rightly know. . . .'

'We found him on the ground, a-sobbing and a-weeping. . . .'

They led him into the house. Servants came running, one of whom was despatched for a physician. He sat in his study, answering none of their questions and staring at them in a bewildered way. Presently he asked for Jenny.

'We've sent for her,' said Romilly. 'She's at the Priors.'

'Ay. Bring her back. Bring her back. But take care of the moon. It's very light. Very late. I must have a word with her. She was perfectly right, you know. Perfectly right. No child should work for Cranton.'

3

EARLY enquiries at the Parsonage next morning brought a reassuring report. Dr. Newbolt had slept well and was, to all appearances, fully recovered. Romilly was quite ashamed at his own dismay when he heard this. Had the old man turned out to be very ill nobody could, at the moment, have asked for his daughter's hand. There could have been a propitious delay. This recovery left no loop-hole for retreat. The awkward dilemma must be faced; how far must a man of honour deem himself committed by the scene in the garden last night?

Marriage with Venetia might be a diverting fantasy. Any obligation of that sort was a disagreeable fact. If there was none it would be wiser to avoid her for a while. Yet personal enquiries at the Parsonage, later in the day, would have to be made; to omit them would be outrageously uncivil, save for a very valid excuse. Within half an hour Romilly discovered a regard for Latymer so strong that it obliged him to accompany the poor fellow as far as Severnton, on the first stage of his journey. Dr. Newbolt might, in the meantime, take a turn for the worse. Seizures are unaccountable things. By Friday he might be very ill indeed.

Friday's report was a disappointment. The physician now pronounced his patient to be perfectly recovered and doubted whether there had been any seizure at all.

Dr. Newbolt, on Thursday, had refused to keep his bed. He would not even remain in the house. He had insisted that he must revisit Cranton's and would have ridden over if Mrs. Brandon had not intervened. On learning of his obstinacy she had insisted that he should at least be driven over in her chaise.

'I suppose I ought to call today,' said Romilly, when he had heard about all this.

Charlotte declared that it was not in the least necessary, whereupon he set off at once, still in the greatest confusion of mind. At one moment he thought that it might be a very good thing to marry Venetia. At the next, that he must now do so, whether he liked it or not. And then, again, that nothing said by either of them on Wednesday night could be, or ought to be, taken seriously.

He chose the road through the village, the more formal approach to the Parsonage, a route which he generally avoided since it involved recognising and nodding to so many people. Today there was a confounded amount of nodding to be done since the entire population seemed to be standing at doors or hanging out of windows. They were all staring up the road. Yet there was nothing to be seen save a puny boy carrying a large bundle and a small fiddle. He too seemed to be going to the Parsonage, and the appearance of Romilly, striding after him, created, apparently, an enormous sensation. More and more villagers flocked into the road to gape at them. Romilly heard a woman at a cottage door call to someone within:

'Quick! Quick! Come and look! Here's the both of them. Here's Squire himself!'

Quickening his pace he caught up with the child a few yards from the Parsonage gate, and wished him good day. For that he got a hard black stare, but no audible reply. The face was oddly familiar although he was sure that he had never seen the lad before.

'Do you live hereabouts?' he asked.

'Ay.'

'I don't remember seeing you. What's your name?'

'Dickie.'

'Dickie what?'

'Cottar.'

The name had some echo. He could not locate it.

'And where do you live?'

'With Miss Jenny.'

'What? Miss Jenny Newbolt?'

'Ay.'

'At the Parsonage?'

'Ay.'

'How long have you been there?'

'I han't been there yet. I'm a-going there now. Parson, he sent for me so soon as he came out of his fit. For to clean their boots.'

'You have a fiddle, I see.'

'Ay.'

'Shall you play it to Miss Jenny?' asked Romilly, smiling.

'Ay.'

By now they had reached the house. Without another word the boy went on, round to the kitchen door.

Romilly paused for a moment before ringing the bell. Awkwardness or insolence? The little encounter had been oddly disconcerting. The name of Cottar was not completely unfamiliar. But he was sure that he had not heard it for many years. He must ask Ellen. And then, as he rang the bell, he thought of Slane St. Mary's as having some connection with the name. The Cottars might have been Knevett's people, which would explain the scowl and the surly replies. But in that case he had better not ask Ellen.

A servant took him to the study where he found Dr. Newbolt walking up and down in manifest agitation.

'Come in, my dear Romilly. Come in! I'm very glad to see you. Very glad indeed. We have much to discuss.'

Good God! thought Romilly, remembering his own quandary. She must have told him already. She'd lost no time. Had she also written to her brothers?

'Sit down! Sit down! You'll be shocked. I'm sure you had no more idea of it than I had. That man Cranton, you know, is a monster. An inhuman beast.'

No, no! All safe. This hullabaloo has nothing to do with her.

'What has he been up to, sir?'

'I saw him yesterday. You must know that on Wednesday . . . by the way, I must thank you for your kindness that evening. . . .'

'You quite startled us. We feared . . .'

'I made a very shocking discovery that evening. Wednesday evening. . . . I am now talking about Wednesday. I'll tell you . . .'

The story was hard to follow. Mrs. Hollins, Sukey, Tommy, jiggers, saggers, candles, a bowl of soup, and the possible origin of the expression 'poised' were inextricably confused. Dr. Newbolt confessed that, when he awoke on Thursday morning, he had wondered whether it might not be a kind of dream.

'But I was determined . . . yesterday I rode over . . . no . . . stay . . . your mother was so kind as to . . . I drove over . . . I saw this fellow Cranton.'

He paused and gave one of those wild stares which had been so alarming on Wednesday night.

'He . . . he . . . he owns to the whole of it! Not a trace of shame. Perfectly cool. Asked me why he should employ men and women for work which children can do at half the cost? Says he treats them as well as anybody else. What's to be done? How are we to deal with him?'

'In what way, sir?'

'There will be, of course, an outcry when these facts are known. But how shall we set about it? Should we begin by consulting a lawyer?'

'You think he may have broken some law?'

'Of course he has. He is making slaves of these people. Slavery has been abolished in these islands. Any man, once he has set foot on British soil . . . Somerset's case . . .'

'Somerset was a black, sir. And, if these people don't like to work for Cranton they can refuse. They are free.'

'That's what he had the assurance to tell me. I wonder you should swallow it. They can't help themselves. I spoke to some of them, before leaving yesterday. They say he won't engage a man unless this man's children work too; that saves him the cost of apprentices. If they were to leave him, and failed to get other employment, they might come upon the parish. And then their children might be taken from them.'

'That sounds,' said Romilly, 'as though the law supports Cranton.'

'Impossible! In this country! In this enlightened age! But, if it is so, the law must be altered. You must agree, I think. Especially since Cranton would never have come here if your father had not sold him the land.'

'I'm very sorry that he sold it. But it's no longer my land. I am not responsible . . .'

'As a Christian are you not responsible? When we encounter misery and oppression, must we not exert ourselves? The matter must be raised in Parliament. You must set your fellow on to it . . . your legislator . . . what's his name? Lestrange.'

Romilly had a borough in his pocket which he had disposed of to a neighbour with political ambitions. When he explained that he could not give such orders to Lestrange the old gentleman began to lose his temper.

'The man's a legislator. You put him up to make laws for us. You would not, I suppose, have put him into Parliament had you thought him unworthy. Have you no sense of your duty in the matter?'

'He's a Tory,' said Romilly. 'That's good enough for me. I should not have put in a Whig.'

'Whigsh? Toriesh? Have they not the same Christian dutiesh? To defend . . . defend . . . Liberty . . . Magna Carta . . . Bill of Rightsh . . .'

The old man was almost choking. Romilly, fearing that another fit might have occurred, retreated in alarm to the bell. But then a promising idea occurred to him:

'Should you not begin by consulting the Bishop? He's a legislator, and should know more than I do on the point of Christian duty.'

This was well received. It had a soothing effect. Dr. Newbolt's cheeks faded from purple to pink again, as he declared that he ought to have thought of this step himself.

'He's an excellent man, I believe,' said Romilly.

'Oh ay, and always very civil. I'll lose no time. I'll go to him at once. He ought to know of it as soon as possible.'

If Bishop Summerfield could not shut the old boy up, thought Romilly, nobody could. He took advantage of the lull to escape, since this was clearly no moment to open the topic of Venetia.

She was, however, waiting for him in the hall.

'How can the surgeon call him recovered?' he said at once. 'He's not himself at all. He can talk of nothing but Cranton. Useless to introduce any other topic.'

'I know. I know . . . Jenny is not uneasy, but I . . .'

She paused for a moment, listening, as though she feared to hear some unwelcome sound. Then she said hastily:

'I think you'd better go now. Don't see him . . . avoid him if you can, till he's over this. He'll want you to join him in some mad scheme, and grow angry if you refuse, and quarrel with you.'

It was almost as though she were pushing him out of the house, and all the while she had that anxious, listening look. If he was eager to be gone, she was quite as eager to be rid of him.

He took the way home by the garden and the church-yard so as to avoid all those staring people in the street. As he crossed the lawn he heard a sound which might explain her discomposure. Somebody, inside the house, was playing the fiddle.

It could only be that surly child. Not bad, he thought, listening. Not bad at all. Better than one might expect. Quite spirited. But why in the world should it trouble Venetia?

4

'I COULD never have believed,' said Bishop Summerfield, 'that a man of education, by no means half-witted, could have contrived to live so long in the world yet know so little about it.'

He said this to his old friend Canon Wilder, to whom he had repaired as soon as he got rid of Dr. Newbolt.

'They're a rustic lot, over on the other side of the forest,' said Wilder. 'And he's lived there all his life, han't he? Got the living very young?'

'That is so. I don't suppose he's come across anything of the sort before. The Brandons are good landlords. They've always treated their people well. There's no great poverty there. I suppose poor Newbolt imagined this to be an universal rule, and thought of a master potter as some kind of squire. He's too old, his mind is too set, for discoveries of this sort. I failed to convince him that, in industry, these evils are inevitable.'

'Nobody told him about Economy?'

'If they did he never listened. I tried to explain to him that economic laws are as inflexible, as fixed, as the laws of nature. We can't alter them. We might as well forbid water to flow downhill.'

'We do that, to a certain extent,' said the Canon. 'We're always defying the laws of nature. If water flowing downhill becomes inconvenient, we build a lock.'

'Wa-a-a-ah!' said the Bishop.

He always made a noise like this when Wilder chopped logic, and had been doing so ever since they were at school together. But an obstinate craving for honesty still drove him to discussion with his old friend, whenever he felt unsure of his position. He growled for a while, and then thought of an answer.

'We don't build a lock when the river is in violent flood. We wait for a convenient season. It is by dint of Economy that we are beating the French.'

'Did you tell Newbolt so?'

'I did.'

'And he said that, in that case, no good would come of it, even if we do beat the French?'

'Yes. How did you guess that?'

'It's what I'd have said myself, if I thought, as he does, that Economy is a subtlety of the Devil.'

'I was obliged, in the end, to tell him not to meddle with matters which don't concern the Church. He's an old man. His language to me I can overlook, though he did call me a Pharisee. But if he says in the pulpit one tenth of what he said to me we shall all be set by the ears.'

'May he say it when we have beaten the French?'

'Wa-a-a-ah!'

'Are you quite easy in your own mind about it?'

'No. When we threw out Whitbread's Bill . . . not that I thought it a good Bill . . . I was troubled by some of the facts which came to light. I daresay something might be done. But it's no work for silly old men who know nothing of the world. Enthusiasts do more harm than good. Newbolt seems to imagine that politicians are philanthropists.'

'Most ungentlemanly,' agreed the Canon, shaking his

head. 'Hodge at the plough had better think so, perhaps. Which is why you won't allow Whitbread to teach him to read. But we have known better as long as we can remember. We should not be here if we had not.'

'Wa-a-a-ah!'

'We should be raising pigs in a tumbledown parsonage at the other end of nowhere. Severnton Close is a great deal pleasanter. We are here because we know that our cathedral, although built by Christians, was paid for by Jews who wanted to keep their teeth in their heads.'

'I never knew that!' protested the Bishop. 'Bless my soul! I don't believe it.'

'You will, when you've read my History of Severnton.'

'Which I can't do until it's written.'

'I'm still digging up facts. So don't say Wa-a-a-ah! And remember that we have always treated our Jews a little better than other nations have. Some did worse than pull out their teeth, whenever money was wanted.'

'We can't be blamed for the barbarity of our ancestors.'

'Our children may say that about us, a hundred years hence.'

'You think that they will be more humane than we are?'

'Probably, in some respects. In others they might shock us. But they will cling, as we do, to the safeguard of inequality in suffering. Belief in that is essential. Without it, humanity might despair. We are protected from the full impact of human agony by the notion that some law ordains it shall never be ours — that the worst disasters are appointed, by Nature, by Economy, by Divine Providence, for others. Suppose some calamity which might threaten all equally! From which no class, no race, no nation, might hope to be immune. Some comet, let us say, which must inevitably collide with this planet and destroy it? In what frame of mind should we endure that?'

'Wa . . . Resignation!'

'I doubt it. I believe that many would convince themselves of their own probable immunity. Some favourable position, some superior foresight and ingenuity, might still preserve them. In which case they would find resignation to the fate of the rest mighty easy. No. We shall cling to inequality until the Last Trump shall sound. If we abolish suffering of one sort, we shall replace it by another, harden our hearts to it and declare that it is inevitable.'

'You had better say all this to Newbolt.'

'Too late. He don't know how to harden his heart — deliberately. He is, in fact, and always has been, as inhumane as the rest of us. But for his own sake, let's hope he never finds that out. Should he ever begin to blame himself . . .'

'Why! There he is! That's the man.'

'What? Newbolt?'

'Down there in the lime walk.'

Wilder joined his friend at the window.

A tree-shaded path ran across the turf of the Close to the cathedral. Up and down it trotted the enthusiast, his wig a little awry, his lips moving in noiseless argument. At one point he paused. Some trenchant fact had occurred to him. He demolished his unseen opponent with it, shaking his finger triumphantly.

'I must say,' murmured Wilder, 'he looks pretty mad.'

'Poor creature,' said the Bishop in a shaken voice. 'Poor old man! God help him!'

'God help us all.'

The cathedral clock struck four, flinging the quarters on the air like a flock of silver birds. Wilder pulled his friend away from the window, adding gently:

'Come to dinner.'

5

NOTHING would convince Tibbie that she had not been turned out to die by the stony-hearted New-bolts. Nor would she allow that a room over the stables could be described as 'her own little cottage'. As for Mrs. Hollins as an attendant, that dirty tramp and her children should never come next or nigh her. She would sooner die in a ditch.

'But she will do far more for you,' pleaded Jenny, 'than the maids do here. You always complain that they neglect you.'

'So they do. Sluts all.'

'Mrs. Hollins will be in the stables too, next door to you. Whenever you ring this pretty little bell . . .'

'I'll ring no bell. She'll rob me right and left. Your Papa is out of his senses to bring her here, and that's what all the village says.'

'She has nowhere else to go. Cranton turned them off.'

'And for why? Folks don't get turned off for nothing.'

'You should be sorry for her. You never had so hard a life yourself.'

'I'd have been ashamed, at her age, if I couldn't keep myself. I got my own bread from the time I was seven years old till the Lord struck me down paralytical. And there she is, eating your Papa out of house and home, likewise her brats, what can't keep themselves either.'

'They'll be put to work. Sukey is to weed the garden.'

'She don't know weeds from seeds. A fine thing it will be when all folks as don't relish hard work can look for free lodging with the gentry.'

Jenny shook her head sadly. She had never expected this scheme to answer. The Hollins family might be lodged above the stables, to the scandal of the entire village, but Tibbie would never be persuaded to join them. Compulsion would be cruel, and she had even ventured to tell her father that kindness to Mrs. Hollins did not justify cruelty to Tibbie. He refused to give up a plan which had struck him as solving two problems at one stroke. It provided employment for Mrs. Hollins, and might ensure better care of Tibbie. There seemed to be no other work available for the widow. The servants, already irritated by the introduction of Dickie Cottar, insisted that she would never be fit to work in a gentleman's house. The farmers wanted no strangers in their fields. Dr. Newbolt had at first placed hopes upon a mangle. He had heard that a widow with a mangle might always keep herself. But it appeared that no mangling was required in Stretton Courtenay.

For the children Satan had found plenty of employment. Having nothing to do, for the first time in their lives, they could not keep out of mischief. They broke the cucumber frames, let the pigs into the gardens, over- ate themselves and were noisily sick in church. Sukey had publicly used a term for an apron so obscene that village matrons were obliged to whisper it behind their hands: '*She called it a — cover!*' Even Dr. Newbolt had left off patting their heads, which Jenny, after a shocked examination, had been obliged to shave.

'It has to be,' said Jenny at last. 'My father has ordered it . . .'

'Then he must carry me out himself. No one else will. They'd be ashamed to do it. There's not a soul in the village would lift a finger to drag a poor old woman from her dying bed.'

'He said you were to be in the stables, with all your things, by four o'clock.'

And if she was not, Jenny would be the whipping boy. Her father would blame her; he had begun to believe that she was in a plot to frustrate him. She decided that Dickie and she could at least make a start by taking over Tibbie's belongings piece by piece, leaving to the last the problems of the great chest, the bed, and Tibbie herself.

She went downstairs to find Dickie who should have been swabbing the flags in the kitchen yard but was not. Nor was he to be found in the garden. It was too bad of him to play truant again: she had enough to endure without that. Going round by the outhouses she heard his voice raised in emphatic declamation. It seemed to come from an empty pig-sty.

'Thou shalt not covet thy neighbour's HOUSE! Thou shalt not covet thy neighbour's WIFE! Nor his servant nor his MAID, nor his ox nor his ASS, nor ANYTHING that is his!'

'Dickie!' she called.

The recital stopped. He crawled out of the pig-sty followed by the three Hollins children. At the sight of them she gave a little scream. Their bald heads were now concealed under rakish wigs made of cobwebs.

'What have you been doing?' she gasped.

'A-learning the twelve holy commanders,' explained Sukey.

'But your heads . . .'

'I done it,' said Dickie. 'Folks poke fingers at them for that they're bald. Now they look like Parson.'

'Run back to your mother,' she told them, 'and wash your heads.'

They scuttled off and Dickie defended himself.

'You told me to be kind to 'em.'

'But you shouldn't neglect your work, or you'll be sent away.'

'Parson won't let me be sent away.'

'He's trying to help you and Mrs. Hollins. We must do all we can to . . .'

'They say he's moonstruck. They say it was a full moon when they found him in that fit.'

'Don't interrupt, Dickie. We must help him in every way that we can, for he is trying to be kind. It's right to be kind.'

'Not much profit in being right, if folks think you moonstruck.'

'Only very ignorant people think so.'

'The gentry think so too. My father don't come here no more.'

'Dickie! Who . . . who do you mean?'

'Why . . . Squire Brandon! Bless you, Miss Jenny, didn't you know that?'

'You must never say such a thing. Never!'

'Other folks say it. I've heard it said so long as I can remember.'

'Listen, Dickie! If you say it you'll have to go away. You really will.'

'Aw, Miss Jenny. I wouldn't say it to nobody but you. Any trouble from me and he'll have me put away. My granny, she's told me that often enough.'

Jenny sat down on the pig-sty wall, feeling suddenly that the world was too much for her. A tear rolled down her cheek and she exclaimed:

'Oh dear . . . what shall I do! Everything is too difficult. I've tried to help you, Dickie. . . .'

Instantly remorseful, he seized her hand and squeezed it.

'Ah now, Miss Jenny! Don't! Don't! I'll do all you say. I'll do any work I'm put to. I never knew you'd be vexed at me for them wigs. I thought you'd be pleased.'

A little cheered, she dried her eyes and smiled at him.

'You made them very cleverly. Where did you find so many cobwebs?'

'I got 'em from the rafters in the big barn. But they don't answer, they dwine away so quick. Thistledown would serve better if I could find some way so it shouldn't fly off.'

'Tow,' said Jenny. 'A tow cord unravelled makes a very good wig: we used to do that for charades. I remember . . . a . . . a boy I used to know . . . made a very . . .'

A bellow from the house interrupted this discussion. Dr. Newbolt had discovered that Tibbie was not yet in the stable loft. Jenny trotted off to be rated soundly for this disregard of his orders. He went himself to find the gardener and the groom, who looked sullen but dared not defy him outright. Tibbie's possessions, including the chest, were carried away. Driven on by her father, Jenny removed the coverings from the bed. Tibbie's shrivelled form was revealed in a calico bed gown, her feet sticking out of the end of it as gnarled as a couple of walnuts.

'Parson said take her on a hurdle,' muttered the gardener. 'We have it at the stair head.'

'Lay a finger on me and 'tis assault,' snapped Tibbie.

'She's in the right, I believe,' said the groom. 'She could have the law on us.'

Dr. Newbolt, when this was reported to him, decreed that Tibbie should remain where she was till she came to her senses.

'She's too old,' wailed Jenny. 'She has no senses to come to. She'll take cold, lying there. It may kill her.'

'One can't help these people if they won't do as they're bid. She can lie there till she chooses to be carried to pleasanter quarters.'

'But, sir . . .'

'Do as I tell you.'

Jenny disobeyed him to the point of putting a rug over Tibbie who lay rigid, with closed eyes. Thus she continued for the rest of the day.

'She's an ungrateful old woman,' declared Venetia, when she heard of it at dinner. 'Few families are so kind to an old servant as we are.'

'Jenny,' he said crossly, 'seems to think that Tibbie should be allowed to do as she pleases.'

'Jenny would have all poor people do as they please. I believe she thinks that they, not we, should make the laws.'

'A Pantisocracy? Eh? That won't answer, my girl.'

'They have one in America,' said Jenny, goaded into reply.

'Together with slavery. Remember that. Tibbie in America would be black. Bought and sold. No rights at all.'

Venetia took the opportunity to find some fault with Dickie's work, but beat a swift retreat when she saw that this displeased her father. In all these turmoils she managed to remain aloof. She never protested against the importation of Mrs. Hollins, agreed with all that he said, and managed skilfully to suggest that Jenny might be responsible for failures and obstacles.

The night turned chilly and a wind was getting up. Before going to bed Jenny looked in once again on Tibbie, to encounter the same mute defiance. She meant to remain awake but fell at once into an exhausted sleep from which she was roused to a racket of thunder and rain. Someone was shaking her.

'Miss Jenny! Miss Jenny!'

'What is it?' she cried, starting up. 'Dickie!'

'Miss Jenny . . . Tibbie's gone.'

'What? Not . . . not . . .'

'Gone out of her bed. Gone out of the house.'

'Impossible!'

'Her bed's empty. Go up and look.'

She hurried to put on a dressing gown.

'Wait till I strike a light. But who could have . . .'

'She went of her own self, I believe.'

'She can't move. She hasn't moved for years.'

While she found the tinder box and lit a candle Dickie explained. He slept in a little cupboard of a room next to the kitchen. The servants' door, he said, had been left open for Kitty who had gone to dance at the Coach and Horses, which he trusted Parson would never come to hear of. He had heard a strange shuffling noise going along the passage and out into the garden. At first he had been too frightened to investigate. When he nerved himself to do so he found the door not only unlocked but swinging and all the rain coming in. He peeped out. By a flash of lightning he had seen something like a great long old snake wriggling away into the bushes. This, he believed, was Tibbie, pulling herself along by her hands and dragging her paralysed legs after her.

Jenny, by this time, had run up to the garret with her candle and discovered that Tibbie's bed was indeed empty.

'The stairs! How could she have got down the stairs?'

'Maybe she just rolled herself down.'

They ran down themselves and out into the downpour which immediately soaked them to the skin. By the next flash they located Tibbie lying under a lilac bush. She said:

'I've bested the lot of you, I believe.'

'Oh, Tibbie! How could you? Run, Dickie, and fetch Mrs. Hollins.'

Jenny crouched shivering by Tibbie who remarked that when she had rested herself she would get on to the village. Some kind soul would take her in. Not all hearts were as hard as Parson's.

'You'll probably get on into your grave,' snapped Jenny. 'You'll have caught your death.'

'Thanks to you if I have.'

Footsteps and laughter were heard. Kitty came tripping along the path under a very large umbrella held over her by a very large young man. At the sight of Jenny, rising up from the bushes in a long white dressing gown, she gave a squawk and fainted into the arms of her swain.

'Put her down,' commanded Jenny. 'Put the umbrella over her. And help us. Nothing will be said about this tomorrow. But we must get Tibbie into shelter. Oh . . . here are Dickie and Mrs. Hollins.'

Amongst them they lifted the truant up and carried her to the stables. She was surprisingly heavy. It was all that they could do to get her up to the loft, amidst shrill squeals from the Hollins children, who had run out to join this frolic. All three were stark naked although Jenny had provided them with nightshirts.

Kitty's sweetheart was then dismissed with a renewed promise that no trouble should ensure for him or her. Jenny, shivering, her teeth chattering, removed the soaked bedgown from the withered old body, whilst Mrs. Hollins warmed a blanket. They rolled Tibbie up in it and put her by the fire.

'I'll have her bed sent over as soon as I can tomorrow,' said Jenny. 'I wish we had cordials. I had better fetch...'

'Naught better than a drop of gin,' said Mrs. Hollins, 'and that I've got.'

'Gin? Oh, I don't think Tibbie would ...'

'The poor man's medicine,' asserted Mrs. Hollins, producing a bottle. 'You'd better have a drop yourself, and so had I, after that soaking. Now, Mrs. Lockyear, ma'am.' She shook Tibbie. 'Have a sup of this, do! 'Twill keep off the chills.'

Tibbie took a sizeable sup and grunted approvingly.

'That's good sense,' she said. 'But they'd never give it to you at Parson's, not if you was perishing for it. Naught there but gruel and pap!'

The bottle was offered to Jenny, who shook her head, Mrs. Hollins then took a swig, smacked her lips, and announced:

'Old people should ought to have what they fancy. That's what does them good. Eh, Mrs. Lockyear?'

'You're in the right, Mrs. Hollins, ma'am.'

Jenny left them agreeing that gruel and pap never did nobody any good. She went home, rubbed herself dry again, and went to bed. But she could not get warm. All night she lay shivering, as the rain slackened and the storm died away.

Tibbie turned out to have taken no harm from the night's escapade. The poor man's medicine might have preserved her. When her bed was taken over next morning she was still taking doses of it and appeared to be on the best of terms with Mrs. Hollins.

It was Jenny who had caught her death.

6

AFTER a month of amiable neutrality Venetia appealed to Charles, her banker brother, for intervention at Stretton Courtenay. Her account of matters there puzzled him very much.

'I should not have believed a word of it,' he said to his wife, 'if it were not for these letters which my father has been writing to the newspapers.'

'Only one, surely?'

'Only one that we saw. I believe that there were others.'

'And only to expose the Slave Trade.'

'My dear Eliza! I sometimes doubt if you can read.'

'I protest it was all about black slaves.'

'Not all of it.'

Charles went to his desk and found the cutting.

' "In the cotton fields of America," ' he read, ' "the little piccaninnies sport and gambol about their mothers' knees . . . the overseer who would lift his impious hand to Woman would be an object of universal execration. . . ." Hmph! I doubt if my father knows much about the cotton fields.'

'No indeed. They flog the poor black wenches with a calabash, while the dandies look on and make brutal jokes.'

'I think you mean *in a calaboose*. And some of *our* dandies don't object to seeing a woman hanged. "In the cotton mills of Britain infants of tender years, torn from their natural protectors, sleep for six hours in twenty-four. Their beds are never cool. As one party is driven back to toil another takes its place . . . in the iron foundries . . . splashed by molten metal . . . nor does any inquest sit on such deaths. In the mines. . . ." You'll observe that he quotes no authority, no places, no dates. Nay, here's something of that sort. "Are we to accept the defence for these barbarities offered, six years ago, by the employers of Burley, in a protest against legal protection for infant apprentices: *Free labourers cannot be obtained to perform the night work but upon very disadvantageous terms to the manufacturers.*" Ha! Ha! Somebody should have told them not to say that; it don't sound well.'

'But where in the world did your father hear of all this? I thought it had only been the potters.'

'Venetia says that he has been writing to that friend of his, Eccles, a curate down in Lancashire, and has learnt some particulars about the children working there which disturb him dreadfully. She claims that he grows very extravagant, and gives money away right and left.'

'She'd grudge his giving a flannel petticoat to an old woman. We all know what Venetia thinks he should do with his money.'

'Yet I suppose I had better go, though I can't for the life of me see why Jenny should not engage a knife boy. Venetia hints at some scandal too shocking to be disclosed.'

'You can't believe a word Venetia says. Depend upon it, her real reason for summoning you is something very different.'

'At least I can talk to Jenny. She has some sense.'

'Not much, or she'd stand up for herself, for our sakes as much as her own. Who will suffer most, if Venetia gets everything and Jenny is left without a penny? We shall, for then we shall have to keep her.'

'If it ever comes to that she can take a good deal off your shoulders with the children.'

'I'd sooner hire a governess. To have Jenny at every meal! She looks so dismal, poor thing. A governess dines upstairs.'

'If Venetia were to marry well Jenny might go to her.'

'Venetia will be in luck if she marries at all. She's no favourite with the men.'

'Come now, my love! Such a very handsome girl . . .'

'When we were there at Christmas I noticed that she sat down a good deal of the time at the Freemans' ball. Men, when they see her, press for an introduction, but they seldom dance with her more than once.'

'Is that really so? How very strange!'

'Not strange at all. No matter how handsome a woman is you men are frightened of her unless you can persuade yourselves that she's good-natured. Your father is the only person in the world who believes that Venetia is good-natured. I daresay we shall see her sitting down at dances twenty years hence, whilst everyone wonders that she did not marry.'

Eliza was against his going, since she was quite sure that Venetia would turn out to be the only gainer by it. But he had begun to feel uneasy and set off next day for Stretton Courtenay, hoping to talk things over with Jenny. In this he was disappointed. Jenny was in bed with a violent cold; she had had it for some time and could not throw it off. He went to see her once but she was so hoarse and languid, so totally unfit for conversation, that he did not stay long.

So far as he could see, there was nothing very much amiss in the Parsonage. His father was a good deal altered, subdued and thoughtful. He spent much of his time reading his Bible with anxious and earnest attention, as though he had never studied it before. When Charles mentioned the letter to the newspaper he waved the matter aside:

'Say no more of it. Nothing has come of it. No notice was taken by the public. I was a fool to expect it. I must take some other course, for which I hope to find Divine guidance.'

'Ah yes! I hear you have been to Summerfield.'

'It was not his guidance that I mean. There's nothing Divine about that fellow.'

This pre-occupation with the Bible was, perhaps, a little disturbing. In the matter of Economy Charles thought that Bishop Summerfield would be the safer guide. It would be a bad thing for bankers if rich men should take seriously to thoughts of camels and needles' eyes.

On the other hand the establishment over the stables won his approval. Jenny should never have been burdened with the care of Tibbie and only Venetia would grudge the hire of some person to undertake it. The scheme appeared to prosper. He visited the stables and thought that he had never seen his old nurse so cheerful and contented. She declared that she wanted for nothing. She was, of course, a good deal less clean and neat than she had been at the Parsonage and it struck him that she might be decidedly tipsy, but to this he preferred to turn a blind eye.

There remained the mysterious little knife-and-boot-boy. He questioned Venetia and whistled when the facts came out.

'But the Brandons? They don't allow it?'

'Oh no. They've never taken the slightest notice of the rumour.'

'I should have thought that our engaging the child would suggest that we think nothing of it, either. How do they all go on at the Priors, now that Brandon has come back?'

She hesitated and then said:

'Not very well, I fear. We . . . we've seen a good deal of him. And a situation has arisen . . . I'm anxious to consult you. My father is so . . . I need somebody to advise me.'

Ah! he thought, now we are coming to it. Eliza is always right, where other women are concerned.

'Mr. Brandon asked me to marry him,' she said, 'on the evening when my father was taken ill, coming home from Cranton's.'

'What? Romilly Brandon?'

'There's only one Mr. Brandon,' she said, smiling. 'I told him that he must speak to my father, and he said that he would do so immediately. He waited, hoping to see Papa that evening. But then they brought him home so ill. Nothing could be done or said, either then or two days later, when Mr. Brandon called again. Papa was still too ill to attend to him. So that nothing was settled. And . . . since then . . . I've heard nothing from him. He's never come again.'

Thought better of it, concluded Charles. I don't wonder.

'If he'd got Papa's consent, should you have accepted him?' he asked.

'Yes,' said Venetia, a little impatiently.

It had been a foolish question to ask. She would jump at it, nor could anybody blame her for doing so. The match would be an excellent thing for everybody, since the Stretton living would assuredly, in such an event, go to Stephen whenever their father should die or retire. Stephen's future was at the moment unpromising. He held a poor living and had little prospect of finding a better one. Venetia might have got her brother down to secure Brandon for her, but the man was worth securing from the family point of view.

'I hardly know what to think,' she said. 'He may have changed his mind. Or there may be some mis-understanding. I'm sure his sisters would prevent it if they could. I've wondered whether I ought to consult my father, but I feel your opinion counts for more, just now.'

'Should you like me to have a word with Brandon?'

'I think that I . . . that we all . . . have a right to know how matters stand.'

'Certainly. I'll deal with it. I ought, in any case, to call. If he means to abide by his offer I'll see that any misunderstanding is cleared up. If he has changed his mind, nothing, I suppose, can be done about it. The less said in that case the better. You've been wonderfully prudent, Venetia. Nobody need know.'

For all that, he thought, as he set off on his errand, Brandon was not going to get out of it very easily. Venetia might be a liar but she would not have invented this story; she must have got Brandon to commit himself.

Romilly was immediately aware, when his visitor was shown into the library, that an interval of respite was over. This formidable banker was going to make his mind up for him. They measured one another warily whilst exchanging enquiries as to the health and prosperity of all the Brandons and all the Newbolts. They had not met for many years. As boys they had been pretty friendly, although Romilly had secretly resented Charles' faculty for getting his own way, and Charles had secretly despised Romilly's chronic indecision.

Do I deny that I made her an offer? wondered Romilly. I'm not sure that's true, and I don't care to tell lies. Do I tell him I've changed my mind? Have I? He looks confoundedly sure of himself. I shall cut a very poor figure unless I take the initiative.

'You've come, I hope,' he said, smiling, 'to tell me what I am to do about Venetia? I expect you've heard all about it from her. But your father's illness . . . I've had no opportunity of speaking to him. When I called on him to do so he was obviously unable to attend to me, and she told me that I had better wait.'

'He's perfectly recovered now,' said Charles drily.

'Is he indeed? We'd heard reports . . .'

'Very much exaggerated. There's no reason at all why you shouldn't speak to him now.'

He forbore to express any opinion of the match. He knew, and Romilly knew that he knew, enough to invalidate the usual civilities. This long delay could only mean one thing; the fellow had intended to slip out of it but lacked the assurance to say so.

'It might be better,' he added, 'if you speak to him whilst I am still at the Parsonage. Then, if by any chance he proves unable to attend to things, I can act for him.'

'Ah yes. How long shall you be there?'

'I shall remain as long as my family has need of me, but I shall be glad to get off as soon as I can, for I'm a busy man.'

'I see.'

'If you have no other engagement today, come back with me and see him now.'

Ten minutes saw them walking back across the park. Charles felt an irritation which he recognised as familiar. He had often, in the old days, forced Romilly to some course of action and then experienced, not triumph, but the impatience of one who has shot a sitting bird.

'How is your elder sister?' asked Romilly suddenly. 'I think I heard that she has a very bad cold.'

'Yes. It still seems to be unusually severe.'

'I'm sorry.'

'Venetia thinks she is beginning to throw it off.'

'She's had it for some time, surely?'

'Yes. I don't know how long. It was still very heavy when I came.'

Romilly sighed and said no more. Charles began to be a little sorry for him. To be obliged to marry Venetia would be a misfortune for any man, although Brandon had only himself to thank for his situation. He might already have begun to guess what she was, and had better be marched to the altar before he guessed any more.

He ushered the condemned man into his father's study. Dr. Newbolt looked up impatiently from his Bible but smiled when he recognised Romilly.

'I'm very glad to see you,' he exclaimed. 'I fancy you've not been here since you advised me to go to Summerfield. As it turned out I might have spared myself the trouble. He's a very ignorant fellow, you know. He don't know what he's talking about. He's all for this Economy. Since then I've written to my friend Eccles, down in Lancashire. It seems they suffer shockingly from Economy in the north. . . .'

Charles retired and went to find Venetia. She was on the stairs, talking to the maid Kitty, who carried an untouched breakfast tray. It seemed that Jenny could not be roused to eat anything.

'Much better let her sleep,' said Venetia.

'If you'd just go up and look at her, Miss . . .'

'Later. When she wakes.'

Venetia waved Kitty away and turned to Charles with a questioning look.

'You've not seen Jenny today then?' he exclaimed.

'No. I'll go later. Well? I see you brought . . .'

'You don't spend much time with her, do you?'

'My dear Charles! Kitty waits on her hand and foot and would tell me directly if she wanted anything. But this isn't exactly a moment when I'd wish to catch Jenny's cold.'

He saw her point. A lady with a bad cold has a poor chance of fixing a reluctant suitor.

He took her into the garden and gave her an account of his interview with Romilly, making no attempt to spare her feelings.

'I think he'd have been off if I hadn't brought him to the point. And if I were you, Venetia, I'd exert myself to keep on the right side of the Brandon ladies. You can do so if you wish. I've never known you fail to secure anything you wanted. It won't be comfortable for you, you know, living with all of them up there, if they dislike you. It's not as if Brandon himself is particularly . . . manageable.'

She assured him tranquilly that all difficulties of that sort could be smoothed over. The Brandon ladies might prefer to live elsewhere.

'I'm very much obliged to you, Charles. You shan't

find me ungrateful. And there's just one more favour that I have to ask — quite a small one. Then your exertions on my behalf will be over. When he leaves my father I shall go back with him to the Priors. We should tell Mrs. Brandon and the girls immediately. Could you be so very good as to call for me, half an hour later? I'm sorry you should have to walk across the park twice in one day, but it will leave us time to call on the Arbuthnots, on our way home.'

And to ensure that the whole village knows the news before sunset, he thought. Brandon will find himself at the altar before he knows what o'clock it is.

'How many of his sisters are there now?' he asked.

'Only Ellen and Amabel. Charlotte has gone home and taken Bet with her. Why . . . here he is! They've not been long about it!'

Romilly was coming from the house. Charles made off hastily, wondering what Eliza would say to all this when she heard of it. He was not quite sure what she would think.

'I'm the happiest of men,' announced Romilly, joining Venetia. 'Your father did not pay me very much attention, he had so much to say about the Bishop. But I have his leave to address you. What a determined fellow Charles is!'

'It was time something was settled. If you had wanted to be off you could have gone away. You could have gone to some races and stayed there till the danger was over.'

'There are no convenient races. Except Cheltenham. And that don't begin till tomorrow. What are your commands for me?'

'To take me to the Priors. We must tell your mother at once. If we don't, Charles will take more steps. He's hiding in the raspberry canes, in case I should cry for help.'

'Just as you please. I'm sorry Charlotte has gone.'

'It must be the first time in your life you ever wished her here. But I'm sorry too. We should enjoy telling her, I think.'

That would have been a pleasure they could share. His spirits rose a little as they set out for the Priors. Her freedom from cant and humbug was a great point in her favour. She did not demand that he should play the lover. He owed her nothing save a wedding ring and might, with a clear conscience, do as he liked. In order to make that point perfectly plain he decided that he would, on the morrow, go to the Cheltenham races, and stay there as long as it suited him. He must begin as he meant to go on. If he stuck to that he might do very well. She was amusing. She made him laugh a good deal on the walk with a description of the gin palace now flourishing over the Parsonage stables.

She's probably as good a wife as I deserve, he thought.

They found his mother and Ellen writing letters. The old lady received their news with tearful agitation, kissed them, sobbed, and declared that she had always seen how it would be. Ellen wished them joy but could not entirely conceal her dismay and surprise.

'You come just in time,' said Mrs. Brandon, after a pause. 'We are writing to Mr. Latymer, Romilly. May we tell him?'

'Writing to Latymer! How does that come about?'

'Oh, I've engaged to write to him regularly, poor young man. He misses letters from home so much. It was Ellen's scheme, and a very clever one, don't you think? May we tell him? He'll be so much interested.'

'Oh yes, ma'am. Everybody is now going to be told. Where are Amabel and Miss Wilson, and Flinders and George . . .?'

'We can trust your mother to tell them,' said Venetia. 'But, for a formal announcement, shouldn't we wait until you get back from Cheltenham.'

Everyone looked startled.

'He goes to the races tomorrow,' she explained, rising and making ready for departure. 'I expect he'll neglect us for ever so long. I should be quite sunk in my spirits if you had not been so kind.'

Having kissed them both she tripped off.

'I never said that I was going to Cheltenham,' he protested as soon as they were out of the house.

'No. But you made up your mind to go, on the way here. I saw it in your face. Pray go, if it will make you easy.'

'Ah well . . . you keep a broomstick in the vestry.'

'You may hand me to it now. It's coming over the bridge to take me home.'

She pointed to Charles who was, upon her instructions, coming to take her away.

Mrs. Brandon and Ellen were meanwhile each giving her own version of the news to Latymer. Mrs. Brandon wrote of Venetia's beauty, her cleverness, and dwelt much upon the value of old acquaintance. Ellen wrote:

'What can I tell you that Mama has not told you already? Only this: I wish that I could learn prudence. Pray forget what I said formerly about a person that is now to be my sister. I mean to forget it all quite. You scolded me then, for talking too much, and you are justified.

'Now that Charlotte is gone Miss Wilson is at leisure

164

to attend to our education. We are continually at lessons. Here is something very important which I learnt before breakfast this morning. It will be of the greatest support to me, I am sure, on my journey through this Vale. If anybody asks me how the ancient Romans made their ink I shall be able to reply immediately: Gum! Gall! Lamp-black and sometimes a dash of alum!'

7

SHE could have climbed out of the deep pit into which she had fallen if only she had been able to breathe. They had tied a scarf over her mouth and nose which she could not tear off. Sometimes she knew that there was no scarf; she was losing the power to breathe. Even so, she sometimes got her head and shoulders over the top of the pit, which was lined with spruce boughs. Then she saw Xamdu, its cool waterfalls, its twisted rocks, its mild, pensive people. But at last she slipped right down to the darkness at the bottom, where it was icy cold, not burning hot any more.

How long she lay there she knew not. The darkness thinned. Her window was glimmering in the light of dawn. She heard a bird singing, and thought: I'm dying. Somebody should be with me.

She needed nobody. But in a well-ordered household no one is left to die alone. She had done her best, and she had failed. The neighbours would be shocked. Her father, who took the Sacrament to the humblest of his flock, would reproach himself. For his sake she must not die until the morning. She must continue to see the light until they came.

She fixed her eyes on the window. The light grew stronger. Again she heard the sleepy chirping of awakened birds.

The pale square flickered, faded, and was gone for ever.

PART IV
THE BEREAVED

I

'I HEARD the bell toll when I was dressing,' sobbed Amabel. 'I wondered who . . . but I never dreamt . . .'

'We must go at once,' said Mrs. Brandon. 'There might be something we could . . . that poor old man! And Venetia! Our . . .'

She tried to say *our dear Venetia*, but could not. She added doubtfully:

'So young . . . unused to nursing. She'll feel it dreadfully.'

'But fancy thinking it a cold,' cried Amabel, 'when it was inflammation of the lungs!'

'Ought we not to send for Romilly?' suggested Ellen.

'At Cheltenham?' Her mother looked startled. 'Why yes . . . now that we are to be connected . . . and he will want to be with Venetia . . . to comfort her. . . .'

There was a short silence. They were all crying but their tears were checked by the effort to imagine so unlikely a scene. Venetia demanding comfort? Romilly supplying it? Impossible!

'The people in the village will miss . . .' mused Mrs. Brandon. 'She was so good to them. But we shall all miss her.'

Shall we? wondered Ellen miserably, wishing very much that they should. But she could only think of a great ugly bonnet bobbing along the street, and recall the qualm of boredom with which one stopped to chat with Jenny Newbolt. She had been a good woman — a very,

very good woman. There was no doubt about that. Ought not goodness to be missed?

'If they never knew how ill she was,' exclaimed Amabel, 'I daresay she never got the Sacrament! How shocking!'

'She stayed for it last time,' said Ellen.

She had stayed herself, kneeling alone, because in five years there are sixty months, and she must kneel alone sixty times, and now there would be only fifty-nine before he and she might kneel together again. What a sad letter she must now write! 'You will be very sorry to hear ... you will remember how kind and obliging she was at our little ball ... we are all miserable.' But I am feeling so much which I can never tell him because I have not the words. I'm miserable because we shall forget her so soon. Life is sad ... sad ... because it is so much sadder than we are.

The three ladies drove down to the Parsonage, where they found everything in confusion. The cook, who received them, said that his Reverence had gone to the stables, summoned by an urgent message from Tibbie. Miss Venetia was locked in her bedchamber and would answer nobody.

'I don't know where to turn, madam. I don't indeed. There's Kitty in strong hysterics! It's very hard, madam, that all the blame should be put on the poor girl. She's not very bright, but she did all she could for poor Miss Jenny, and she's young. She's not accustomed to sick bodies. She never thought but it was just a cold. And now Miss Venetia has turned her off!'

'Have you sent for ...'

'Oh yes, madam. Word has been sent to all the young gentlemen. Poor Mr. Charles! He'll hardly have got home, before he gets the express.'

'How ... how does Dr. Newbolt take it?'

The Bereaved

'Dazed, madam. Han't spoken a word since Kitty come screaming downstairs this morning, like a mad thing, to say she found Miss Jenny . . . Oh dear, oh dear! . . . all alone, madam! All alone!'

'He'll feel it shockingly.'

'To be sure. We all shall. Miss Jenny was . . .'

The woman paused, and then said, as everybody was saying, that Jenny had been so very good.

'I shall go upstairs to Venetia,' announced Amabel. 'Perhaps she would answer me.'

She ran upstairs. Ellen surmised that Venetia was merely an excuse. 'Have you seen the corpse?' was a question always asked by Amabel on these occasions.

Seized with a sudden nausea Ellen ran out of the house and across the garden into the churchyard. On the far side of the laurel hedge, lying on the grass beside a flat slab tomb, she saw a boy.

That boy! she thought, stiffening. She had heard, of course, that he now worked at the Parsonage. Amabel had made a great pother about it and had written the news to Charlotte and Sophy. They had snubbed her for her pains, pointing out that, since there was no atom of truth in that vulgar scandal, the fact that the child now cleaned Dr. Newbolt's boots need excite no comment. But it had excited a good deal, all the same, although nobody ventured to mention it to Mrs. Brandon.

She was about to turn back when he raised his head and gave her a look so full of misery that she felt it like a blow over the heart. With a stifled cry she sat down on the grass beside him and whispered:

'Oh, you poor child! No wonder you should grieve. She was very kind to you.'

He nodded and presently gasped out:

'I wan't kind to her. I never minded her as I should.'

'We all feel so. When some person dies whom we've loved. I felt so when my father died.'

'I loved her. I did. But I never took her part when folks laughed at her. But I loved Miss Jenny.'

'We all loved her.'

'Nay. Nobody loved her. They let her die. There an't nothing good left in the world, now she's gone.'

'Dr. Newbolt . . . you must do all that you can for him. He will miss her so much. In that way you can still do something for her.'

'I would. I'd tend him. But I'll not be let stay here now. Miss Venetia will see to that.'

This seemed very probable. Ellen wondered if she could not herself do something for Jenny by helping the child. She then remembered that a good many people believed him to be her nephew. It was an awkward business. But then a brilliant idea occurred to her.

'Should you not like to go to sea? To join His Majesty's Navy?'

Dickie's opinion of His Majesty's Navy, expressed with some force, annoyed her so much that she grew less sorry for him.

He was not a respectful child, she thought, as she went back to the Parsonage garden. No decent village child would use such language. But then, she remembered, he was not exactly a decent village child. Moreover, he might believe her to be his aunt. He ought to be sent away. Before Rom gets to hear about him, she thought. Rom is so unaccountable. One never knows what he might do.

Amabel knocked at Venetia's door and begged for admittance. When no answer was returned she went down the passage to another door. For a few seconds she listened. There was no sound within. The village women must have finished their grim task. She opened the door and peeped into the darkened room.

It was there, straight and narrow on the bed, rigid as the frills of the cap standing up round the long chalky face. She stared at it avidly. Then, remembering decorum, she knelt down and repeated the Lord's Prayer.

This duty performed she rose, looking about the room, remembering former occasions when she had been there. There was a visit long ago, when, as a very little girl, playing with Venetia in the garden, she had fallen down and cut her knee. Jenny had brought her up here, bathed and dressed the cut, and consoled her by showing her a secret drawer in a little desk by the window. There had been nothing in it. Jenny, when Amabel had wonderingly asked why not, had laughed and said that perhaps, some day, she might find a treasure worthy of it.

She had seemed like quite another person then, thought Amabel in surprise. Twelve years ago. She must have changed after Mrs. Newbolt died. That tall laughing girl was as unlike the woman they now mourned as the woman was unlike the thing lying on the bed.

Crossing to the window, Amabel pressed the spring which Jenny had showed her so long ago. The little drawer sprang up. It was so thin that it could hardly have held more than the letter which now fell out of it.

So she did find something to put in it after all! But what could it be? A love-letter? Jenny Newbolt!

Pulling the curtain aside, Amabel peered at the direction. The letter was sealed and addressed to Romilly Brandon Esq.

Romilly! Why should Jenny write to Romilly? Why was the letter never sent? Ought he not now to have it? He never would, if she put it back into the drawer. Nobody else knew its secret. Would he get it if she now put it on the dressing table?

Footsteps were coming along the passage. She pushed the drawer back and slipped the letter into her pocket. When a servant came in with a jug full of white roses, Amabel was once more kneeling at the foot of the bed.

THE house had become very dangerous. It was full of secrets, memories, and truths hitherto lying in ambush which might now pounce on a man and endorse what Tibbie had said. Tibbie was a drunken, doting old creature; no attention need be paid to her. But it might be better not to return to the house, because upstairs . . . upstairs . . .

Dr. Newbolt set off on a ramble across the fields. He must protect himself. He must return to the thoughts of yesterday which had been, still were, immensely important. Only yesterday he had made his great discovery, and it was imperative that he should communicate it at once to the Archbishop of Canterbury. Humanity must be informed of the identity . . . the rider of the Black Horse in the Apocalypse . . . for weeks he had known himself to be upon the brink of a momentous revelation, and yesterday the crucial words had leapt out at him. '*A pair of balances in his hand.*' '*A measure of wheat for a penny, three measures of barley for a penny, and see thou hurt not the oil and the wine.*'

This, your Grace, is Economy, followed by Death . . . (Death! Death! Death! Gone! Never . . . never . . .) . . . Death on a pale horse, and Hell following after. It is therefore impossible to maintain that Economy does not concern the Church. Sent as a plague to mankind, doubt- less . . . the sudden appearance of this Phantom of which we never heard in former years . . . the insensibility to human suffering which it has bred . . . reason, compassion, Christian principles, all challenged . . . an universal blindness . . . (Blindness! Blindness!) . . . my task will never be accomplished if I allow my mind to be disturbed. . . . (*There's none so blind as those who won't see. Her heart was broke before your very eyes*) . . . what comes next? The injustice. . . . (*No need to seek injustice at Cranton's. There's been enough of it under your own roof.* No man has ever set more store by justice than I, Tibbie. I have always . . .) . . . We are told, your Grace, that these inflictions are to fall upon the fourth part of the earth. Undoubtedly the Continent of Europe. Buonaparte rides a white horse, so we are told. It has long been allowed that the red horse brings war and slaughter. After these two . . . Economy with his scales, sparing neither woman nor child . . . (*Weep for any child you would, save your own.* Jenny! Jenny! My child . . . dead . . . gone . . . gone . . . *All for that greedy young one, and she who gave you her life to be left to charity at the last* . . . these people are very ignorant. 'Tis the custom . . . an unmarried daughter . . . one does not make the same provision . . .) Are not these, gentlemen, the counsels of the devil? Economy bids us exclude thousands of helpless creatures from all claim to mercy . . . (I can give her nothing now. Nothing. Nothing. Nothing. Nothing. Nothing. Nothing. Had she lived . . . part should have been hers . . . I had not considered . . .) In my first letter I shall not mention the White Horse of the Corsican. No, no! That shall be revealed later. But not too late. (Too late. Too late. Too late. Too . . .) That's a very terrible thing. Eccles must be told of this discovery. He pays too little attention to Economy. This scheme of his for teaching the poor things to read, what should that do for them? At least, he says, they may feel that they have a friend. Ay, there's something in that. I believe she would have been all for it. She taught that boy to read. And we must be doing something, must we not? Shall we lie supine beneath the heels of this black horse? No, no! Holy Scripture never bids us do that. Eccles would do more if he had the means. Her portion . . . I believe that my mind might be clearer, I might address His Grace more forcibly, if some part of what should, in justice, have been hers . . . I'll write to Eccles . . . her portion . . . if I devote her portion . . . Venetia will never be in want. She marries a rich man. In justice, perhaps, the whole should have been Jenny's. . . .

So soon as he had made up his mind to write to Eccles he felt able to go back to the house. At some point on his long ramble he must have come to the conclusion that he had, indeed, been unjust. He could not have said exactly when he had admitted the fact. He had left Tibbie denying it. He came home accepting it. And, in that case, he must make what reparation he could before venturing to condemn the injustice of others. He would offer Jenny's portion . . . the provision which he should have made for her, to Eccles for the maintenance of a Ragged School.

He had meant to write at once, but he came home so much exhausted that immediate effort was impossible. He sat down and fell asleep. The day was over when he woke. It was twilight. He had not been given his dinner. Jenny should have . . . *Jenny!*

The jar of remembrance made him dizzy. He crept to the door calling feebly for Venetia, who came, carrying a candle.

'I've had no dinner,' he complained.

'We've been keeping it for you, Papa. We thought it better not to wake you.'

'Very well. Very well. I'll have it now. I must write a letter. I'm writing to Eccles. I am going to give him Jenny's portion, the money I should have left for Jenny. For those schools of his. I think she would have wished it.'

'She would certainly have wished it,' agreed Venetia. 'Will you come to the dining parlour, Papa, or shall something be brought to you on a tray?'

He asked for a tray and went back to the composition of his letter. In time, he thought, he would be able to take comfort in Venetia, but not until he felt easy in his mind in the matter of justice to Jenny, such justice as it might now be in his power to observe.

They were taking a long time over his tray. He waited for forty minutes before ringing his bell. The servant who answered it denied all knowledge of the order. Nor would Venetia, when summoned, allow that he had asked for one. He had been asleep whenever she looked in. He must have dreamt that he woke up and talked to her and asked for a tray.

3

THE express, bringing the news of Jenny's death, reached Charles barely an hour after he had got home. He set off again for Stretton Courtenay immediately, and his wife would have gone with him if one of the children had not been suffering from earache. He was sorry to leave her behind; he felt that she would have been a support in any further transactions with Venetia.

At Severnton he waited at the Three Crowns, until the London coach came in, in case either of his brothers should be travelling on it, and in need of a lift to Stretton. Neither Stephen nor Harry would be likely to travel post.

They both turned up and Stephen annoyed Charles by exclaiming at once:

'Ah! It did occur to you to wait for us!'

Harry made a face at Charles behind Stephen's back, and then pulled his mouth down, remembering their errand.

The three brothers drove on together. For a mile or so they agreed that it was a sad business, that they had never been so shocked in their lives, that poor Jenny had been the best of sisters, and that they trusted there had been no neglect. But they brightened a little when Charles told them of his recent visit and of Venetia's engagement. Stephen even broke into a chuckle, cut it short, and said in some confusion that his wife had foretold as much.

'As soon as we heard Brandon had come home: Depend upon it, says Henrietta, that puss will marry him and be richer than any of us.'

'That's very likely, in any case,' said Charles. 'My father told me something, just before I set out for home the other day, which startled me considerably. If my carriage hadn't been waiting . . . but I had to go. He said that he means to give her twenty thousand pounds.'

The other two exclaimed and Harry said:

'That must be pretty near all he's got.'

'I fancy so.'

'Upon my word! That's going too far,' cried Stephen. 'We always knew she'd get more than her share. But that she should get *all* . . .!'

'Exactly,' said Charles. 'The money was most of it our mother's. It was left to him absolutely, but I'm sure she would never . . . It should have been tied up in some way for the benefit of all her children.'

'Has he made a will?' asked Harry.

'I don't think so. I gather he means to give her the money on her wedding day.'

'And when is that to be?'

'Nothing is settled yet about that, so far as I know.'

'Still, there's not much time,' pondered Harry, 'if anything is to be done.'

'It cannot be very soon, now,' said Stephen, with some satisfaction. 'Not when we are all in deep mourning.'

'Whenever it is, that's what he means to do,' said Charles. 'You can remonstrate with him if you like. Personally I never found any argument answered with my father.'

They all began to look more gloomy than ever.

'D'you think he might be a little . . .' Harry tapped his

forehead. 'I've heard rumours. Han't he been writing some very odd letters to the newspapers? I never saw one, but a fellow in our chambers . . .'

'We saw it,' said Stephen. 'Henrietta said at once: His mind must be disordered. And he had some kind of seizure, in May, didn't he?'

'He had a fall,' said Charles slowly. 'But I believe they think nothing worse.'

'How did he strike you, when you were there?'

'Altered. Unlike himself. But rational enough. Nobody could claim, I think, that he's unfit to have the care of his own money.'

'Lunacy cases are always tricky,' agreed Harry. 'But supposing he grows worse? Eh? This shock . . . this bereavement, it remains to be seen how he sustains it.'

'Venetia will see that he sustains it,' grumbled Stephen. 'At least until her wedding day!'

'If he should . . . grow worse . . .' said Charles, '. . . if it should become necessary . . . what's the law, Harry? When there is no will?'

'I can't say offhand. I must look it up. But I believe it would be locked up until his death and then divided equally amongst his children.'

'Five thousand pounds apiece.'

'No, Stephen old boy, only four. You forget Frank.'

'He don't need money. He's as good as a Nabob already. However, we must keep a sharp look-out. If Venetia is concealing any alarming eccentricities . . . Henrietta says she's damnably clever.'

'We knew that a long time before you married Henrietta,' said Charles. 'Yet, it's an odd thing, one can never put Venetia in the wrong. She does nothing. It's those about her who take leave of their senses; they do stupid,

sometimes unscrupulous, things, which always turn out
to her advantage. Don't you remember when you stole
that strawberry jam, and she ate it? You got the whipping,
Venetia got the jam.'

'I remember nothing of the sort. But in this case her
interest is perfectly clear. She'll persuade us, if she can,
that my father is rational. We must judge for ourselves.'

They thought this over as the great oak trees of Slane
Forest sped past them. Charles at last exclaimed:

'We used not . . . we never . . . now that Jenny is gone,
things are suddenly very bad. We are the worse without
her.'

'Ah, poor Jenny,' agreed Stephen. 'We must never
forget her goodness to us as children.'

'I don't mean that, exactly. Some . . . some tie has
gone with her. While she lived we never talked . . . quite
as we are talking now.'

'She was goodness itself!'

'Yes, Harry, she was. Now it has gone, and we are
the worse.'

'You mean,' said Stephen, 'that to discuss money at
such a time . . . perhaps you are right. We'll drop the
subject . . . at least until after . . .'

It could be safely dropped. They understood one
another well enough. Nothing more was said about their
father's state of mind until Cranton's pottery, in all its
ugliness, burst on them as they went down the hill.

Charles then said:

'That confounded place! All the trouble began there.
This pother about infant apprentices.'

'Is it true he's got some of them at the Parsonage?'

'He's hired the mother of some of them to nurse Tibbie.
And he has engaged a . . .'

Charles broke off and looked thoughtful.

'Engaged a what?'

'A knife-and-boot boy. Who will, I imagine, be sent packing now that poor Jenny . . . I must say I sympathise with Venetia over that. The child is a by-blow of Brandon's.'

This interesting topic kept them busy until they were entering Stretton Courtenay. Here their bereavement became more inescapable. Villagers watched them with long faces. They grew solemn and alighted at the Parsonage with becoming decorum.

Tearful servants took their hats and told them that Miss Venetia was in the breakfast parlour. They found her, not in tears, for she had never been known to weep, but more agitated than they had ever seen her. She kissed them each in turn and spoke more quickly than usual.

'I'm so very sorry, you've come too late to see her. The coffin has been closed. But you'd better go up directly. My father is there.'

'How does he take it?' asked Charles.

'Better than one might have expected.'

In silence they trooped up through the darkened house. Not one of them but had some memory of Jenny's room, visited only whenever they had wanted anything. Not one of them but wished that he had thanked her oftener.

At the foot of the coffin knelt an outlandish person in a bright pink coat. Charles recognised it as one of his own, worn long ago for hunting, and left behind at the Parsonage. A narrow, bald head turned. A ravaged face peered at them.

'Good God!' whispered Harry.

Does he know us? wondered Charles. I scarce knew him. I must have seen him before without a wig. But that coat . . .

'What day is this?' asked their father.

'Wednesday, sir.'

'Then you've come in time. We don't lay her away until tomorrow. Kneel, if you please. We must pray for forgiveness.'

They knelt round the coffin and he quavered the Sacramental Confession. Charles felt it to be appropriate enough. Stephen was shocked, and, as soon as he could, began to repeat, in a determined voice, a more suitable petition.

'Eternal rest give unto her, O Lord.'

His father gasped, almost as if in protest. After a moment's hesitation, Charles and Harry took up the response.

'And let Perpetual Light shine upon her.'

'May the souls of the righteous, which die in the Lord . . .'

'Rest in peace.'

They then knelt in silence until Harry, who felt that he had had quite enough of it, scrambled to his feet. The others rose and followed him out of the room.

'I think that I shall go for a little saunter,' said their father. 'It's a sweet evening and I don't like this dark house.'

'Should you not change your coat, sir?' ventured Charles.

'My coat?' He glanced down at it. 'Ah! That must surprise you. But I have no other, you know.'

They exchanged glances.

'I've had the misfortune to lose my keys. My closets and chests are all locked. I can't get at my clothes. Or my wigs.'

'We'll find the keys,' said Charles, conducting the

old man to his own quarters. 'Could the women not find them?'

'I consulted Venetia . . .'

'Here they are! Look, sir! All here, in their locks. You may open your closets quite easily.'

'Come back, have they? Venetia said I must be mistaken.'

The old man pulled off the gay coat, which was far too large for him, and Charles hunted for a wig.

'I'm glad that Stephen conducted the service,' said Dr. Newbolt. 'I could not have ventured. Perpetual Light, you know, can be a very terrible thing. I once . . . but the thought of it doesn't appear to alarm him.'

Charles persuaded him that they had not just been burying Jenny and that the funeral was on the morrow.

'But Stephen will . . . will . . .' he cried anxiously. 'I don't feel as though I should be able . . .'

'No, no, don't exert yourself. Nobody expects . . . Stephen will do it all. If I were you, sir, I should lie down for a little. You look exceedingly tired.'

'Ay. Tired to death. I shan't go for a saunter. I think I'll go to bed.'

'And I'll tell them to bring you something . . . a warm drink . . . Then you might be able to sleep.'

Having seen to this Charles joined his brothers, who were eating cold meat with very long faces.

'Venetia,' said Harry, 'declares she knows nothing about the keys.'

'They were all in their locks when we went to his room. I hope he remained in the house.'

'No. That's the worst of it. He ran out in that clown's rig, over to the church, to parley with the grave-diggers. Half the village saw him.'

'Yet Venetia insists that he is taking it calmly,' broke in Stephen.

The worse! The worse! thought Charles again. Without her we are baser. So much disregarded, yet so powerful! A part of what we were and are no longer.

He wondered why human creatures should imagine themselves as so distinct from one another, each a complete entity, defined by an unalterable character. He saw the Newbolts as elements in a crucible, each continually altering and modifying the rest, and the nature of the whole determined by the most powerful agent. Withdraw it, and all would be transformed.

And it's so, he thought, in all communities. Half of what we do is really done by others; what befalls them befalls us. 'We are members one of another.' He said:

'He wants you, Stephen, to officiate tomorrow.'

'Thank God for that!' said Stephen. 'I hope we may get through it without any distressing exposure.'

4

THEY got through it with tolerable decorum, although Romilly's absence provoked comment. The messenger sent to Cheltenham had been unable to trace him. Dickie Cottar's behaviour also attracted attention. He took up a solitary station midway between the gentry, grouped round the grave, and the villagers, grouped respectfully in the background. The cobbler, who was a wit, suggested later, amidst guffaws, that the boy must have thought he should play proxy for Squire.

Dr. Newbolt, neatly dressed and supported on either side by Charles and Harry, gave no trouble. Yet, within a week, it was generally reported that he had lost his wits and that his family were seeking to put him in a Bedlam. The red coat had been but one incident. He screamed out in the night. He would not drink his chocolate, declaring it to be poisoned. And all had witnessed his eccentricity on the Sunday. He would not preach from the pulpit, declaring himself to be unworthy. In the address which he then gave from the chancel steps, Perpetual Light, infant apprentices, *peccata mundi*, and the Four Horsemen of the Apocalypse were piteously confused.

Opinion ran strongly against Venetia. It was said that she had lost no time in turning Kitty off before the gentlemen should arrive and ask questions. And many shook their heads over Parson's alleged madness. Keys which vanished and then returned? If that was a delusion might it not have been a 'two-legged delusion'? Who was to say that his chocolate did not taste bitter? Miss Venetia, to be sure, had taken the cup and drunk it off, but she had not left a sip for any other witness.

These mutterings in their most lurid form were epitomised by Sukey Hollins.

'Miss Jenny,' she told Dickie, 'was murdered dead because she was sorry for poor folks. And old Parson will be put away, for that he brought us out of Cranton's. They puts away anybody that goes against 'em.'

Dickie did not contradict her. He half believed it and he was debating his own future. Common sense, together with some adroit eavesdropping, had assured him that he would shortly become an infant apprentice himself, hundreds of miles away, unless he scarpered. He had made up his mind to run off and join the Walking People. That was a hard and dangerous life but the only life he knew which offered freedom. He hoped to get his victuals by playing the fiddle; there were always pence for a fiddler. His playing had improved of late. Jenny had driven him to practise every day and had taught him a number of country dance tunes. He would have been off immediately after the funeral if he had not felt some responsibility for Jenny's father. The old man had been kind to him and was now, so Dickie suspected, in great danger. They were driving him into a Bedlam amongst them. A little vigilance at keyholes made that perfectly plain, for they talked of nothing else. The gentlemen were all declaring that he was crazy. Miss Venetia, she was against them but only because she wanted to get all the money, or so they thought. Dickie felt that his old friend would have been in less danger if the gentlemen thought he had his wits, and the lady had advocated a Bedlam.

Life at the Parsonage had somewhat altered Dickie. Good food and plenty of sleep might account for it. He had grown sturdier and bolder. A closer observation of the gentry and their ways had aroused in him a dormant spirit — that spirit which Jemmy the Finger was to condemn, five years later, as likely to get him hanged before his beard sprouted. He was by no means prepared to allow that his own fate, or Parson's fate, could be settled out of hand by others. On the contrary he felt an impulse, proper only in his betters, to alter the course of events, if he did not happen to approve of it. He thought that something should be done, and that he should do it.

He decided to take Parson with him when he ran away. With his fiddle he might make shift to keep food in their bellies, and Parson might have his value among the Walking People. He could baptize their infants. He could marry them, from time to time, thus giving any tramper's woman the right to call herself an altar mort and to turn up her nose at a mere walking mort. Church weddings were expensive and over-permanent. The trampers generally took new partners once a year, and a parson who fell in with this custom, against which Dickie could see no objection, might be very welcome in the Cold Harbours.

Having formed this resolution Dickie sought out his patron. He began by stating his fears for his own future.

'Don't alarm yourself,' said Dr. Newbolt. 'I promise you shall never leave us. I won't suffer it.'

'But, sir . . . you might not be here yourself for very long.'

'I shan't die yet,' said the old man sadly.

'Nay, but ... I beg your pardon for speaking of it ...
but they're plotting for to put you in a Bedlam.'

'What? What?'

''Tis the truth. All the village knows it. There's a-many
says you an't in your right mind. Day before Miss Jenny
was put away you wore a red coat.'

'I ... I ... I had lost my keys. What nonsense is
this?'

'They say you was deluded. And then the chocolate ...'

Dickie broke off, nearly silenced by the face of misery
before him. But these things must be said. He forced
himself to continue the list of eccentricities, item by item.

'Perhaps I might be a little ...' admitted Dr. Newbolt
at last. 'I've sometimes wondered ... these troubles ...
all so new, so unexplained ... But they would never shut
me up. No, no! They would let me stay here. I do no
harm to anybody.'

'An't there a law that a parson must have his wits?
You might be forced to go, for to make room for another
parson.'

'Yes ... yes ... I had thought of that, in any case. I
doubt if I'm fit, nowadays ... Stephen ... but Stephen
would keep me here. He would never ...'

'You'd not be master, though. I'd be sent northward.'

'Never. I should never agree to that. Don't be uneasy,
Dickie. My wishes will be attended to. And don't speak
of such things again. You forget your place. You are only
a child. You don't understand ... all this is vulgar gossip.
You must pay no attention to it.'

Dickie retired. He had made a beginning and broken
the subject.

On the next day a stranger came to the Parsonage, a
physician from Severnton, said to be an acquaintance of

Harry's. This person strolled coolly into the study and asked a number of questions, professing a strong interest in the Four Horsemen. Dr. Newbolt might have suspected nothing, and chatted freely, had he not now been upon his guard. Dickie's warning supplied an inkling as to the drift of these questions. He gave short answers.

In the end the sinister visitor took himself off. For nearly an hour after that he sat talking to Charles, Stephen and Harry in the breakfast parlour. It occurred to Dr. Newbolt, waiting uneasily to hear him go, that they had all now been at Stretton Courtenay for ten days. Why did they stay? The funeral was over. There was nothing for them to do. They were all busy men. Why did they not go home?

I'll just stroll by the window, he thought, feeling that this might be a little ungentlemanly, but that he must set his mind at rest. He did so and heard the stranger saying:

'. . . as well treated there as he is here. They take none but men of family. In my opinion, a private establishment seldom answers. There is not the same vigilance, and the expense . . .'

Dr. Newbolt walked away again. He returned to his study where he was taken with a trembling fit which lasted for a long time. The visitor was gone before it was over.

'That was a surgeon from Severnton,' said Dickie, bringing in the newspaper. 'He'll come again. He an't sure yet. You answered him so cleverly.'

'Perhaps . . . perhaps . . . I might be . . . my children! My children! Why? They would never . . . I don't know what to think. I mustn't think only of myself. I must consider their happiness. But . . .'

'You'd best scarper. I shall.'

'Scarper?'

'Be off to some place they'll never find you.'

'I never heard that word before.'

''Tis a word they have on the roads. The Walking People they have their own way of talking. I've learnt it, listening to 'em.'

'Do they indeed. Scarper! Tell me some others.'

'Why . . . they call a man a homey, and a drink a bevvy, and a bed a letty. And when they says eggles, that's a church.'

'Eggles? *Ecclesia!* Homo . . . lectus . . . scarpare! Why, Dickie, this is Latin. Was once Latin.'

'Maybe,' said Dickie impatiently.

'It must be very old. It must come from the time when people going from one country to another could all understand one another, since all spoke Latin. Can you tell me more?'

Dr. Newbolt became so much interested that it was difficult to keep him to the point. At last Dickie said:

'The Walking People, they could tell you more. They an't so bad when you get to know 'em. I've a mind to join 'em. They goes where they likes and does what they likes. That's more than you could say for most poor bodies. Scarper . . . or run off . . . it's what I shall do this very night. And . . . oh, sir . . . I wish you'd do the same. I don't like to leave you.'

'I must seek advice, I think. I must consult Eccles. That's a friend I have, in Lancashire. I've been expecting to hear from him. I wrote to him, some time since, on a business matter. I wonder I don't hear from him. I think . . . I think I'll go to Eccles.'

'Do *they* know where he lives?'

'Oh yes, I think so.'

The Bereaved

'Then they'll come after you. They'll never come after me, that's sure. There'll be no enquiration for me. But you . . . if you want to scarper you must fox 'em. There's a trick that would serve, but it wants money. Have you a few guineas about you, sir?'

'Not very many.'

'But there's some laid up somewhere, an't there?'

'In the bank at Severnton. Yes, I must go to the bank. I shall need money, if I'm to get to Lancashire.'

Dickie had heard of banks but did not know what they were. He pictured a great chest full of money buried in some secret place on the banks of the Severn.

'Could you get it easy?'

'Oh yes. At least . . . I believe . . .'

A new idea occurred to Dr. Newbolt. He began to tremble again.

'You'd best get it quickly, then. They don't let mad folks handle money, I believe. Go tomorrow.'

'I fear . . . I fear . . . you may be right . . . I'd never thought of the money!'

'Ride over there tomorrow, before they're astir. They're late risers all. Get your guineas.'

'Yes. Yes. I think I will. No harm in that.'

'I'll be off, soon as 'tis dark. I'll meet you there tomorrow. I've been in Severnton once. Fair time. There's a cross they call Martyr's Cross. Know it?'

'Yes. I know it. But . . .'

'I'll meet you there. Then, when you've got your guineas we may take the coach to Bristol.'

'Bristol? No, no. We'll go north.'

'You'll be all safe if you send 'em a letter from Bristol. Like Billy Bowles done. A letter for to say you've sailed away on a ship.'

'Billy Bowles! That fellow? Who went to America?'

'Not he. They was after him for sheep stealing, and he scarpered and sent a letter from Bristol for to say he'd gone to America. It was true seemingly. They sent to Bristol. There was a writing somewhere for to say he'd sailed in that ship. But he never went only to Cork. That's a place over the sea too, but not so far off. This ship, she puts in at Cork, and Billy gets off. He come back from Cork after the hue and cry was died down, and he got work as a tin miner in a place they call the Red Ruth. Nobody knew till a cousin of his went down into Cornwall and saw him there. That's what you might do, sir. But you need guineas for to go on a ship.'

'I could never do that.'

'Get your guineas first. No harm in that.'

'No, no. I believe I'd better make sure of . . . it will distress them . . . but I could never bear . . . Venetia! She must have been persuaded by the rest. We'll talk of this again tomorrow. When you bring my newspaper tomorrow.'

'But, Parson, I'm off tonight. I've stayed overlong as it is. I'll wait for you by the Cross all day tomorrow. If you don't come, I'll go my ways.'

'No, Dickie! No. You mustn't run off like this. A child of your age! You might come to some harm.'

'I'll come to harm if I stay here. So will you.'

'Never fear. I'll care for you. I'll take you to Eccles. He'll have some scheme for you, I don't doubt. I'll get the money and meet you by the Cross tomorrow.'

Dickie nodded and went off. A pocket full of guineas would, he thought, be necessary, whether they went to Bristol or to Lancashire. He could himself run off, at any time, if the old gentleman proved obstinate.

For the rest of the day Dr. Newbolt sat staring in front

of him. He did not blame his children. He no longer felt able to blame any particular person for the world's sins and the world's sorrows. He had relinquished all effort to distinguish between the innocent and the guilty, and had tried to say so in his address from the chancel steps. These distinctions were, he knew, necessary in the conduct of human affairs, but they are made by the partial and intermittent light in which human affairs are normally beheld. Any alarming premonition of Perpetual Light must make such a task impossible. He had therefore, perhaps, become unfit for participation in the world's work, including the work of a pastor. He must resign the living. He must give no trouble to those still labouring in the field. He must school himself to think and speak as one having no authority.

Yet the thought of a madhouse was more than he could endure. He had seen one once, on a visit to an unhappy friend, and had thanked God when the poor wretch died a few weeks later. Nor did he think himself mad; confused, bewildered, at a loss, perhaps, but not irrational. His memory might be failing; but that was common enough at his age. But these illusions . . . the keys . . . the chocolate . . . the tray . . . the snake in his wig cupboard . . . He began to tremble again. If he could but be sure that they were illusions he would thank God from the bottom of his heart. Madness was very terrible, he must bear it as best he might, but there was another, more terrible, doubt which he could not bring himself to face. Sooner than face it he would . . . what was it the child had said? He would scarper. There was one illusion which he must, at all costs, preserve.

I'll go to Eccles, he thought, and tell him everything. And then knew that this supreme terror could never be divulged to Eccles, or to any living soul. He had ventured as near to it as he dared, on this evening, in his own thoughts. He had ventured too near. He must not see her again, or listen to her caressing voice. He must preserve himself from that, escaping to some place where she could never come, to some existence where he need never think of her. Like Billy Bowles done. Cork . . . Why not?

5

No Stretton news could reach Romilly since he had
decided upon a strategic disappearance, and concealed himself in an inn at Tintern. This was
partly in order to assert his right to do exactly as he
pleased, whether married or not. He also thought it a
very good trick to play upon Charlotte and Charles Newbolt. They would conclude that he meant to slip out of
his engagement. Charlotte would triumph, far too openly.
Charles would pen a challenge ready for despatch so soon
as he could discover Romilly's whereabouts. Both would
look very silly when he eventually returned, perfectly
ready to marry Venetia and blandly surprised that anyone
could have doubted his intentions. Venetia, to do her
justice, would probably enjoy the joke as much as he did.

All this was apparent to Markham, who understood his
master better than anybody else in the world. He had his
own channels of communication with Stretton, and knew
all that had happened, but he thought it better to hold his
tongue until asked for information. The sudden appearance of a blue waistcoat did at last inspire a question.
Romilly, finding it put out for him, asked if it had not
been left behind at the Priors.

'Yes, sir. But we can't well do without it, so I took
the liberty of writing for it to Mr. Partridge.'

'Partridge? H'm. . . . And he sent it? Had he any news?
All goes on much as usual, I suppose?'

Markham hesitated and decided that he had now better speak up.

'Pretty well, I believe, sir. Except that they are distressed at losing his Reverence. He's left the country, it seems. Gone to America, so Mr. Partridge says, and written to his family that he's never coming back.'

'His Reverence? Who . . . you don't mean Dr. Newbolt?'

'Yes, sir.'

'Gone to . . . impossible! Are you sure? You must be mistaken. Partridge must have meant somebody else.'

'No, sir. Dr. Newbolt disappeared very suddenly some days ago. Nobody knew where he was gone. Then the family got a letter to say that he was off to America.'

'Good God!'

After a short pause Markham continued:

'They say his mind was unsettled. Had been for some time.'

'That's true,' agreed Romilly, remembering the infant apprentices. 'But . . . America! I can't believe it.'

Markham went round behind him to brush his coat at the back, murmuring:

'He had a shock, sir. One of the young ladies died very sudden. They say it drove him clean out of his wits.'

Romilly stood very still. He did not ask which young lady. Markham stole a look at him, saw that he guessed, and went off to put some boots away in a cupboard.

'A severe cold,' said Romilly at last. 'She had a cold.'

'Yes, sir,' said Markham, with his head in the cupboard. 'It went to the lungs.'

'When . . . when was it?'

'The day after we came away, sir, I believe.'

'I see. You can go now.'

Markham went into the next room and began to pack the portmanteaux, foreseeing that they would now return to Stretton.

After an interval of stunned stupor Romilly told himself that nothing in particular had happened, so far as he was concerned. He had lost her a long time ago. Death could scarcely part them more. It was very sad; a blow to her father and her family. But for him it signified no momentous change.

He was growing tired of Tintern and toyed for a while with a notion of going north. He had always wished to inspect Hadrian's Wall. They would miss her in the village. Who would bring them baskets? The old man . . . *America?* . . . what had Markham said? He rang the bell.

'What was it, exactly, that you said about Dr. Newbolt?' he asked.

The story, as Markham had learnt it from Partridge, was repeated. Dr. Newbolt had grown so eccentric, after Miss Jenny's death, that his family had taken fright. A surgeon from Severnton had been consulted. It was thought that the Doctor, getting wind of this, had gone off so as to escape a madhouse.

'I suppose . . . I ought to go back . . .' said Romilly.

'Yes, sir.'

That night they got as far as Severnton. In the morning Romilly ran into old Mr. Freeman, father of all the Freeman boys, stamping about the inn galleries. He had come to Severnton on some business connected with a law suit. They breakfasted together and Romilly heard more about the recent scandals at Stretton Courtenay. The old gentleman might have been less outspoken had he heard or remembered the rumours connecting Romilly with Venetia. He repeated all the stories current about neglect, the deaf ear turned to appeals from Kitty, and the lonely death in a summer dawn.

'Not one of them by her! Not one to bid her God speed! What d'ye think of that? Why, she'd devoted her whole life to 'em. A shabby crew, those Newbolts; always were. All save poor Jenny. I've no patience with 'em. So soon as she was gone they turned on the old man. It seems he'd written to some friend . . . was planning to endow a little school for poor children in her memory. Why not? Very right and proper. His own money, wan't it? But Miss Venetia got wind of it; by all accounts she played some very double game, though I don't know the ins and outs of the matter. They had a letter from this friend after the old man had run off, and then it all came to light. And now, so it's said, they're all at loggerheads over a bed-ridden old nurse. Who's to keep *her*? Did you ever hear of anything so pitiful? Stephen declares he won't have her at the Parsonage when . . .'

Mr. Freeman broke off in some confusion, remembering that Stephen's succession to the living could not be taken for granted. Romilly would have some say in the matter.

'Tibbie . . . ?' said Romilly, recalling a shadowy presence in an enormous cap, of whom even he had once stood in awe. 'You mean to say she's still alive?'

'Alive and kicking, thanks to Jenny's care. But I never meant, you know, to put you against Stephen Newbolt. He's not a bad sort of fellow. One must allow for gossip. And you may depend upon it he . . . all the boys . . .

would have showed up better if Venetia . . . she was at
the bottom of it all. She's a sly one, that girl. My boys
never liked her.'

Romilly nodded. He had not yet realised that he must
shortly appoint a new parson. He was trying to remember
what he had been doing at the moment when Jenny
breathed her last. Fast asleep, probably. *Dreaming in
some soft repose.* . . .

'She's buried now?' he asked.

'Who? Jenny? Why, yes. It was some weeks ago, you
know.'

'I knew nothing of it. I only heard yesterday.'

'We supposed not, or you would have been there.'

'You were there?'

'Oh yes. All of us. All came who could, I think.'

Mr. Freeman sighed and added:

'One blames the family. But we felt amongst ourselves
that we'd never made enough of her. We said so, the boys
and I, riding home. She was a very good . . . What?
Are you off? You han't touched your eggs and bacon.'

'I've had all I want.'

Markham was promptly dragged from eggs and bacon
which he would have liked to finish. On all the drive
homewards Romilly was oppressed by an increasing
sense of unreality. The forest trees, the fields, the village
green, were not solid, not actual; they were painted
screens set up to mask vacancy. He remembered such a
sensation once before; he had known it for a moment
in the garden during his first call at the Parsonage. At
the Priors he told Partridge that he would be in the
library and must on no account be disturbed.

Once in that haven he flung himself into a chair.
Nothing, he decided, was very much amiss save for the

dark and the cold. These advanced. Total darkness
threatened to break through the bright screen of sunshine
and green trees; a slow chill was gradually creeping along
all his limbs. To sit still, yielding to their threat, was
intolerable. He went out at last, into the sunlight. He
crossed the park, not defining his own intention, but
aware that he must see for himself.

They had put back the slab on the grave beneath the
yew tree. The new mortar looked white against the
mellowing stones. He picked up a dead daisy chain
which hung forlornly on one corner, and flung it away
into the grass. The cold was now so terrifying that he
looked up at the sun, half doubting that it could still be
there. As he stared a curious tingling in the back of his
neck told him that he was not alone. The yew tree was
staring at him, as trees could and did stare if they caught
a man quite alone. He turned sharply. The shadows
under the upper branches were full of eyes.

'Who's that?' he exclaimed. 'What's that?'

A thin husky voice muttered:

'We seen you.'

Another said, more clearly:

'You threw away the poor lady's flowers.'

Children, he thought, relaxing. Nothing worse than
children. But his own eyes were so dazzled by sunlight
that he could not locate them.

'They were dead,' he said.

'So is the poor lady,' piped a third voice.

'Come down! You can't play here. Come down at
once.'

There was a rustling and crackling. Three dirty little
creatures slid down the tree and stood in a row before him.

'Who are you? Where d'you live?'

The Bereaved

After a long silence the tallest murmured:

'We don't live nowhere now. We got to go away.'

'Right away,' agreed the smallest dreamily. 'Our Mam's a-tying up our bundles.'

'Hugga!' cried his sister. 'Run! She's after us!'

All three promptly took to their heels. There were quick footsteps on the other side of the hedge. Venetia appeared, an angry whirlwind in crisp black.

'If I catch you here again . . .' she cried in a voice which Romilly had never heard before.

Then she saw him and drew up. They gazed at one another over the newly mortared slab. She spoke first, dropping to the habitual low, slow tone.

'What are you doing here?'

'Looking at the grave,' he said simply.

'You could have done that at the funeral. It's too late now to make a fuss about Jenny. You threw her over once, and she cried her eyes out. But that was a long time ago.'

'You knew that?'

'I had eyes in my head. Even in the nursery. I daresay you'd like to believe that she always loved you. It's years since she gave you a single thought.'

'I understand that perfectly.'

'Then pray don't come here again till we've gone. We shall be off very soon . . . as soon as my brothers can settle which of them is to take me home with him. Once we are out of the way you may come and mope over Jenny's grave for the rest of your life, if you've nothing better to do.'

Her voice was still casual and easy. Anyone at a distance might have thought it an amicable interview. She paused and then went on:

'You're not listening. Please attend. I want you to tell your mother that I have broken off my engagement to you. I could never marry you now. I could never live in a place where such stories are told against me. You've heard them, I expect?'

'I've heard some of them,' he agreed wearily. 'As far away as Severnton. Are they true?'

'Quite untrue.'

Her voice sharpened a little and she coloured.

'Charles saw Jenny shortly before she died. He suspected nothing amiss. He's as much to blame as anyone for that disaster. And it was entirely against my wishes that Dr. Colley was brought to see my father. I protested, but I was overruled. But now . . . I can't set foot in the village lest some brat behind a hedge should throw a stone at me. They are all . . . you are all my enemies.'

Her indignation was manifestly genuine. There was in it a touch of bewilderment, as though the feelings of her fellow creatures must always be a little mysterious to her. Up to a point they would think and act as she did, ruled by self-interest, supported by duplicity. Then, suddenly, they would turn on her.

'I'll tell my mother,' said Romilly. 'And she can tell the rest. I shall say that these . . . these dreadful disasters have been too much for you — that you can't bear to stay here.'

'That will make Mrs. Brandon very happy.'

'I don't think I've ever heard her speak of you unkindly.'

'Nor of anybody else.' She gave a slight shrug. 'You've heard plenty from your sisters to make up for that.'

Suddenly and unexpectedly he felt sorry for her, getting a glimpse of the isolation in which she lived — aware of no existence save her own, knowing no tie closer than that of an occasional accomplice. But with this first stir of feeling he suffered another pang so dire that he turned and fled without bidding her farewell.

On his return to the Priors he went to his mother's dressing room and told her of the broken engagement. She showed no great signs of joy but said that it was probably for the best.

'I doubt if you would have been happy. Poor Venetia! What a good thing we told nobody. We were waiting for you to come back. Charlotte thought . . . people would say . . . I can understand her feelings. No wonder she wants to go. But it must be a disappointment for all that; such a good match!'

'She never pretended to love me.'

'Yes, but so few girls marry for love. One can't blame them. They must get husbands. I was lucky. I loved your father. But I don't think Charlotte or Sophy . . . we must make it perfectly clear to everyone that it was Venetia, not you, who broke the engagement. I shall write to Charlotte that you are quite wretched.'

'You can do that with a clear conscience.'

'Indeed I can. We are all wretched. We were so fond of Dr. Newbolt. It's so very shocking.'

For her, for everyone else in Stretton, lamentation over Jenny was no longer necessary. All had been said on that score and Dr. Newbolt now held the field. It was only after an interval of wondering exclamations that she said:

'Such a thing could never have happened if Jenny had been there. She would never have allowed . . . she was . . .'

At a sudden involuntary movement from Romilly she broke off, glanced at him, and said:

'Ah! I forgot. That's news to you too. Poor Jenny! I feel quite ashamed when I remember . . . as though we never valued her enough. . . . No, Ellen, my love! Not now. I'm talking to Romilly.'

'Ellen can come in,' said Romilly. 'I'm never sorry to see Ellen.'

'I only came for my sewing,' said Ellen, who had peeped round the door.

'How are you?'

'Quite well, thank you.'

She spoke a little coldly, ignored his outstretched hand, and went across to get her work-basket. He saw that her eyes were red, as though she had been crying.

'We were talking about poor Jenny,' said Mrs. Brandon, 'and how we know what she was, now she's gone.'

To this Ellen made no reply. There was something almost stubborn about her silence as she gathered her embroidery wools together. She carried the basket to the door and then turned to say:

'What Jenny *was* . . . ought not to be gone. It ought to be here still. She was very good. Everybody says that. Now she's gone everybody laments that there is no convenient good person to see to things. Jenny would never have allowed that poor woman to be sent away.'

'My love! We've been into this before. Giles says . . .'

'Oh, I know she's not one of our people, and not . . . not very deserving. But she had a home of sorts before she was brought here. Now she's turned off with nowhere to go and her children will be taken from her . . .'

'What's this?' asked Romilly.

Mrs. Brandon explained. The Hollins family were to

be turned out of the Parsonage stables. She had wanted to do something for them, but Giles had said that no cottage was available and that the villagers would resent it.

'Jenny would not have allowed it,' repeated Ellen. 'Oh, Romilly . . .'

'Now, Ellen! Don't trouble Romilly just now.'

'Three children?' asked Romilly, remembering the eyes in the yew tree. 'I think I saw them this afternoon. Don't cry, Ellen. I'll attend to it.'

'Oh, Romilly! If you would! Instead of talking and talking about . . .'

'But, Romilly, my dear boy. Giles says . . .'

'Let them stay in the stables till some plan can be made,' urged Ellen. 'Those stables don't belong to any of the Newbolts, now that their father . . . you can give orders about the stables, I'm sure, till you've chosen another parson.'

'I'll send a note down to Charles . . . I'll write it now.'

Ellen, much cheered, brought him writing materials. He wrote a line to Charles, asking that the family might be left where they were until he could arrange for their removal. He was not sure of his own rights in the matter but quite certain that Charles Newbolt had none. When he had finished he gave the note to Ellen, charging her with its despatch.

'And you might tell them to light a fire in my bedroom,' he added. 'I find it very cold here.'

Ellen went and he lingered awhile with his mother, reluctant to face solitude or the night. She told him about the cook's grandchild and a fox in the poultry yard. He scarcely listened, but her soft chatter was soothing.

A Night in Cold Harbour

Night had fallen when he braced himself to rise and leave her. His room was waiting for him. A bright fire danced in the grate. All his clothes were unpacked. His brushes lay on the dressing table and beside them lay a white oblong — a letter, folded and sealed. He picked it up. It was addressed to himself. But not until he had opened and read it could he be certain that he recognised the hand.

6

No explanation was ever found for the appearance of Jenny's letter upon Romilly's dressing table. The servants denied all knowledge of it. Ellen suspected Amabel, and privately taxed her with it, but Amabel stoutly asserted that she had done nothing save pray, on that visit to Jenny's room.

Speculation and enquiry were, in any case, confined to the women. Romilly scarcely asked how the letter had reached him. It was enough that he had it. Within a few weeks of her death Jenny had written to him exactly as she would have spoken ten years ago, with unshaken affection and complete confidence. The long silence was broken. That woman who wandered past him in the plantation might have drifted, beyond recall, out of the path of common human happiness, but she had not forgotten him.

It remained to do as she asked: to claim and protect this child whose story moved him deeply. It might well be his; he could remember nothing of the mother, but some recollection of nights spent at Slane St. Mary's forced him to allow the possibility. Jenny made no claims for it on that score, but her interest and affection gave a strong indication of her private opinion.

Early next morning, without a word to anybody, he set off for Corston Common, only to learn, from Goody Cottar, that Dickie was now in service at the Parsonage.

She had seen and heard nothing of him for weeks. Thither Romilly pursued him, to be informed that Dickie had gone back to his grandmother. Everybody was at first quite positive on this point. Where else could he be? But neither the parlour nor the kitchen could agree as to the date of his departure. The subsequent excitement over Dr. Newbolt had confused their memories. Venetia could not remember seeing him after the funeral. She made it plain that she thought this cross-examination in singularly bad taste, but Romilly was too anxious to mind what sort of figure he cut. Charles furiously refused to have any opinion at all. Harry had gone home. Stephen reminded Venetia that she had been urging them to get rid of Dickie for many days after the funeral. He alone showed sympathy with Romilly's quest and also contrived to inform him that Mrs. Hollins was to remain, undisturbed, in the stables. Romilly was a little softened by his civility, until a casual reference, by Venetia, to the vacant living suggested that there might be a motive for it.

Perceiving that no more could be got from the Newbolts he went home. The idea that Dickie could be quite lost did not as yet trouble him. So young a child could not have gone far; kindly people had probably taken him in. He put the problem before his mother and Ellen, who now heard of the letter for the first time. Their attitude displeased him. They were angry and dismayed. It appeared that they had known of Dickie's existence and had been in a plot to keep it from him.

'You think the child is not mine, and has therefore no claim on me?' he demanded.

'It's not a matter to be discussed before Ellen,' said Mrs. Brandon.

'I fancy she knows all about it. I'd have expected her to support me. My son or not, Jenny asked me to protect him. Is that not enough?'

'I don't wonder the Newbolts were offended. It must have looked so very odd . . . just after the engagement was broken . . . to be going there and demanding . . . they must have concluded . . .'

'That I own to him? If I do, I don't care to have him cleaning anybody's boots.'

'I know what you mean about Jenny, Romilly,' said Ellen in some distress. 'I felt as you do, the day Jenny died; that for her sake . . . I found him crying in the churchyard . . .'

'Crying, was he?'

'Everybody in the parish was crying. But I think he might be a difficult child to help.'

'On your dressing table?' cried Mrs. Brandon, who was always slow in mastering details. 'Who put it there?'

'It must have been found among her papers and sent here,' said Romilly impatiently. 'Difficult?'

'He's not respectful.'

'Why should he be respectful?'

'I advised him to join the Navy and he was very rude.'

'I should be rude if anybody advised me to join the Navy.'

'There's *no* profession . . .' began Ellen hotly.

'He sounds intelligent. Does he look like me?'

'N-no.'

'You don't sound very sure about it.'

'He's small and thin.'

'Natural in a half-starved child of nine. I never asked if he looks like a well-fed man of thirty.'

'My dearest boy,' broke in Mrs. Brandon, 'it's impossible to be certain. Bessie Cottar . . . she'd lost her character a long time before she went to Slane St. Mary's.'

Romilly looked thoughtful. Those two names had been linked in his mind before he got Jenny's letter. But he had at first been so intent on her message that he had not paused to wonder why. There had been some recent incident connecting them. He searched his memory and located it. He saw suddenly the lane to the Parsonage and a child. *A child with a fiddle!*

The discovery jarred him. He had not much liked the boy, who had nothing in common with the interesting little creature evoked by Jenny's appeal.

'Mine or not,' he repeated, with less passion, 'I must find it and do as she asks. I must set enquiries afoot: offer a reward if necessary. I'll go and have a word with Giles.'

'Oh dear! Oh dear!' wailed Mrs. Brandon as soon as he had gone. 'Now it will be all through the country. Everyone will think . . .'

'Don't oppose him,' begged Ellen. 'You know what he is. If we are sympathetic he may be sensible — apprentice Dickie to some good trade. But if we make him angry he may insist on bringing the child here! Treating him like a gentleman!'

'At your age you ought to know nothing about it. Most improper.'

'Not half as improper as heathen gods and goddesses,' said Ellen. 'And I'm obliged to learn about them in Lemprière. Only last week I learnt that the Minotaur was shut up in a labyrinth in order to "conceal the lasciviousness and indecency" of his Mama.'

'But that's education, my love. And it's not true, and we don't talk about it.'

'Why is it education to learn things which aren't true and can't be mentioned? However . . . you must admit that getting this letter has done poor Rom a world of good. He's almost himself again, and yesterday he looked dreadful.'

'Ah yes. It might help him to forget Venetia.'

'Venetia!'

Ellen sniffed. She had never believed that Romilly cared a pin for Venetia and was beginning, moreover, to suspect the truth, though it amazed her not a little. She thenceforth did all that she could to further Romilly's search, suggesting likely sources of information and consoling him in repeated disappointments. These troubled him greatly, as his lively imagination went to work on the possible fate of a nine-year-old child adrift in this wicked world. Local pessimists were eager with horrible suggestions. He could dismiss the idea that Dickie had been caught by the body snatchers and sent to be cut up alive, but there were likelier alternatives which sounded grim enough. Kindly people would have come forward at news of the enquiry. Respectable people would have claimed the reward. If the boy was still above ground he had probably fallen into bad hands.

It was Ellen who thought suddenly of the pottery and of the chance that Dickie might have got work among the children there. The people in the black valley were so much cut off from the rest of the world that nobody might have questioned them. Romilly snatched at the idea and rushed off to Cranton's. He was gone so long that she grew hopeful. But his face, when at last he rode up the drive, promised no good news. It was so blanched and weary that she wondered if Dickie was dead.

'A fruitless errand,' he said, as he dismounted. 'Though I insisted on seeing every child in the place. Come with me . . . I'll tell you about it.'

They went into that part of the grounds known as Mrs. Brandon's flower garden, although she seldom set foot in it. It was some time before he could bring himself to speak. His nostrils were still haunted by the stink of the potters' children and his eyes dazed by peering into stifling caverns where wizened pygmies scampered hither and thither for dear life. This brightness and peace could not entirely banish that other spectacle. Across the gay flowers little shadows flitted. With bird-song was mingled the echoing shouts, the strange clamours of those murky sheds.

When he did begin to talk it was about himself and Jenny. Her name had been continually present in their thoughts, during these days, but seldom mentioned. Now, in the bitterness of failure, he told the whole story to Ellen, who found it hard to comprehend since she had no memory of Jenny which might account for it. Amabel, two years older, might have had a glimpse of a tall, happy girl laughing because she had nothing precious enough to put in her secret drawer. Ellen had been but five years old when that girl was quenched for ever.

'But . . . but . . . how could you have been so cruel to her?'

'Cruel? Ah, child, you could never understand that. You . . . who are all kindness!'

'Oh no! I'm often unkind to people I dislike.'

'But not to those you love.'

'Why . . . that's impossible. Love is . . . it *is* kindness.'

'We don't always know our own hearts.'

I know mine, she thought.

'And when those we love hurt us . . .!'

If Edward were to be unkind to me I should . . . I think I should lay me down and die. But I could never wish him to be unhappy.

'But it made no difference to her, Romilly. Her letter tells you that. Oh . . . I'm so glad you got that letter. I understand now.'

He took it out, for he always carried it with him, and began to re-read it, yet again, with agonised attention.

Ellen reflected that his unkindness had touched many people besides himself and Jenny. But for that, Dickie might never have been born. Father and son might not have fallen out. The river valley might have been saved and Cranton might never have come amongst them, to distress poor Dr. Newbolt.

'Is Cranton's really such a shocking place?' she asked.

'I might not have thought so once. But when every child I saw there might . . . *might* have been mine . . .'

'But all poor children have to work, don't they?'

'Not work of that sort. No wonder they die. They should, if employed at all, have light tasks . . . short hours . . .'

He folded the letter and put it away, adding:

'I shall insist on that.'

'Can you? How can you? Is there some law?'

An idea which he had debated on the ride home hardened into a decision. Jenny's letter had provided him with an Object. *We must challenge misery.* He had failed to find Dickie but he might still obey this behest in another way.

'I mean to buy the place,' he declared.

'What? Buy back the land? Have it all taken away?'

'No. Buy the pottery and manage it myself. I believe I could prove that it's not necessary to employ children at all. Cranton only does so because they're cheap.'

'Manage . . . how could you manage a pottery?'

'You're not very flattering, are you? If Cranton can do it, surely I can. He strikes me as singularly stupid. I saw him today, when I'd done with the children, and told him what I think of him.'

'But would he sell it to you?'

'I think so. He had the impudence to tell me that I could have it and welcome if I thought I could make a profit on it.'

'I've heard rumours,' she said thoughtfully, 'that it does badly.'

'By his lights no doubt it may. He thinks of nothing save profit. I, you see, should be content with a much smaller return on my capital. Three per cent would be quite enough, I think. I could therefore pay higher wages than he does.'

Having digested this, Ellen asked why there could not be a law forbidding people to take more than three per cent interest on their capital. There would then, she pointed out, be more money for wages. Nor could she quite understand him when he explained that this would infringe liberty.

'All laws do that,' she argued. 'But we are obliged to have them, in order to prevent people from doing what is harmful. If it's harmful to take more than three . . .'

'Women don't understand these things. I hope to set the matter right without any need for laws. I mean to set an example which others may follow.'

Romilly rose from the bench where they had been

sitting and began to walk up and down, explaining his idea.

'Gentlemen must take to industry and treat their people with the same liberality and justice which we show towards those who work in the fields. Here are black valleys springing up all over the country. This sweet island will soon be given over to a thousand Crantons. To put a stop to that . . . to lead the way . . . that is my Object.'

Ellen began to think it a splendid Object. She thought of a clean valley full of tidy cottages — an orderly population calling down blessings on Romilly's head every Sunday when they came to church.

'How grateful those poor people will be!' she exclaimed.

'I trust I may give them cause. They shall at least learn that an industrial employer is not necessarily a brute. They may come to know him as a benefactor.'

'And the smoke! What a blessing to be rid of that horrid smoke!'

Her enthusiasm was very welcome but he did not feel able to make any definite promise about the smoke. He had not so far examined any facts about the manufacture of china, but he had a notion that it was baked in a kiln and that kilns must needs smoke.

'There are many improvements, new inventions, which I shall introduce,' he said. 'I shall make a close study of the subject, of course. I shall go into it thoroughly. I hope to hit upon something striking in the way of new designs. I don't mean merely to compete with those people in Staffordshire. I hope, some day, to beat them at their own game. What does Cranton know of taste? No wonder he can't hold his own with Wedgwood!'

A Night in Cold Harbour

The more he thought of it the happier he became. Here, at last, was an Object which might finally content him. It would give him active employment, fill his days, and bless his repose. He might still hope to influence the taste of his age. And he might, in a most striking way, obey Jenny's command. Such a challenge to misery would go far beyond the task she had laid upon him. As a benefactor upon so very large a scale he might be able to forget the fate of one obscure, unlucky child.

PART V

THE BENEFACTOR

I

Five years of studying the Navy Lists cured Ellen of a delusion that Latymer might return to her a rich admiral or, at the very least, the captain of a famous frigate. She was content enough to welcome him as commander of an ancient and insignificant sloop. Such advancement might silence her sisters: they could no longer call him a penniless lieutenant. A modest fortune of prize-money, carefully invested, had already made him richer than Amabel's husband; if the wars would but continue he might end up as rich as Sophy's Mr. Sykes. Only Bet, who had so far failed to get any husband at all, would sneer at him, and she must sneer at a distance since she now lived almost entirely with Charlotte.

It had long been settled amongst them that he should come immediately to Stretton on his next leave. He therefore set off at once for Severnshire, as soon as he came ashore, but he was not sure how long he would stay there. If Ellen would not marry him he would go away again. He supposed that some time must elapse before he could ask her. She might be very much surprised. Ideas of that sort could scarcely have occurred to her on his last visit, for she had been far too young. He must take his time and waste a few weeks in prudent courtship. If he could but win her heart he had strong hopes of gaining her friends' consent. By what he could gather the Brandons were not so prosperous as they had been; Romilly had lost a great deal of money over his absurd pottery which had never produced even the three per cent profit with which he had originally intended to be content. There had been re-trenchments of all kinds — fewer horses, fewer servants, and money had doubtless been sacrificed when Amabel married. They could not, therefore, turn up their noses at a suitor so prosperous as Latymer, if only Ellen would like him well enough.

As he drove from Severnton through Slane Forest he tried to steel his heart against disappointment. Why should she like him well enough? Why should he assume that he might be all the world to her just because, in the course of five years, she had become all the world to him? He knew that she was fond of him, her letters had been so kind, frank and artless; but he feared that her feelings went no further than those of warm friendship. Away at sea he had managed to assume that this was propitious to love. Doubts now assailed him. How, he wondered, does a man get a girl to be in love with him? The thing must constantly be achieved, since most men got married. But, on closer inspection, it was an extraordinary thing to demand.

He had in his pocket a couple of letters, from her and from Mrs. Brandon, which had been awaiting him at Portsmouth. They were doubly precious since several previous ones had missed him. Through a series of mis-chances he had heard nothing of Stretton affairs since Amabel's marriage at Christmas. He took out this latest budget of news and ran over it again, in order to be sure that he had missed nothing.

'We thought you had been at the Cape,' wrote Mrs. Brandon, 'but it seems, from your last letter, that you are in the Baltic. How you do fly about! We fear you may not have got ours for quite a while. This, I hope, will reach you since Ellen says it is to stay in England, in case you are really coming *home*. Remember, if you please, that your home is here; we expect you and will be very much disappointed if you do not come directly. I hope it will be soon. A visit from you will be so good for poor Romilly. He is in very low spirits, now that he has been forced to give up making his pretty china. I suppose it had to be. There is no use in making it if people will not buy it. They are very foolish, for it is superior to any other; Spode and Wedgwood make nothing so pretty. But they say it costs too much and he cannot afford to lose any more money. It is a melancholy business. At the start he was so much interested. He used to be riding over there every day. Now that the pottery is closed he scarcely goes out of the house.

'You will find us very dull and quiet, for we are only three now — Romilly, Ellen and myself. It is too quiet, I think, for poor Ellen. She has nobody young with whom to frolic. Her married sisters ask her to stay so that she may go about a little and meet people, and I have urged her to go, though I should miss her sorely. But she will not stir. And I am glad, for Romilly's sake, since he is exceedingly fond of her. . . .'

This final disaster to Romilly's pretty china was news, but Latymer felt little surprise. He had always thought it a crack-brained scheme, and the accounts of its progress had been dismal from the first. Ellen's letter gave fuller particulars.

'Pray come here as fast as you can and persuade Romilly not to hang himself. His pottery is now closed and all the people have gone away. I am not sure if you ever received our recent letters, so I will explain how it was, and you must forgive me if you know it already. People would not buy Cranton ware. And he made no profit at all, it cost him so much to make, he has merely lost money ever since he bought it. We have no canal, you see. They have one in Staffordshire, which enables them to send their wares away cheaply, and that reduces the price.

'Yet I am sure you will believe that it is not the loss of money which he minds most. Now he is obliged to think that nothing can ever be done, and that it is hopeless to strive against low wages and too much work for the poor children. He was so sure that he could succeed and that others would follow his example. He thinks now that everything will go on getting worse and worse, and that there is nothing to be done, and that the working people must always be very poor and miserable.

'I am, myself, not quite sure whether his scheme had a fair trial. If there had been a canal, and if Romilly had known more about the manufacture of china, he might have been successful. They say now that Cranton himself was going bankrupt, and that is why he sold to Romilly. If he could not make it pay, perhaps nobody could. Romilly did not know near as much concerning the actual work as Cranton did. I am sure that he was cheated right and left. He has only just discovered, for instance, that he has been paying nearly twice as much as he should for coarse salt.

'But the worst hit of all has been the ingratitude of the people. They were not in the least grateful to him. In their eyes he was a master, just like Cranton, and if he paid them better wages this was not because he wished to be their benefactor but because, for some reason, that suited him. At the last, in hopes of keeping the business going, he was obliged to ask them to take lower wages and they were furious. He told them that it was in their own interest but they did not believe him. One man said they could mind their own interest a great deal better if they could send their man to Parliament, as he can! Worse than this, they tried to form an association amongst themselves, to which all should belong, and which could call them all off work, if they were in any dispute with Romilly! That is quite against the law. He could have had them sent to prison. But he would not. He merely sent men to seize their papers and records and had them burnt. Even at the end, when the pottery was closed, they could not see that he had been right. They went away cursing him and saying that they had been better off with Cranton who could at least give them employment. I quite hate them for treating him like this.'

Latymer felt some sympathy with the potters, just as he would have been sorry for the crew of a man-of-war, bought and commanded by Romilly. Fools they might be, but their folly was more excusable than his. A man might as well set up as an admiral without ever having served as a midshipman.

Yet for all that, reflected Latymer, it must be a dead bore to have nothing to do. He wished that Brandon would go into Parliament and make a pother about the Pay Office. That was a scandal which deserved exposure, nor was it necessary that the men should be so shamelessly cheated. It was what he himself would do, if he were in Brandon's shoes. He would go into Parliament and there keep his mouth shut until he knew which way the wind blew. He would collect some other fellows who thought as he did, and then, when it was in their power to oblige some bigwig, they would begin to bellow about the Pay Office. Even in Parliament it must be supposed one must wait for a wind, but Brandon might not have the sense to know it. He'd put on all his canvas in a dead calm, thought Latymer, and then blame the British Constitution because nothing came of it.

The carriage came out of the forest and stopped at the top of the hill for a drag to be put under the wheels. Home! he thought, looking with a lifting heart at the fields and woods below. And he leant out, as he had leant five years before, to survey the river and the black valley. It presented a more melancholy appearance than ever, now that it was silent, rotting and deserted. The tumble-down hovels had been homes of a sort. Those who had lived there were now perhaps homeless, turned away to drift off through the forest in search of a new master. He was glad when the second turn of the road hid that desolate scene.

As his thoughts swung back to his own affairs, his own future, he began to smile broadly. His horses' hooves, on the level road at the bottom, beat out a merry tattoo. Happy Latymer! Happy Latymer! they seemed to say. Latymer! Latymer! Happy, happy Latymer!

These smiles must be controlled when he arrived at the house. It would never do to walk in with the face of an accepted lover. A great deal of work remained to be done. She might . . . there was no certainty . . . *She did! She must!* . . . Happy Latymer! Happy Latymer! But I shan't pull a long face neither. That won't do. And when I see her I doubt if I can help . . . there's the green . . . no cricket today, only geese . . . it was evening before, and now it's afternoon . . . there's the lane to the Parsonage . . . the poor old gentleman . . . the beauty . . . she never told me why that was broken off . . . a new man now . . . what's his name? Wilmott? If all goes well he'll be the fellow who . . . *with this ring I thee wed!* . . . I wish it had been the old man, though . . . a strange story . . . sad . . . that other sister who died . . . Happy! Happy! . . . The park wall. Less than a mile now. I must take this grin off my face.

He had got it off when they stopped at the lodge gates and gave a positive scowl at the keeper who opened them. He kept this up as he bowled through. After fifty yards the carriage stopped. A white dress, a straw hat, sparkling eyes, living, breathing bliss sprang in beside him. She was in his arms.

Oh happy, happy, happy, happy Latymer!

2

'PULL the check string,' said Ellen when they got to the bridge. 'Tell him to turn to the left and drive round the park a few times.'

After a third circuit of the park Latymer asked how soon they could be married.

'At once, of course.'

'Don't they have to call banns?'

'No. Not if there is a special licence.'

'Where do they keep them? Special licences?'

'I believe the Archbishop of Canterbury has them.'

'I always thought a wedding took a great time to . . . clothes! Shan't you have to buy clothes?'

'I have clothes. I've always had them, ever since I was born, so they tell me.'

'And people! One invites people. They all come to breakfast.'

'They can eat their breakfasts and wish us joy in their own houses. If we wait for a day when it will suit Charlotte and Sophy and Bet and Amabel to come and eat breakfast with us we may never get married.'

'But your mother! What will she say?'

'Perhaps we'd better find out. Tell him to stop driving us round the park and take us to the house.'

'Even if she consents she might think we should wait until . . . we must be guided by her wishes.'

'Poor dear! We'll be the first people who ever were!'

'And Brandon . . . your brother?'

'He'll be all for cutting out that breakfast. It was he told me to go and meet you at the lodge gate. I wanted him to come too, but he said that if I went alone it would be a great time saver.'

'Ellen! I can't believe it! I thought that it would take weeks. I was wondering how to set about it.'

'Weeks! Oh dear, what a bore that would have been.'

'But, my darling . . . when did you . . . how soon did you . . .'

'Ssh! We've arrived. And we have all the rest of our lives, you know, for "how soon did you . . .?"'

'My business was settled the very first evening.'

'So was mine. When Charlotte asked you to change your room and we . . .'

'*Ellen!*'

'Oh fie! You'll shock Partridge.'

Partridge was on the steps, smiling a discreet welcome. George, who came forward to take the portmanteaux, grinned broadly. There were now but the two of them, since William had departed to better himself and had never been replaced. Latymer found it impossible to control his smiles when he met so many on all sides. Crossing the hall, he looked up to see Mrs. Flinders smirking at him over the gallery rail. Then he was in the drawing-room where Mrs. Brandon first smiled and then wept, as she embraced him. But it was from Romilly, who had meanwhile been kissing Ellen, that he got the strangest smile. It was full of good-will and affection, yet it gave him a pang, reminding him of some very sad occasion, as yet unidentified.

'We thought we heard your carriage quite a while ago,' said Mrs. Brandon. 'But then it seemed to turn away, beyond the bridge.'

'We drove round the park for a little,' said Ellen.

'What a waste of time,' said Romilly.

'Ellen and I . . .' began Latymer solemnly.

'Don't tell me!' implored Romilly. 'Let me guess. What *can* you and Ellen have been up to?'

'I knew how it was as soon as I saw their faces,' said Mrs. Brandon. 'Oh, my dear Edward!'

For Ellen's sake, thought Latymer, they ought to be more prudent than this! This is no way to dispose of her.

'Perhaps, ma'am,' he suggested, 'I should talk to Brandon . . . to Romilly . . . he . . . you . . . must want to know. My prospects . . .'

'Yes, to be sure. Charlotte and Sophy would scold us for going on too fast. Romilly is the proper person . . . go into the library with him, and mind you tell me what you say to each other, so that I may write it to the girls. Oh, my dearest Ellen . . .'

The two men went into the library. Romilly produced a decanter. He then took up a position on the hearth-rug and said in a menacing voice:

'Now, my good man! How much money have you got?'

Latymer told him and he wrote it down, explaining that Charlotte, Sophy, Bet and Amabel would want to know to a farthing how much it was.

'Now it's your turn. You should ask me how much Ellen has got.'

'I shan't.'

'Oh, very well! The gentleman is, in any case, believed to have found that out before he offers. But you should

230

make some demand — suggest that you get it all if you
marry her. Whereat I shall say: On the contrary. We
expect a settlement for her. Charlotte and Sophy will
think very meanly of us if we don't haggle.'

'We'll certainly make a settlement.'

'Ellen has four thousand pounds in the three per cents.
I wish it had been more, but that's her portion, under my
father's will. If I'd not made ducks and drakes of my own
money I should have been delighted to give her more.
But there it is. She's no great catch. I think you could
look higher.'

'Look higher than Ellen!'

'Quite so. If ever a man is likely to be happy . . . but
I don't think she'll meet any more likely to deserve her.
And han't she grown into a beauty?'

'You think so? I don't find her changed. She's just as
I'd always thought of her.'

'When do you mean to get married?'

'Why, we were discussing that when we were . . . were
. . .'

'Wasting time? Well, if I were you, I should march
her off to church as soon as possible. You want to spend
as much as you can of your leave together.'

'If your mother wouldn't think that too . . .'

'I'll answer for my mother.'

'How does one get hold of a special licence? Do you
know?'

Romilly did know and offered to put the matter in hand
immediately. He sat down to write a letter which
Latymer's driver could take to Severnton, whence it
could be sent on by express. As he took up his pen he said:

'Have some more port. We must be shut up here for
at least forty minutes, if we are to satisfy Charlotte and

231

Sophy. Sit down, do, and get your breath. You look positively blown.'

It was not merely the suddenness of his good fortune which took Latymer's breath away. He had never known that it was possible for any man to be so happy. It seemed to him that he had spent his life in a parched desert, drinking by thimblefuls, and supposing such an existence to be tolerable. Now, having come upon a river, he had fallen into it, was drowning in bliss.

'Place of birth? Date of birth?' said Romilly without looking up. 'In what Parish Register? Particulars of parents, including mother's maiden name.'

'Good heavens! Will the Archbishop want to know all that?'

'I doubt it. I think he'll merely want guineas. But we won't risk a delay by failing to send any necessary particulars.'

'How many guineas?'

'The bride's family come up with those. Ellen won't cost us as much as Amabel did. We save a breakfast, and a good deal of Brussels lace.'

Latymer gave him the particulars and thought how greatly he had changed. He looked far more than five years older. When not smiling he had an aspect of settled sadness, probably now so habitual that it might only strike a stranger. In the old days he had often been moody, but this was nothing so transient; it indicated the prevailing hue and tenor of his thoughts. The failure of the pottery could not entirely account for it. There must be some more deep-seated, more abiding, sorrow. That broken engagement might explain it if he had been genuinely in love with the beauty. Yet Ellen had never seemed to think so.

232

Otherwise nothing at Stretton Priors had altered. The roses blooming in the flower garden outside might have been there ever since that last evening when seven couples had danced from sunset to moonlight. It was hard to remember that those petals had fallen five times, to be blown away by the autumn gales. Above the fireplace hung a great old picture by some unknown Dutchman, which had given them all a great deal of trouble to take down. Romilly's grandfather had bought it, asserting that it must be elevating since the subject was scriptural, but Romilly, Latymer and George had disagreed with him. An adipose woman, naked and very blue as to flesh tints, writhed amidst some bed-clothes. A gentleman dressed from head to foot in black velvet, a feathered hat on his head and a white ruff round his neck, ran from her in pious horror.

'I see you've still got Potiphar's wife,' said Latymer. 'How is the Brandon Arabian? Is he still in the dining-room?'

'The horse? Oh yes. He's always been there, you know.'

'You meant, at one time, to throw him into the canal.'

'Did I? I'd forgotten that.'

Having finished the letter, Romilly rang the bell and gave orders for its conveyance. Again there was a marked alteration in his manner. Not only did he give orders less abruptly, he asked if they had given the man something to eat. Five years ago the fellow would have been packed off, dinner or no dinner.

Yet it was that smile which disturbed Latymer most. During dinner he was very cheerful, laughing at them, teasing them, and skilfully curbing his mother's inclination for tears. He seemed to rejoice with them, as a man

233

may do who has so completely relinquished all hope of happiness for himself that he can view felicity in others with an easy genial detachment.

No early opportunity for comment on this occurred. Next morning he took Latymer and Ellen to the Parsonage to call on the Wilmotts and to explain the business of the special licence. Later he went off on some errand with Giles, leaving the lovers to walk home together.

'Romilly! He's changed out of all knowledge,' began Latymer at once. 'What is it? What has happened to him? When he smiles he reminds me . . . I could not remember at first, but I remember now . . . he reminds me of a poor fellow, our first officer on the *Ariadne*, who had seen his wife and children drown before his eyes. Is it all this business of the pottery? Surely not?'

'No. It's not only that. Although, if that scheme had been a success I think it would have been a comfort to him. But the whole story is something which I could never write in a letter. Besides, I ought not to have told it to you unless we were engaged. Even so, it's very hard to explain.'

Latymer found it hard to understand. The little that he could recall of poor Jenny Newbolt cast no light on it.

'And then there was the loss of the little boy. He searched and searched. He had enquiries made all over the country. Never a word! He fancied, still fancies, such terrible things. I think he threw himself into the pottery scheme partly to make amends. He felt that he had caused great misery and could never now set it right, but he still hoped that somebody might be the better, if he exerted himself. And that was all a failure too.'

'I don't quite understand. Did the boy go with the old gentleman?'

'Oh no. Not together. There was no connection. Dickie ran off first. I suppose immediately after the funeral. And Dr. Newbolt went some time later.'

'And what became of the other daughter? Venetia?'

'I believe she went to India. Charlotte, who always manages to find things out, Charlotte says so. They sent her out to the brother who is in the East India Company. I daresay she has married a Nabob.'

'Poor Brandon. That escape is the only piece of good luck he's had. And I don't suppose he suffers less because . . .'

He hesitated and she finished for him:

'All his own fault? I know. Yet he's so good. So kind. You saw how he played backgammon with Mama last night. He does that every night, though it must bore him dreadfully. He would never have been so patient in the old days.'

'Nobody could have been kinder to me.'

'Or to me. If it were not for him we should never have met. He's been a benefactor to us.'

'Yet I don't suppose he would have brought me here if he'd foreseen the future. It's enough to frighten one . . . some chance action, taken without thought, may have such tremendous consequences for other people.'

'Yes, indeed. You and I, happy for the rest of our lives, thanks to him. And the people at Cranton's, for whom he sacrificed so much, turned off to starve, cursing him and shaking their fists at him.'

'Oh, I don't suppose it was as bad as that.'

'But it was. He was riding through the forest and he met a party of them coming away, with their wives and

children. And when they saw him they cursed him. And
some of them sang a song. He says it's a song the convicts
sing. *Here's to You and Yours.* You know it?'

'Yes. I've heard them. They sing it in the carts going
down to the hulks. It makes one glad to think they're
being taken to the other side of the world.'

'Is it so bad? What does it say?'

Latymer pondered and then said:

'I believe it runs something like this:

> Here's to you and yours,
> And here's to us and ours.
> Look well to you and yours,
> For if it's in our powers
> We'll do as much for you and yours
> As you for us and ours.'

She shivered, and hoped that those songsters would go
a long way off.

'He goes out so little now,' she lamented. 'He hardly sees
anybody. He has nothing to do. Nothing to think about.'

'Yes, poor fellow. He must be lost without an Object.'

After a moment's hesitation she went on.

'Edward . . . dearest . . . should you . . . I was wondering if you would think it very strange . . . I believe it
might do him a great deal of good. To ask him to come
on our wedding tour.'

He did think it very strange, but saw that she was
eager for his sympathy.

'By all means, my darling, if you think it would cheer
him up. But wouldn't he think it an odd invitation?
One doesn't generally take an extra man on these
occasions.'

'I know. One takes a girl. A bridesmaid. Charlotte took Sophy and Sophy took Bet. Amabel ought to have taken me, but she got out of it by saying she owed it to one of her new sisters-in-law. People will expect us to take Bet. Do you want to take Bet? I don't.'

From what he could remember of Bet she was the last person whom he desired to take. This custom of a travelling bridesmaid struck him, for the first time, as absurd and a nuisance. To have some smirking, simpering Miss continually at one's elbow, just when one has at last got one's girl to oneself must be intolerable. Ten to one she would get up confoundedly early in the morning. A man would be more likely to enter into a bridegroom's feelings. He would take himself off pretty often, to inspect old ruins. The bride's brother would be far less trouble, in most cases.

Not that he could see why he and Ellen should be obliged to take anybody at all. Other girls, torn from their families, and sent off with a strange man, might need a sister or cousin to keep them company until they had been broken in to the married state, but he and Ellen were not strangers.

'Why do they take a girl?' he exclaimed. 'One would have thought that an older woman ... a married woman ...'

'Oh no. If the husband turns out to be very disagreeable it puts the wife in spirits if she has a girl with her, to whom she is superior, you know, because she's married.'

'Good God!'

'Sophy told Amabel that she would have run away from Mr. Sykes within forty-eight hours if Bet had not been with them. She felt obliged to put on a good face before Bet.'

'And what if I turn out to be disagreeable?'

'If Romilly is there he'll call you out. I believe he would be very much pleased if we ask him. And we might trust him to leave us alone a great deal.'

'In that case let's ask him.'

A faint shadow fell upon Latymer's spirits. It was soon thrown off, but he felt for a moment a qualm of uneasiness which only very fortunate men can permit themselves to feel. Had he been less certain of his own happiness he would have denied that he felt it. But he was secure enough to glance at the enormous risks run by his sex amongst these supposedly tender creatures.

3

THE invitation gave great pleasure to Romilly. After some show of protest he accepted, resolving that they should not have cause to repent of it. He would keep out of their way and run errands for them.

The thought of losing Ellen was hard to bear, for he had grown exceedingly fond of her. During those years of slow, paralysing disappointment her affection and good humour had made life endurable. Stretton would be very dreary without her. He had lost touch with all his old friends and had found no new ones. The local gentry thought him a fool. He had run out of Objects. The charge in Jenny's letter, which he kept over his heart, was still paramount with him: 'We must challenge misery, even though it is always too strong for us. We must still defy it and cry out against it.' But, having failed with his pottery, he could think of no further challenge save to shut himself up and do nothing at all, lest he might do more harm. Backgammon with his mother of an evening was safe enough; she would be very unhappy if he went away and she would miss Ellen cruelly. There he could perceive a clear duty, and he shrank from anything more positive. He had been born with money, power and considerable capacities. Yet it seemed to him that he had lived for half his allotted span with no positive record save one of injury to others.

The young couple planned to make a tour in the West, a part of the country which Latymer had never explored. The wedding took place with all possible despatch and they set off from the church door to Salisbury where they were, at Romilly's suggestion, to spend a day or two quite alone. He himself escorted his mother on a journey to visit Amabel, near Winchester, before he joined them.

In Salisbury he found them, absent, smiling, sleepy, and unable to say whether they had yet inspected the stone carving in the cathedral chapter-house. At his suggestion they decided to dawdle their way into Dorsetshire.

'We have no obligation to get as far as St. Michael's Mount,' he pointed out one morning when, as usual, they apologised for a delayed start.

'You said you'd like to see it,' remembered Ellen.

'It can wait. I merely want to find out if it looks towards Bayonne.'

'It don't,' said Latymer. 'I've seen it from the sea. I should say, at a guess, that it looks towards Trinidad. Who says it looks towards Bayonne?'

'Milton. "Where the great vision of the guarded Mount looks towards Namancos and Bayona's hold." We can settle for something nearer, you know.'

'The Cheddar Gorge?' remembered Latymer. 'They say one should see that.'

Into Somerset therefore they went. Romilly looked at the Cheddar Gorge. Ellen and Latymer looked at one another.

This they were able to do without interruption since Romilly established himself as their courier. He chose the rooms at the inns, ordered the dinner and paid the bills. He made Ellen's comfort his care. At Glastonbury they were disturbed by people singing and dancing in a great barn just under their windows. Ellen expressed a fear lest this shouting and stamping should go on all night; it was, so a waiter told them, a frolic got up amongst the inn servants since two trampers, one of whom played the fiddle, were sleeping in the stables. Romilly at once sent down a couple of guineas, one for the fiddler, with a request to go away, and the other for the disappointed dancers that they might drink the lady's health. Ellen and Latymer were grateful to him, but thought this liberality excessive. A complaint to the landlord would have been a cheaper way to silence the fiddler.

They went from Glastonbury to Bridgwater, where it rained. In better weather they came to Porlock, which all voted to be a sweet place. Ellen and Latymer were beginning to emerge from their first dazed dream. They sometimes took notice of the scenery. They answered questions intelligibly and laughed at jokes, whereas they had formerly been disposed to laugh for no reason at all. They became more energetic: having decided to drive over Exmoor, they scrambled up to Dunkery Beacon.

Romilly was a little sorry to see this first stage of the tour coming to an end. For a while their happiness had transformed them into creatures inhabiting some other world. As though possessing already the substance of things hoped for, they had shed the defences, the tones, the gestures, the caution, the compromise, needed for existence on this earth. Such felicity it was almost in his power to share since it had nothing in common with the workaday contentments and satisfactions which, as he believed, could never now be his. They were, in themselves, a challenge to misery, and he rejoiced to behold them. Strangers, sojourners, exiles in the wilderness, they raised a song of home. Now the glory was fading. They were becoming themselves, Latymer and Ellen, an excellent couple, good-humoured, honest, courageous, warm-hearted and energetic — likely to thrive in the wilderness.

At supper, on the day that they had climbed Dunkery, an argument sprang up amongst them. Latymer mentioned a Captain Collet, under whom he had served, and Romilly remembered meeting this man in London.

'A very pleasant fellow,' said Romilly. 'I liked him extremely. But I should have thought he had too much sensibility . . . too much for keeping strict discipline?'

'Sensibility!' snorted Latymer. 'You might call it that. He thinks nothing of flogging his men. Flogs as often as any commander in the Navy, I fancy. But never sees it done.'

'Do you see it done?' asked Romilly earnestly.

'Why, yes. It makes me sick. I never have a man flogged if I can avoid it. But if I think such a measure necessary I've no business to be so nice that I won't see it.'

'And you do think it necessary?'

'Yes. In some cases.'

'H'm! The rack and the stake were once thought necessary.'

'That was in the olden days,' said Ellen, 'when everybody was quite barbarous. Now we are enlightened.'

'Someday we may be thought barbarous.'

'If anyone thinks Edward barbarous they will know nothing at all about him.'

'Edward! Yes. We'd better leave Edward out of it. But not all captains are as humane as he is.'

'Some are great brutes,' agreed Latymer. 'Their men are out of luck to be serving under brutes. But that's not to say flogging is unnecessary.'

'So necessary that power must be given to brutes?'

'I think,' said Latymer, 'most men would sail under a flogging captain sooner than with one who failed to know his business. Whole skins wouldn't profit them much if he very humanely drowned 'em all by accident one fine day. Flogging captains an't the most unpopular.'

Romilly could believe that, remembering how he had himself very humanely deprived his potters of their livelihood. Cranton might have been a brute but was, from their point of view, a better master.

'It's the way of the world, I suppose,' he said sadly.

'I don't think this world is such a bad place,' protested Ellen. 'People who deserve to prosper and be happy generally are so. Don't you think so, Edward?'

'No,' said Latymer. 'I can't say that I do. A man's luck and his deserts don't always square. It's mostly luck in this world, you know, Romilly. A man must take his luck as he finds it. You can't alter luck by legislation.'

'An excellent philosophy for those whose luck is good.'

'Why, what would you do about it? Abolish bad luck by Act of Parliament?'

'No. I suppose not. But . . . the necessary . . . the inevitable . . . must these for ever be taken for granted? We tolerate evils which we have declared to be inevitable. Don't we do so because toleration suits us? Ought not the inevitable to trouble us? To be continually on our minds? Even though we can see no remedy?'

'I don't think so,' said Latymer. 'We should be fit for nothing if we trouble ourselves to no end. When it's in our power to do good, we should exert ourselves. When we can do nothing we'd better harden our hearts a little.'

'And so continue to believe that nothing can ever be done? Here's Ellen claims that we are enlightened.

243

Who enlightened us? Those who cried out against barbarity, against the rack and the stake, gave themselves no rest, gave others no rest, until these horrors were abolished. They cried: Intolerable! Until the rest of the world began to say: Unnecessary!'

Ellen was ruffled because she thought that Romilly had criticised the Navy and had accused Edward of barbarism. She said, a little sharply:

'And who is to make all this pother about flogging in the Navy? You'd not like it if Partridge took to giving himself no rest and you no rest. A fine thing you'd think it if your morning chocolate never appeared because Partridge was bawling "Intolerable!" down in the pantry. You'd turn him off.'

'*Touché*,' agreed Romilly good-humouredly. 'We can't spare Partridge for work of that sort.'

'Only people who have nothing better to do . . .' began Ellen, but a quick look from Latymer silenced her.

Edward is too kind, she thought impatiently. He won't defend himself. Here he is, leading a hard and useful life, often in danger, dependent only on himself and his own exertions! Whilst Romilly, who can do nothing in the world save make himself miserable, presumes to . . . it's too bad! Poor Rom! Not his fault. As Edward says, the wonder is that he should be so amiable, spoilt as he was. But he should recognise which is the superior. And now Edward will reason with him as though he were talking sense.

'I think,' said Latymer, who had been pondering, 'that Partridge might count for more than either of you suppose. He might sit on a jury.'

'Juries can be barbarous,' objected Romilly.

'To be sure. But they speak for their age. I heard an

odd thing on the coach coming down to Severnton. Some people were talking of a case . . . I think it was at the Gloucester Assizes. A fellow stole a horse, for which he should have been hanged, for most horses are worth more than forty shillings. But he wan't hanged, for they brought it in . . . what was it? Fraudulent conversion, and that, it seems, is not a hanging matter. The owner, it was said, asked him to hold the horse, upon which he made off with it. And a man on the coach, a lawyer, says: Oh yes. If it's fraudulent conversion the jury is more ready to convict. They don't like to hang a man for forty shillings. If the goods can be fixed as worth less, they'll convict for theft. If not, they're liable to acquit, whatever the evidence.'

'To hang a man for forty shillings,' said Romilly, 'they begin to find that intolerable?'

'It seems so. We hang in order to check theft. But the boot may turn out to be on the other leg if Partridge thinks the penalty unnecessarily severe. He lets the thief off. Milder measures would serve better. If the law comes to be changed, that may not be entirely because your gentlemen in Parliament are sorry for thieves. It might be in order to safeguard property.'

'But did the man steal the horse?' asked Ellen, who was puzzled.

'I gather that he probably did. The story of the owner entrusting it to him was pretty thin. But the jury decided to believe it.'

'They would have thought very differently if it had been their horse.'

The two men exchanged glances and smiled. Suddenly she felt that she, not Romilly, was the third party: they had some understanding from which she was excluded.

She disliked this and said no more until later, when she was alone with Latymer. Then she exclaimed:

'You can't really agree with Romilly? To make a great to-do over sad things which can't be helped, of what use is that?'

'Very little immediate use. But I think that feeling comes before judgement. People who cry out: Intolerable! may be very tiresome, but they might serve some purpose, even if they can't, themselves, suggest any remedy. The men, and the measures for that, come after.'

'Oh? I see. Unhook my gown, will you?'

Latymer unhooked her gown but his mind seemed to be somewhat off the business. She found herself growing quite cross.

'In that case,' she said, 'Romilly's task in life . . . nobody can accuse him of neglecting it! To distress himself and everybody else. If he feels away hard enough perhaps someday nobody will be flogged and nobody hanged, and poor children will be put to school instead of to work.'

'Poor Romilly! Why are you so hard on him?'

'Because . . . because you seem to agree with him, not me!'

'Then it's I who should catch it.'

'I daresay. But I'm a woman, you know, and therefore unreasonable. And I begin to see why one doesn't take another man on one's wedding tour.'

4

ELLEN was rarely out of temper. This little burst of peevishness sprang from reluctance to believe that the first bliss was over. A fortnight ago Latymer would have been so completely preoccupied with herself that he would not have pursued the discussion. He would have smiled vaguely, agreed with Romilly, and changed the subject. This enchantment could not last. She knew that. But she thought it hard that it should end so soon, merely because he took it into his head to remember a discussion on a coach, driving down to Severnton. She wished Edward and Romilly to love one another because she loved them both. She could see little reason for any other tie between them.

A growing intimacy, a mutual regard, would have pleased her better could she have understood it. But she had had little experience of men, their ways, and their attitude towards each other. Her world had been entirely feminine, and in that world argument was not thought to be very civil. If possible one agreed with people; to differ was slightly hostile. Love and friendship demanded a perfect concord in opinions. Argument for its own sake, as a means of reaching the truth, puzzled her very much.

Next day they went to Watchet and argued without stopping, nor could she make out which was in the right. In sympathy she would have been all for Romilly, had he been disputing with anybody save Edward. He was against the Americans, as was very right and proper, since Britain was at war with them. Latymer, although perfectly ready to fight them whenever and wherever he should meet them, maintained that they had good cause for resenting the British attacks on their shipping, and that it was not necessary, when fighting, to regard an opponent as totally in the wrong. On the contrary, he maintained that one fought better if one had a high opinion of the other fellows. They broke off occasionally to tease Ellen, but that did not mend matters. She grew quite melancholy and scarcely said a word on the drive home. Latymer thought that the scramble up Dunkery, the day before, must have been too much for her. Romilly guessed the truth and explained it in private to his brother-in-law, when they got back to Porlock.

'She's not used to us and our ways. If she had another woman, they could laugh at us, but she's odd man out, which is a little hard on a bride. Go off by yourselves tomorrow, and talk nonsense. I'll ride over to Minehead and tell you whether it's worth a visit.'

To him the argument at Watchet had been stimulating. It had been a long time since he had attempted to discuss anything with a sensible energetic man. The effort roused him from the lethargy into which he had sunk, secluded and moping, like a sulky child. During his day at Minehead he forced himself to scrutinise, more dispassionately than he had ever done before, the history and causes of his failure at the pottery, and to examine a certain readiness to believe that, since he had failed, nothing could ever be done by anybody. His own melancholy struck him as less excusable after a fortnight spent in Latymer's company.

All day he rode, up hill, down dale, into villages, and by the sea shore, scarce knowing where he went. All day he was tossed this way and that by a debate in which the second voice spoke for that self in him which had been paralysed from the day of his breach with Jenny. He had chosen then to turn his back upon truth, and now, when he sought it, he was baffled. He had lied to himself too long.

He returned to Porlock baffled, believing that he had accomplished nothing. Yet he must at some point on his ride have hit the target, for he found himself putting it all quite clearly to Latymer, late that evening. Ellen had gone upstairs to bed and the two men took a short stroll towards Porlock Weir before parting for the night.

'I've been thinking,' said Romilly, 'about those potters.'

'Why go on doing that?' said Latymer. 'That's over and done with. No mending it now. Think of something else.'

'I might, now that I know what the trouble really was. You know . . . I'm afraid of poor people. So it was all cant to set up as their friend. They knew it. They knew they owed me nothing. Do you understand what I mean?'

'They don't like charity,' said Latymer. 'You can't blame 'em. We should dislike it.'

'Ay . . . charity . . . benevolence . . . philanthropy . . . mighty fine names all of them for a guilty conscience. They say the weak fear the strong. I believe the strong fear the weak a good deal more. D'ye know what my mother said when she heard that those fellows thought they should send their own man to Parliament?' Romilly laughed. 'She's a very honest woman, my mother. She

249

said: "That would be very disagreeable for us. There are so many poor people. They would soon get all the power. And then they would take our money from us." '

Latymer laughed too.

'So they would,' said Romilly. 'If they had the chance.'

'Oh. I don't know. They might set out to do so. But they're lazy devils. Nine men out of ten are bone lazy. And it would be no easy task. We know how to hang on to money, and power, better than they do. Sooner than exert themselves they'll let others rule them: they'll let us grow rich, so long as their own lot an't too hard.'

'They might find leaders who don't fear exertion.'

'They might. Until these leaders collar the money. They'd only change masters.'

'You think so badly of the human race?'

'Badly? No. But only one man in a hundred, one in a thousand, perhaps, likes exertion or undertakes it unless he's driven. Those who do rule the rest. It's easy enough to wail that something should be done. To say that something shall be done . . . a man don't say that unless he's bred to it.'

'Then you think they could be no better ruled than they are now?'

'I don't say that. But they mayn't care to be better ruled if it's likely to cost them trouble. They may bawl about liberty and justice, but they must be pretty desperate before they'll walk a mile to secure either.'

'They need . . .' said Romilly earnestly, 'first of all, perhaps, they need . . . affiance in each other. That must be fostered. But how? Only if they get leaders of a peculiar cast. Risen from amongst themselves, but bred, as you say, to see that something is done.'

'Men of that sort, if they have the wit to escape the gallows, end by making themselves a pretty fortune. We knight 'em and they give no more trouble.'

'Yet there might be some who would refuse. . . . I don't despair. In any case I think better of my potters. They weren't fools. They said what I'd have said in their shoes. They reason as I do.'

Latymer forbore to say that they might be fools all the same. He went up and told Ellen that his brother-in-law seemed to be on the mend.

ELLEN's spirits were quite restored by getting Latymer to herself for a day. She was remorseful over her own petulance and sorry that Romilly should have missed a delightful excursion.

'We found some scenery,' she reported, 'which is as good as anything out of a book. It's truly romantic. You must see it. I'm sure you would like it extremely. We wished you were with us every other minute. We must go again and you must come.'

'What is scenery out of a book like?' asked Romilly.

'I mean it's not like England.'

'That it's not,' agreed Latymer. 'Though it's not quite like any place I've seen in any other part of the world either. I don't know why. Ellen's right. It's very poetical. We left the carriage at a farm and followed a lane by a stream. Then we went through a gate. . . .'

'And as soon as we were through the gate it was like walking into . . . into . . . a book . . .' put in Ellen.

'The stream suddenly plunges down, straight into the sea, through thick trees. One can hardly believe trees could grow on a cliff side so steep.'

'But we never got to the sea,' interrupted Ellen, 'though we went down and down and down. There it was, always just as far below. We could see it through the tree trunks at our feet. I don't believe anybody has ever got down there. Thousands and thousands of feet. . . .'

'No, Ellen. Scarce one thousand. . . .'

'And it looks so strange and dark down below. . . .'

'That's because the cliff faces due north. I doubt if the sun ever . . .'

'Edward will never allow anything to be romantic. He always has some explanation.'

'But I do allow something unusual about this. I've said it's poetical. I should write poetry about it, if I were a poet.'

'You must come, Romilly. We'll go there again tomorrow and take you.'

He went, but with some reluctance, for his mind was still upon his potters. A new Object had begun to take shape. Lestrange, growing gouty and continually disappointed in his hopes of getting office, had begun to talk of giving up Parliament. In that case his seat would again be at Romilly's disposal.

A political career had never appealed to Romilly, but he was now considering a notion of taking this seat himself for a time, while he looked round for some person whom the potters might have regarded as their own man. He had learnt too much to hope that they would ever consider him as a trustworthy representative, sincerely though he might attempt to fight their battles. They would accept nobody whom they did not feel to be one of themselves, nor would it be an easy task to find a fellow with all the necessary qualifications. Latymer's comment also stuck in his mind. He might find some promising candidate who would then make use of the opportunity to feather his own nest. Upon the whole he was inclined to dismiss the scheme as springing merely from vanity, the need for self-justification, and the old impatient desire to be doing something.

In low spirits he drove with the others along a rough track leading westwards over the cliffs from farm to farm. At the last of these farms they left the carriage.

'Now!' cried Ellen, skipping along the lane. 'Listen! You can hear it, how it suddenly plunges roaring down.'

'I doubt if it often roars,' said Latymer. 'I daresay it's often a mere trickle. But there was heavy rain last week, you remember, and a lot of water is coming down off the moor.'

'When does the poetry begin?' demanded Romilly.

'When we get through the gate,' promised Ellen. 'Once through the gate and you feel that poetry is true.'

'An't it true anywhere else then?'

'Oh, you know what I mean. Nobody could make poetry out of this lane.'

'I can think of some which suits this lane very well.'

'Then it can't be an agreeable sort of poetry.'

'It's not. It's confoundedly disagreeable and I wish I could describe it as untrue:

> At thirty man suspects himself a fool,
> Knows it at forty, and reforms his plan;
> At fifty chides his infamous delay;
> In all the magnanimity of thought
> Resolves and re-resolves — and dies the same!'

'Oh, pray stop! Here's the gate.'

They passed into the cool shadow of the woods and the poetry began.

There was no end, no measure, to that descent. Nothing moved save the falling water. No wind stirred in the ravine. All was bright and motionless, like a painted scene. Sunlight striking down picked out, here and there, a bush of green and gold, vivid against the shadow. The falling water woke a thousand echoes as though there had been many streams, not one. Voices from long ago, he thought dreamily, telling of things to come. Far below was the dark sea floor, seen somewhere formerly, and long forgotten. Ellen was right. Seen in some book.

'You'll agree it's romantic?'

Since he did agree he wished that she would not use the word so often.

Now the stream had vanished. It sang through caverns made by strangely curved, writhing rocks, also seen before, long ago. When they came to the water again Ellen sat down on a mossy rock to rest.

Latymer climbed about, leapt across the clamouring water, and stood looking at it pensively.

Romilly remembered.

'Lord Carn!' he shouted. 'But you should be sitting cross-legged.'

When Latymer came back he explained:

'There was an old book. *That was the book.* Jenny's father had it.'

They gave him a startled look. He never spoke of her, if he could help it, although they knew that he continually thought of her.

'This is the scenery. A palace . . . built by . . . no . . . no . . . it was a screen. An Eastern screen at Corston. When Grandmama was there. Ellen! You must remember it?'

'Oh, Romilly, she died before I was born!'

'Did she? I forgot. This is the same. Water falling. Rocks. Caverns. The twisted trees. The dark sea at the bottom. But the fellow who built the palace, he was in a book. *The Travels of Purchas,* or some such name.'

'But that was the book Dr. Newbolt lost!' exclaimed Ellen. 'He was always talking about it.'

'We . . . we used to fancy that we might, by some spell, find this place. We were sure . . . *we were right!*'

'It was a great while ago then?' asked Latymer, puzzled.

'Oh yes. Children. We were children.'

Tears started to Ellen's eyes at the sound of his voice. He looked round him with a recognising, joyful stare. They both saw, for a moment, the man he should have been. Then he set off hurriedly down the path as though expecting to meet someone.

The shadowy sea below drew no nearer. He could not tell whether extreme joy or extreme grief had hold of him. At such a pitch the one could not be distinguished from the other. Yet the unity of all experience had become plain; he knew that one moment in existence, completely filled, embraces all. He had passed beyond time and was no longer alone.

Later he knew that such felicity is only granted at a hard price. Reassurance so complete must erase all lesser sources of consolation. She had dispensed with them and so must he, returning to life like Lazarus, who dwelt for three days in the light and was then recalled to grope his way through mortal shadows grown doubly strange. Being once gone from this place he might never return, nor must he linger there for long.

But before he went he smiled and said quietly, as though she had been standing beside him:

'Oh may we soon again renew that song!'

The shadows had altered when at last he came up the path. Boughs that had been bright had lost their colour and the sun caught the falling water in fresh places.

The other two were nowhere to be seen. They must have grown tired of waiting. He toiled onward and upward. So soon as he had passed through the gate the sound of singing water died away, behind and below him. He had returned to this wild world. The future stretched before him, a straight and empty road. Whither it led he knew not, but he was aware that his own choice had ceased to be of importance. There would be no further detours in search of an Object.

At last he saw them standing by the carriage, so deep in some argument that they did not hear him coming. Ellen looked rebellious, Latymer resolute. When they heard him they turned with grave and anxious faces, but they said nothing. Each seemed to be waiting for the other to begin.

'I'm sorry,' he said hastily. 'I had no idea it was so late. Shall we go?'

Ellen turned towards the carriage but Latymer said: 'No.'

'If we stay now,' she protested, 'we shall be late for dinner. We can tell Romilly on the way back, and if he thinks . . .'

'We've made a discovery,' said Latymer. 'I believe you might like to talk to the people at the farm here.'

'It's only the book,' said Ellen impatiently. 'That book Dr. Newbolt lost. After you went down the ravine I remembered that it was in some place hereabouts he lost it. At a farm, he used to say, near a stream like this. He lent it to a person at the farm. We wondered if it could be the same farm. When we came up, just from curiosity, we enquired.'

She paused, glanced at Latymer, and continued:

'We asked the people at the farm if a gentleman had left a book here, ever so long ago. We never thought . . .

it was just a whim . . . so very long ago. Fifteen years.
But it seems that it was this farm. They remembered.
They said a gentleman who stayed here once left a book
behind. He said it was not his. It belonged to an old
clergyman, who would be calling for it.'

'Then is it here still?' asked Romilly.

He was puzzled by her manner and by a stern expression
on Latymer's face. There was obviously more in this than
a lost book. It was something which Ellen did not want to
tell him.

'No,' said Latymer. 'That's the strangest part. It's
gone. The old clergyman . . . he came at last, and asked
for the book, and took it away. Three years ago.'

'Dr. Newbolt came? Then . . . *three years!* Impossible!
It's far longer than that since . . . Can he have come back
to England?'

'Looks like it.'

'You think we should let the Newbolts know?'

They did not answer that. They were looking at one
another. Then, in a sudden burst, Ellen came out with it.

'They said . . . they said he's still wandering about in
this part of the country. And . . . and . . . they said he's
not alone. He has a boy with him. A boy who plays the
fiddle. And . . . oh, Romilly! he's called Dickie. They
say the boy is called Dickie.'

'Dickie?'

He stood at a loss for a second or two before her meaning broke on him.

'*Dickie?*'

Without another word he turned and set off wearily,
doggedly, towards the farm.

'I hope that satisfies you,' said Ellen to Latymer.

'We must have told him.'

'I suppose so. But you don't understand. Now he'll be off on some new . . . this tramper's boy . . . he'll get up some romantic notion . . .'

'I think,' said Latymer, 'that he's done with the romantic tack. He looks sober enough to me. He'd thought that business of the boy was finished, and here it is cropped up again. It's bound to be a nuisance. But he feels, as I thought he would, that something should be done about it.'

'On our wedding tour!'

'If he wants to stay here, making enquiries, we'll go on without him. I'm sure he'll wish that.'

'Oh dear! Oh dear! I know how it will be. He'll pin such hopes on that tramper's boy, only to break his heart all over again.'

'Ah no. His heart may be safer, now, than you suppose. As safe as mine is.'

Latymer smiled at her, took her hand, and pressed it to his breast. He added:

'Only one thing to be done with a heart, you know. When we heard him speak of her this afternoon we knew what he's done with his. I never quite believed it before. I thought it one of his romantic notions. But I believe it now.'

'Oh, so do I. But she's dead. Poor Romilly! She's dead.'

'And keeping it safe for him in a better place than this. That's what you'd do for me, and I for you, if ever . . . if we came to be parted.'

'Up in heaven?' hazarded Ellen. 'Does it say so in the Bible?'

She had sometimes been a little troubled by her own reluctance to go to heaven and play upon the harp for evermore. The suggestion that there might be something else to do was startling but pleasant.

'It says that love is the only thing we can take with us. Faith and hope we only need here. And . . . I've had occasion to observe . . . I've often wondered at it . . . the confidence and fortitude with which love, genuine love, endures bereavement. . . .'

A little surprised at himself, he broke off. Ellen gave a contented sigh at this reminder that her Edward, so brave, sensible and clever, was also very good and religious.

EPILOGUE: MORNING

EPILOGUE: MORNING

JEMMY THE FINGER started awake, aware that somebody was whispering. The hut was pitch dark but a grey no-light glimmered in the doorway.

'What's that? Who's that? Hannah?'

'Ay,' whispered a voice. 'That sailor, that Hughes, he's gone.'

'Gone? Where? When?'

'Porlock, I reckon. After that Gaujo. He went out must be half an hour since and he an't come back.'

'The bastard! I suspected . . .'

Jemmy rose and went out into a world which hung between night and day. The road, the moor, the wide vale below, were all visible by a light which had, as yet, no declared source. Hughes was nowhere to be seen.

A moment later Dickie and Hannah came out of the hut. The three stood peering at one another.

'Come morning,' said Jemmy, 'we'll see his lordship's back. How's Parson?'

'Still breathing,' said Dickie. 'If I'd known I'd have knifed that . . .'

'Then it's as well you was asleep. We don't want no knifing in Cold Harbour.'

'We'd best scarper,' said Hannah.

'I shan't. I shall stay with Parson. I owe him a leg, I believe.'

'They'll take you for perjurating.'

'Na-a-ah! I wan't sworn. And the gentleman asked for a body I'd never heard on — a reverent doctor or some such. How was we to know?'

They went back to the hut and roused the sailors. After listening for awhile to their comments Jemmy said:

'Save your breath. You'll never see that cully of yours no more. News on the roads goes faster than a coach and six. Parson has friends amongst us, and there'll be plenty, twixt Porlock and Bristol, wanting for to meet the man who sold him. Plenty!'

'Ay,' said Hannah. 'And it will be known that he carries ten finches.'

'He'll ride off safe in the gentleman's carriage,' muttered one of the sailors.

Jemmy spat.

'That's not their way with an informer. They pays him, but they thinks better of the poor sods he sells. And they show it.'

He then advised them not to go east, as they had intended, lest Hughes should set the Press on them. They had better, he said, go down to Dulverton and scatter. And he charged them with a message to Ptolemy Boswell, at Dulverton, to come up with a tilt cart to Cold Harbour. Hannah told them where Ptolemy was to be found, but reminded Jemmy that the gypsy would expect pay.

'I . . .' began Dickie, but was quenched by a look from Jemmy.

'Say I sent the message. I knows Ptolemy and he knows me.'

The sailors collected their bundles and trudged off. Their footsteps died away down the hill. Silence fell once more upon the hut.

'If our luck holds,' said Jemmy, 'Ptolemy might get here first. 'Tis a long step to Porlock. Hughes might be forced to wait before he gets word with the gentleman. The Quality don't rise early.'

'Nor they don't go nowhere fasting,' said Dickie. 'Squire Brandon will call for something to eat first.'

'Then I'll bide here,' said Hannah. 'No need to foot it to Dulverton. I can ride in the tilt cart with the corpse.'

'There an't no corpse yet,' snapped Dickie.

'There'll be one. Ptolemy or the Gaujo, 'twon't be no living man they takes away.'

She bent over the fire to blow it up but Jemmy stopped that. It would be better, he said, for the gentleman to find an empty hut and cold ashes. Signs of recent habitation might encourage him. Ptolemy must take the tilt cart back to Dulverton through by-lanes. She grew rather sulky, being too dull-witted to comprehend anything between careless security and blind panic. After grumbling a little she curled up and went to sleep. Dickie and Jemmy went to sit in the doorway. They were all hungry, but this did not trouble them since they were scarcely aware of it.

The world was brighter now. Day had conquered night, and colour had returned to the scene.

'What does Ptolemy want with a mort like that,' wondered Jemmy. 'I'd not walk half a day with her.'

'Shall you come down with us to Dulverton?'

Jemmy shook his head and said that he must be on his way into the White Horse country as soon as he had seen his old friend clear of this.

He suppressed an impulse to invite Dickie as a walking partner. A fiddler was a good cully to have and the boy was sharp-witted. He might do well in Jemmy's line of business, carrying word of contraband over the roads. Now that old Lucy was gone new links in that chain would be needed. But there was something about Dickie which promised trouble. He might quite easily have knifed Hughes, had he caught the man slipping off. Parson Purchiss kept him conformable, thought Jemmy. Nobody else will. He'll be for the High Toby or some such caper. Born to be hanged. That's his dukker, come by chance as he is. Too high for us. Too low for Quality. Wild and venturesome, without guineas to pay for his free way of thinking.

'If Ptolemy knows you've a guinea,' he said, 'he'll want the whole of it in his hand before he stirs for Dulverton. A crown's plenty. Tell him you've a crown and that you'll pay him by and by. I'll be there, if he gives trouble. In Dulverton you may change your guinea.'

'I'm obliged to you. A good friend you've been.'

Down in the valley below a cock crew. Jemmy, after a while, said:

'I wish you'd be as good a friend to yourself.'

'What d'ye mean?'

'If that gentleman is minded to do aught for you, and I've a notion he might, give him a civil answer.'

Dickie brooded on this in silence and said at last:

'He'll get the answer he deserves.'

'You know him?'

'Ay.'

'And he knows you?'

'No. He'd never look so low.'

'He was asking for you, wan't he?'

'Hark! Is that Parson stirring?'

The old man had begun to gasp and cry for air. Between them they carried him out and laid him on the heather where he seemed to breathe more easily. They sat down on either side of him, waiting and watching. Presently the sun rose in splendour. The sky was full of lark song.

'Where d'ye reckon they go?' asked Dickie mournfully.

'Out like a candle. That's my notion.'

'Mine too.'

'But you've had schooling. They learnt you about Jesus and the good place?'

'That's a tale they tell us for to keep us down. We lick their arses and we go to heaven. We give trouble and we go to hell.'

'This Jesus? They say he was a poor labouring man. What's the truth of that?'

'True enough. He was a carpenter. But he wan't suffered to speak his mind for long. He gave trouble and they nailed him to a cross.'

'They think a deal of him, all the same, don't they?'

'Dead, they like him pretty well. They write what they please of him, in their books. How should we know true from false?'

'Parson bid you get more schooling. There was one he named last night, that might be a friend to you.'

'Eccles?'

'Ay. That's the name. Who's he?'

'A gentleman. I'll own no gentleman as a friend.'

'You're too fierce against 'em, Dickie. I likes a gentleman. A true gentleman. Free and affable.'

'Who put them over us?'

'How should I know? We might have worse over us.'

Dickie shook his head and exclaimed:

'There was never but one of them in the world I'd have trusted. And she bade me have no dealings with Squire Brandon. Is that a cart on the road?'

'I see none.'

'Down by those haystacks.'

'Your eyes are sharper than mine.'

They sat watching. In a few minutes Jemmy saw it, and declared it to be Ptolemy's tilt cart. They called to Hannah, who came blinking from the hut.

'Parson's luck!' she said. 'We might be sure he would get clear off.'

Their hopes rose so high that Dickie suggested Parson might get over this bad spell. He might not be dying after all.

'Ah no! He carries all the signs. Look at his nose, child. As sharp as a . . .'

'Hark!'

All stood rigid at Dickie's cry.

There was a sound now in the air besides the lark song. It came from the moor behind.

'Horses,' groaned Jemmy. 'Wheels. We should have known. There's more time gone by than we thought.'

Ptolemy would arrive too late. They were sure of it before the carriage came bowling down the hill. Dickie leapt up and stood threateningly between Parson Purchiss and the road.

'Put up that knife,' implored Jemmy, retreating with Hannah to the hut. 'D'ye want us all hanged?'

'They shan't touch him.'

Dickie, however, put away his knife as the carriage drew up and Squire Brandon got out of it.

For a second or two he stared uncomprehendingly at the bundle of rags on the heather and the youth standing

on guard over it. Five years had passed since their last
and only meeting in the Parsonage lane. He did not
immediately recognise that puny child in this young
ruffian. When he did so his first thought was that he had
come too late.

'Cottar?' he said doubtfully. 'Dick Cottar?'

A jerk of the head from Dickie was the only answer.

'You know who I am?'

Another jerk.

'I've come . . . Dr. Newbolt . . . Good God! Is . . . is
this . . .'

He advanced a step, at which Dickie shouted:

'You keep off!'

'Is it true then? Is he dying?'

'He's dying. Can't you let him die in peace? Han't
he been tormented enough?'

Hannah, crouching in the hut with Jemmy, whispered:
'Who's the other Gaujo then?'

'There's only the one,' said Jemmy. 'That's Dickie.
He's got two ways of speaking. I've heard it before. I
reckon it comes from walking with Parson.'

Curiosity overcame Hannah's alarm. She poked her
head out of the hut. The slight movement caught
Romilly's eye and he immediately came towards them.

'You fool!' muttered Jemmy.

They were, however, a little reassured by Romilly's
mild greeting. He recognised them as having been in the
hut the night before, but did not reproach them.

'Is the old man really dying?' he asked. 'The boy
won't let me go near him.'

'He is for sure, sir,' said Jemmy. 'There's naught to
be done for him. He was a-dying last night and we all
knew it.'

'But he can't lie there.'

'There's a cart bringing. Some of his friends are coming for him.'

'The Poor People,' put in Hannah. 'We'll see he wants for nothing. We'll put him away as we does our own. Parson Purchiss we calls him. When the gentleman come asking for a reverend doctor we was all in a blunder.'

'Don't think I blame you,' said Romilly. 'That fellow who came to me this morning might be willing to sell him. You would not. I honour you for it.'

Hannah and Jemmy had nothing to say to this. Nobody had ever honoured them for anything before in the whole course of their lives. Hannah thought him as unaccountable as any other Gaujo. Jemmy noted that he had been right as to a gentleman's opinion of an informer.

'I only discovered four days ago that these two were in the country,' explained Romilly. 'We had supposed Dr. Newbolt to be out of England and we never knew the boy was with him. Since then I've had news, in various places, of a couple seen on the roads, who might be the same people. But I could meet with nobody who had spoken to them.'

That was not surprising. Tradesmen and farmers might know the pair by sight, and say so readily enough. Those who had had dealings with Parson Purchiss would hold their tongues.

'I only want to make sure that he is comfortable and cared for. Do you think you could persuade the boy that I mean him no harm?'

'Ah,' said Hannah, 'he's a poor, low ignorant kind of boy. A tramper's boy. Not right in his wits.'

'No,' said Jemmy quickly. 'He's got all his wits. He's as sharp as a pin. A fine spirited lad, sir. Good for a better life than this. But he thinks, d'ye see, that he's doing the best for his friend. It's a-many years he's been caring for Parson.'

They all went back to Dickie, who scowled at them.

'Now, Dickie,' whined Hannah, 'speak civil. The gentleman means kindly by you.'

'I'll speak as I please,' said Dickie. 'Kindness can't be forced on us, low though we may be.'

'That's true,' said Romilly sadly. 'That much dignity is still preserved to every human creature.'

This rejoinder shook Dickie a little. After staring for a moment he moved aside, muttering:

'Look at him, if you like then. See for yourself . . .'

Romilly knelt in the heather. He looked at a face changed beyond all recognition, not only by approaching death but by shock, sorrow, heartbreak, and five long hungry years.

He remembered another face seen in the pulpit at Stretton . . . pink and smiling between white puffs of wig . . . strawberries and cream . . . 'Remember to bow to the Bishop.'

'He's weeping,' announced Hannah. 'Oh, the kind gentleman!'

'I expect you are right,' said Romilly, without looking round. 'He chose his own friends, and would wish to die amongst them. You spoke of a cart?'

'Away down the hill,' said Jemmy, pointing.

Ptolemy, catching sight of the carriage standing by the hut, had scented trouble and halted. He was coming no further up the hill until he knew more.

'But his family,' said Romilly, rising from his knees, 'must be told of it. They must have news and proof of his death. You seem to be a sensible man. Go down to that fellow with the cart . . . what's his name? Where does he come from . . .?'

'Boswell, sir. He comes from Dulverton.'

'Tell him I shall drive over to Dulverton later today, and stay there until . . . desire him to send me word where . . .'

'His family!' Dickie broke in. 'Much they care. They were for putting him into a Bedlam.'

'Be quiet, Dickie. This is no business of yours.'

'Nor of yours neither. None ever cared for him but Miss Jenny, and she's gone. She . . .'

Dickie broke off, checked by the look Romilly had given him.

'Yes. She's gone. That's why I'm here, you know. She wrote me a letter desiring me to seek you out.'

'Miss Jenny? Miss Jenny did? When?'

'A letter given to me after she died. I set off at once to find you, but you'd already run off. I could never get word of you till now. I have her letter with me. You may read it if you like.'

'Miss Jenny! And she bid you own to me?'

'No. But she thought that I should set right any wrong that might have come to you through me.'

'You can never do that.'

'She thought that I could. What she thought should be attended to. Don't you think so?'

'It never was. They treated her as if she was nobody. They never minded what she thought.'

'Did you?'

After a pause Dickie shook his head.

'No. Not always.'

'You could now. Nothing can be forced on you, of course. You are old enough to choose your own life. But if there is any trade or profession . . . some kind of life which you could wish for yourself . . . I think she would tell you not to refuse my help in the matter. That was what she suggested in her letter.'

Dickie hesitated, frowned and said sharply:

'Not now. That must have been all of five years gone. Too late now.'

So much had been clear to Romilly the moment they met. He had intended to forgo those fanciful schemes for adopting the child with which he had once consoled himself. He would stick to Jenny's sensible advice. But five lawless years had left their mark. He could not imagine that Broadwood's, or any respectable firm, would make much of Dickie now. Yet to abandon him without an effort was impossible.

'Is there nothing . . . nothing you want to do, to be?' he said urgently. 'Save play the fiddle at fairs?'

This got him a grim smile.

Sweet Jesus! thought Jemmy, who had been listening with close attention. For two pins the young donkey would come out with his gilliteen. If he don't fish up the word so quick as he did last night it's because he thinks the gentleman will laugh at him.

Mockery was, indeed, the thing which Dickie most feared at the moment. If he could but say that he wished to play the fiddle at fairs for the rest of his life, he might be left in peace. But he had a notion that he owed the truth to somebody, although he could not have said to whom. At last he got out, a little breathlessly:

'If I could, I'd put down the tyrants.'

And cursed himself for the childish sound of it, and waited for his enemy to laugh.

Romilly did not laugh. His face grew grim and hard as he strove to quench the flame which had flickered up in his heart. No, no, he told himself. No more nonsense. A chance word! The boy was merely repeating something he had heard said.

'That's a creditable ambition,' he commented coldly. 'Which tyrants in particular?'

Grimness suited Dickie, who spoke up more firmly.

'The gentry. And the lords and the judges and the parsons. What are they but tyrants, even though they mean well? They set themselves up to rule us. I'd have none rule us save men of our own choosing.'

'You think you'd choose better?'

'Maybe not. But we shan't be full men till we do.'

'And how do you mean to set about it?'

'Get poor people to hang together as close as the gentry do. Once we do that we may call the tune, for they can't fare without us and they know it.'

'And who has put that idea into your head?'

Dickie looked surprised.

'It must be in anybody's head that has thought for five minutes.'

'Perhaps. But to think for five minutes is hard work. I should . . .'

My duty, remembered Romilly, checking himself. What is my duty to the boy? If he really wants to think, put him in the way of thinking? And leave him to think for himself?

'You can do nothing of that sort,' he said, 'without long and arduous preparation. Moses was able to deliver his people from Pharaoh because he submitted to be

274

brought up in Pharaoh's house. And, even so, his own people gave him a great deal more trouble than the Egyptians ever did.'

Having delivered this comment he turned away and strolled off for a little, telling himself sternly that he must build no hopes on the boy, never regard him as an Object.

'You can't chop logic with a gentleman,' said Jemmy to Dickie. 'He's winded you, I believe.'

'He's setting a trap for me,' said Dickie.

'To be sure he is. Shivering in his shoes. You're a lion broke out from the circus, and he's seeking for to pare your claws.'

'*He* knows better than to laugh at me.'

'If you was like to be any danger to him and his you'd have asked him for a new fiddle and held your tongue.'

Romilly came back to them and Dickie turned on him at once.

'If you think you'll stop my mouth with your schooling . . . Is that what you're after? You'll get me to go with you . . . thinking to win me over . . .'

'I should probably do so very easily,' said Romilly coldly. 'Moses could have remained in the house of Pharaoh and had a mighty pleasant life of it. When the time came, he went into the wilderness. But there an't many men of that mettle.'

Dickie flushed at the imputation and was not soothed when Romilly added hastily:

'Not that I blame you. I blame myself for taking you seriously. For God's sake let's drop it. Is there nothing else you can think of? Consider of it. This is not the time to . . .'

He turned again to the gaunt form lying in the heather and drew in his breath sharply. The old man's eyes were open. He seemed to be conscious of his surroundings. Romilly and Dickie fell on their knees on either side of him. A faint whisper came to them:

'Romilly . . . dear boy . . .'

'Sir . . .' cried Romilly, seizing his hand. 'Oh, sir . . .'

'You've come . . . for Dickie? God bless you! A great load off . . . what should become of him? A good boy. A son to me . . . a very fine man if . . . you may be proud . . . Dickie!'

His left hand moved feebly, and Dickie took it.

'Go with him, Dickie. Bear with . . . his ignorance. No greater than yours . . . tell him what you know . . . ask him . . .'

They waited, linked by his ebbing life, but heard no more save a long sigh and:

'Patience . . . patience . . .'

His eyes closed and the grasp on their hands slackened. Jemmy, who had been standing close by, turned away and made a significant gesture to Hannah.

'He said some holy words, I believe,' hazarded Hannah. 'Now he'll go.'

'He's gone. But they don't know it yet.'

'Gone?' Hannah nodded and immediately supplied the conventional comment:

'Gone. His time comes and he must go like another. Parson Purchiss is no more.'

'Get off and tell Ptolemy to bring the cart.'

'He said for you to go.'

'Get off and don't chatter. He'll pay you well.'

She went down the hill reluctantly, for she would have liked to see what Dickie and the Gaujo did next. Had they risen and danced a jig she would not have been surprised.

Jemmy, who understood a little of what had passed, also wanted to see the end of it. He was aware that the decision must lie with Dickie, who might, if he chose, drive off with the gentleman and never know hunger again. That they were father and son was plain enough. There was some physical resemblance, but that was nothing to the likeness in tone, stance and gesture. And a handsome pair they would be, thought Jemmy, so soon as the boy had been got into better toggery.

But he was not sure now how he himself would choose, were he in Dickie's shoes. It was not, as he dimly perceived, a matter of guineas, a soft bed, and plenty to eat. Some stern and arduous task was involved, viewed by both with reluctant hesitation, and offering no pleasure or profit to anybody, so far as he could understand. Dickie might have hoped for a gayer life, if shorter, on the High Toby.

Hannah had got to the bottom of the hill before either of them stirred. It was Romilly who said at last:

'We can do nothing more for him now.'

He broke the link which had for a few minutes fused three lives. He crossed the thin old arms on the breast. Then he lifted his eyes to this young creature preserved and confided to him by Jenny's love.

Neither time, nor wrong, nor death could quench that love. He knew that he had it still, and that it would dwell on him to the end of his days, as it dwelt upon Dickie. With humility, but with sudden confidence, he held out his hand. Dickie took it.

Within an hour all were gone. The gypsies had taken the cart south to Dulverton. Father and son drove north to Porlock. Jemmy trudged east to meet the people who waited for word from Mother Squires. Cold Harbour was left silent and deserted until evening, when others came, passed a night in their lives there, and were gone in the morning. Now the hut is gone too: nothing remains save a few stones lying in the heather.

THE HISTORY OF VINTAGE

The famous American publisher Alfred A. Knopf (1892–1984) founded Vintage Books in the United States in 1954 as a paperback home for the authors published by his company. Vintage was launched in the United Kingdom in 1990 and works independently from the American imprint although both are part of the international publishing group, Random House.

Vintage in the United Kingdom was initially created to publish paperback editions of books bought by the prestigious literary hardback imprints in the Random House Group such as Jonathan Cape, Chatto & Windus, Hutchinson and later William Heinemann, Secker & Warburg and The Harvill Press. There are many Booker and Nobel Prize-winning authors on the Vintage list and the imprint publishes a huge variety of fiction and non-fiction. Over the years Vintage has expanded and the list now includes great authors of the past – who are published under the Vintage Classics imprint – as well as many of the most influential authors of the present. In 2012 Vintage Children's Classics was launched to include the much-loved authors of our youth.

For a full list of the books Vintage publishes,
please visit our website
www.vintage-books.co.uk

For book details and other information about the classic
authors we publish, please visit the Vintage Classics website
www.vintage-classics.info

www.vintage-classics.info

Visit www.worldofstories.co.uk for all your
favourite children's classics